Don't Look Too Tasty

First published 2024

Published under licence by Brown Dog Books and
The Self-Publishing Partnership Ltd, 10b Greenway Farm, Bath Rd,
Wick, nr. Bath BS30 5RL, UK

www.selfpublishingpartnership.co.uk

ISBN printed book: 978-1-83952-838-5
ISBN e-book: 978-1-83952-839-2

Cover design by Andrew Prescott
Internal design by Andrew Easton

Printed and bound in the UK

This book is printed on FSC® certified paper

MIX
Paper | Supporting responsible forestry
FSC® C013604

Don't Look Too Tasty

PGH HANNAFORD

BROWN DOG BOOKS

For Emma, Rory, Niamh, Stephanie and Clare:
my daughters, my heroes.

Acknowledgements

Writing is necessarily a solitary pursuit. When the time comes to let others into the world we create, it can be scary. I want to thank the people who encouraged and supported me along the way; they know who they are. I will single out two in particular: Joe Barnes, editor, for knocking out my excessive fondness for hyphens and commas, and my daughter, Emma, for providing the illustrations introducing each part of this story.

Introduction

Here's the thing: I no longer know what day it is. I often don't know where I am, but lately I've been trying to make sense of it all. I found this manuscript the other day, in an old biscuit tin under my bed, along with some chocolate digestives and half a packet of Jaffa Cakes. I don't know what it was doing there. I don't know why there would be biscuits under my bed. Who does that?

The manuscript was in my handwriting, and I remember a lot of what's in it, but I don't remember actually writing it. There were a couple of sketches too; the type of thing I did in my 'comic-book' phase. Maybe I kept a journal or a diary. I mean it looks like I wrote this as a memory, so maybe I haven't caught up with that part of my life yet.

PART ONE

MR NEWTON

Chapter One

It all started when Mum and Dad made me move schools. I didn't want to, but Dad had gone crazy – well, he'd stopped going to work after that incident when he punched the window-cleaner guy. Mum had gone back to work when she didn't want to and we'd had to move towns. So, I was at a new school.

'Hi … I'm Elemenope.' The little red-haired girl stuck out her hand like a businessman on the telly.

'Hi Penelope. I'm Martha Gibbons.'

'I know. My mum said to look out for you. But my name's Elemenope.' She was whispering. Was her name a secret?

'That's what I said … Penelope.'

She shook her head and said, 'Everybody does that. I don't know why; it's a perfectly understandable name. It's the letters of the alphabet; you know … *LMNOP*.'

I said, 'Oh … sorry … I get it now.' I still had to think about it.

'Liquorice allsort?' I asked her, holding out the bag I'd smuggled out of the house. There weren't many left, but

I thought it was polite to ask anyway. I'd eaten most of them on the way to school while Mum ranted on about how I was going to love my new school and not letting me speak so I could munch away without getting caught.

'No thanks, Martha. I don't eat sweets before lunchtime.'

Suit yourself, I thought, *there won't be any left by then!*

Mum was doing her fake 'everything's-going-to-be-OK' smile. She was talking to a big version of Elemenope and they were both nodding in our direction.

Elemenope said, 'I'm supposed to take you under my wing, like a mother hen.'

I snorted. Elemenope was freckly, with great waves of really red hair, and I could imagine her as a hen. The problem was her size: barely half mine.

'Come on, Martha,' whispered Elemenope, 'I'll show you where the lockers are.' I didn't know it at first, but Elemenope whispered all the time; like she was telling a secret, and that was a problem, because I couldn't tell whether she was or wasn't. I had to put it in context. Obviously, the location of the toilets was not a secret (that would be weird), but when she told me about taking money from her Mum's purse, well, surely that was a secret. Tricky.

Elemenope showed me a two-pound coin and said, 'We can share something at the tuck shop. They do cream buns.'

My mouth watered. I said, 'My old school didn't have a tuck shop.'

She said, 'There isn't usually one here either; it's just for this week … some kind of fundraiser. Mum doesn't approve, so I took this from her purse when she wasn't looking.'

'My mum's the same. She'd give me another *fat-girl* lecture and I'd just go hungry.'

If Elemenope said anything I couldn't have heard it over the clanging of Big Ben. There was a really tall, ridiculously skinny, lady in a long dress heaving an old-fashioned brass bell. Her face was a triangle of red fury. Elemenope grabbed my hand and pulled me to a group of kids starting to form a line.

'What's going on?' I realised the whole school was doing this. There were six neat lines and all sound had stopped; nobody was talking anymore.

Elemenope shook her head at me and whispered behind her hand, 'That's Mrs Gnash … stay out of her way. She's horrible.'

We started to march – well the other kids did – I tried to copy them. I tried again to ask Elemenope what this was all about, but she put a finger to her lips and shook her head. I glanced at the lady in the long dress as I walked past, trying to keep in step; she looked like the Statue of Liberty's ugly sister. Her huge eyes followed me. I felt like a slice of pizza must feel before it gets eaten.

I looked away. I tried to be a robot, but that made me slow down and I felt a shoe kick at my right heel. It was the boy behind me. Was he doing this deliberately? Was he one of *those* kids? I turned around and saw his face, rigid with fear. His eyes stared straight ahead as he focused on walking in a straight line.

I stopped, so he walked right into me. That made the kids behind him walk into him, and then there was a pile-up. It was my fault, I knew, but it was all so unexpected. All that discipline was just not normal.

The tangle of frightened kids happened right at the doorway into the long school corridor. Why were they frightened? They should all have been laughing. Then I heard the whistle and the Statue of Liberty was in my face.

'Who is this new, large child?' Her voice made me think of insects. I couldn't speak, but I couldn't help staring at her. Her eyebrows wriggled like they had a life of their own. She thrust her triangular face further into mine … eww! Her breath stank. No wonder everybody was scared of her.

Slowly we all got up off the ground, out of each other's legs and faces. The line reformed and we marched into our classroom. That's when I saw him for the first time; at least I thought it was a him.

Chapter Two

It was bad enough having to start at a new school with new kids, new teachers, new toilets, new rules. It was a long list of new. But nobody, old or new, could ever have expected Mr Newton.

He was standing at the front of the classroom, to the side of the desk, staring at us. Was he staring? How could I tell? His face was all wrong. It was a mask, and he was wearing a hat – indoors. Elemenope took my hand and whispered, 'Don't stare; that's Mr Newton. Don't stare at Mr Newton.'

Just as we settled in, there was a breathy sound, like a loudspeaker crackling, then a voice said, 'Good morning, children. Welcome to class five ... we're going to have a great year.' I looked for the speaker, but I couldn't see one.

Elemenope whispered, 'That's his voice. Weird, right?'

I listened hard to the sounds that made up Mr Newton's voice. I'd heard something like it before. Then it hit me: Stephen Hawking. Dad was watching a documentary a little while ago, and this man in a wheelchair was using a machine to talk for him; it sounded exactly like Mr Newton's voice. So, I knew it wasn't his real voice. I had to try really hard not to stare; it was way too strange.

Mr Newton, or rather his voice machine, told us about the daily routine: we would have a school assembly and a separate class assembly. There was a time slot for English and one for maths. I was resigning myself to another boring school year when he said something about ancient Egypt that sounded remotely interesting. And there was this new thing called 'rainbow maths', which sounded terrible.

'Let's get off to a rocket-propelled start,' said the machine voice. It seemed strangely apt. 'A rapid-fire maths test to sweep away the holidays.'

I groaned out loud. Mr Newton, who was looking over me to a chart on the back wall, slowly tilted his head so he was looking straight at me. I couldn't look away. The mask was rigid; I had no idea what it was made of. Plastic maybe, but it was a really good skin colour. It was *too* perfect; there were no spots or marks. And it was smooth, like a doll's face, not rough and scratchy like my dad's.

The voice said, 'Martha Gibbons, isn't it?'

'Yes, Mr Newton,' I squeaked.

'Well, Martha Gibbons, it looks like you get to go first.'

Normally, when an adult spoke to me, I could pick up clues, which was good because I couldn't always trust the words. There was the facial expression: maybe their eyes didn't agree with their mouth. And the tone: friendly, critical, angry. I couldn't tell what was going on, because the machine just sounded the same. Was I in trouble, or was he teasing me?

'Six times seven?'

I was blank; I couldn't think; I started to sweat. He started to tap his gloved fingers on the table.

'Fifty-six.' I knew it was wrong.

Mr Newton didn't blink. How could he? His eyes seemed to be swimming behind the mask. He pointed to my left. Elemenope said, 'Forty-two'.

He kept pointing at her and said, 'Seven eights?'

'Fifty-six,' she whispered.

He didn't respond. He pointed to a boy in the back row as he said, 'Nine nines?'

'Eighty-one,' yelled the boy.

Mr Newton changed hands and pointed to another boy, 'Six sixes?'

That boy yelled too, 'Thirty-six.'

It went on and on. He pointed at every kid in the class. Sometimes they got two questions in a row. I couldn't see any pattern to it, but my heart was beating so hard I could hear it in my head. I knew all my times tables; we did them to death at my old school. So why couldn't I remember them? I sat still, terrified of another question.

Suddenly it was over; the noise had stopped. I realised my eyes were screwed shut. It was too quiet. When I opened my eyes, Mr Newton was nowhere to be seen. Just as I started to relax, I felt a cold, leathery finger touch the top of my head. It felt wet. Three gentle taps in time to the machine words, 'So you see …' I froze. '… Martha Gibbons, it's very straightforward in this class. I teach – you learn. I ask – you answer. Simple.'

I wished it was a normal voice. I really wanted to think he was just teasing, but I couldn't tell.

As Mr Newton walked back behind his desk, his legs, or at least his baggy trousers, seemed to be out of time with his feet. I must have been hallucinating with fear and confusion.

'Did you see that? Tell me you saw that.' It was the loudest whisper yet from Elemenope.

'What?'

'That ... didn't you see it? He pulled his watch out of his pocket, but his hands are still on the desk. How did he do that?'

I was sure I was going to be sick. I couldn't answer. I put my hand up and asked if I could get a drink of water. Mr Newton pointed at the door and said, 'First right, ten yards, second left ... enjoy, Martha Gibbons ... water is important.'

The first day of school is universally horrible. It doesn't matter if it's your old school and a new term; it's always horrible. But when it's a whole new school it's extra bad. And when your teacher's a weirdo? No hope. I'd never been a clingy kid, but I stuck to Elemenope like chewing gum to a shoe. That first day I went everywhere with her.

* * * * *

Lunchtime was not so bad: jacket potatoes with cheese, pizza which was better than Mum's home-made, and a slice of chocolate cake. I had seconds. Of everything.

The afternoon was endless. I tried to keep my head down and not stare at Mr Newton. He got us started on our Egypt project: I liked the sound of that. Dad had lots of books about history in his bookcase. It's a lovely bookcase, with glass doors and row after row of beautiful books. I thought about working on the project with Dad, now that he was around all the time.

'Martha Gibbons!' Oh no. What did he want?

'Yes, Mr Newton?'

'What are we studying in this class, Martha Gibbons?'

'Err … Egypt, Mr Newton.' My voice was shaky, my head was wobbly; I'd been daydreaming.

'Yes … Egypt. We're talking about pharaohs. It's not art, is it Martha Gibbons?'

'No, Mr Newton.'

'So why do I see a drawing in your workbook? Is it a drawing of an Egyptian pharaoh?'

I looked at the page in front of me. It was not just a drawing; it was a whole comic-book series. There was my dad getting a book out of his bookcase. There was me sitting beside him, reading to him. There was a big close-up of him smiling (something I couldn't recall seeing in ages). The last one wasn't finished; my pencil was still touching the shading I was doing to give the book depth. *Guilty. Absolutely caught in the act.*

I had nowhere to go, so I lied, 'Actually it is … it's a

picture of me as a slave, reading a papyrus to Ramses the second.'

Mr Newton came closer and peered over my shoulder. 'That looks like a book. The Egyptians didn't make books, did they?'

He had me there, but I had to keep going. 'No, Mr Newton, but they made papyrus … that's a kind of paper. They used plants to make it and it really was just like paper, and they used to write on it. Their writing is called hieroglyphics; it was pictures and symbols. They didn't really have an alphabet. And …'

'Take a breath, Martha Gibbons. Maybe you should be taking this class.'

My face was on fire. Every kid in the class was staring at me. But at least it felt like I wasn't in trouble anymore.

* * * * *

When the bell rang, I stood up to pack away my things. Elemenope had already piled up her books and was making for the lockers. I dropped my pencil case, and everything spilled on the floor. My hands were shovelling pencils, felt-tips and erasers into the open zipper of the unicorn case I'd been given for my birthday, when I saw the shoes. They were scuffed and completely overhung by folds of dark grey trousers. The cuffs wriggled. Was there a little puddle under one shoe? Gross.

The machine voice came from above, 'Martha Gibbons ... when you've collected yourself, could we have a word?'

'Yes, Mr Newton.' My voice was strangled; I was bent double and it was getting hard to breathe down there.

I sat back on the chair to catch my breath. All the other kids were wandering out to be picked up, and Mr Newton stood beside me with his arms folded.

'Tell me, Martha Gibbons ... did you study ancient Egypt at your last school?'

I shook my head, 'No, Mr Newton.'

'Can I ask, how you learned what you told us in class?'

'I read about it.'

'On a computer, I suppose ... something like Wikipedia?'

I'd never heard of that, so I shook my head. 'No. In a book. Actually a few books. Dad has lots of books, but I borrowed a really detailed one from the library. It's so interesting. Not just the pyramids, but what they believed in. Do you know, they used to shove tiny hooks up the dead person's nose to pull out their brains? It must have taken ages – and they put the dead person's organs in special jars; they're called canopic jars. Then they wrapped them to make a mummy. It was amazing.'

'So ... you read books ... you go to a library. Interesting.'

I was waiting for more. None came. I sat there, waiting for Mr Newton to ask me another question, but he just stood there. I wanted to go, but I didn't ask – at least not out loud.

Mr Newton said, 'Yes, Martha Gibbons ... you can go now.'

Chapter Three

'How was school honey-bun?' Dad had a new pet name for me every day.

'OK,' I said without thinking. It was my go-to response. Then I stopped and looked at Dad; I wondered if he was genuinely interested, and I remembered my drawing during the Egyptian class. 'Actually, it was a bit weird. Make that a whole lot weird.'

Dad looked at me and gave that head-tilt that meant he really was listening. I decided I liked having Dad around, picking me up from school. It was better than when he used to go to work all the time. He kept looking at me, so I knew there was a question coming, but I beat him to it.

'Well, I met a girl called Elemenope. She's weird; she whispers all the time. And there's something scary going on with this teacher who looks really fierce, Mrs Gnash I think she's called. Oh … and my teacher doesn't have a face.'

Dad kept looking at me. He didn't blink; I knew he'd heard me.

I said, 'No ... seriously ... he doesn't have a face. He wears a mask. And a hat. And gloves. Oh, and his voice is a machine.' I was gabbling and Dad did his *OK, well-that's-a-load-of-nonsense* laugh.

I couldn't stop. 'His name is Mr Newton and he creeps me out.'

'OK, missy. Maybe you need something to eat.'

I hadn't even noticed we were home by that stage of our one-sided conversation. I headed for the kitchen table and saw Isabella for the first time. She was colouring something in *my* spot at the table. There was a plate with no biscuits on it, and crumbs all over. I was starving; she had a faceful of food that should have been mine. I lost it.

'Get out of my place!' I yelled right in Bella's face. I went for her hair, but she pulled away just in time and my hand knocked over a glass of milk that shouldn't have been there in the first place.

'Hey – stop that now!' Dad shouted at both of us.

We both said, 'It's her fault,' fingers pointing wildly. Nobody did anything to clean up the mess and Dad suddenly looked like he was going to cry.

Bella and I said, 'Sorry,' more to Dad than each other, and I got the dish cloth from the sink and started wiping up the milk. Dad was kind of growling in his throat. If there was one thing we all knew it was how much Dad hated spilt milk. He'd told us, actually he'd shouted at us, often enough.

He started to say it; but I beat him to it, 'I know, I know – you hate spilt milk. Yes, I know it smells if we don't clean it up properly.' He was looking at me. I could see him counting under his breath.

Why was everybody so tense? I was the one who'd had the weird day. I was hungry, so I grabbed some biscuits from the tin Mum thought she'd put out of reach: three ginger snaps and some kind of fruity flapjack. I presumed it was one of those healthy things Mum was trying to sneak onto my plate. It was surprisingly OK.

I poured myself some milk, but I was shaking, so I spilled some. Bella opened her mouth to tell on me and I rounded on her. I knew her. I grabbed the pencil she was using, and put just enough pressure on it to see it start to bend. I won; she shut her mouth. I flashed her a big smile as I handed the pencil back, gulped the milk and walked out of the kitchen.

'Oh, Dad … Bella just spilt the milk again.'

Chapter Four

Michael said, 'I still say Mr Newton's an alien.' Michael was an oversized boy; he was a head taller than anybody else in our class. He had an even bigger brother in year six. The problem was Michael took everything his big brother told him as the gospel-truth. And the problem with that was Michael's big brother was an idiot.

'That's rubbish,' said Hakeem, 'and do you know why?' He peered through his glasses and didn't wait for an answer. 'I've read every report about so-called *aliens*, and there's no proof. It's just a lot of idiots wanting attention. If there were aliens, why haven't they been in contact? Why aren't there spaceships coming and going? They don't exist, that's why!'

'Well, there are aliens. And he's one of them.' Michael looked down at Hakeem, and then me and Elemenope in turn. 'Why else would he wear a mask? He's got an alien face, that's why.'

'Why aren't you playing football, like you normally do?' asked Elemenope.

Michael sighed, 'Well, I'd rather be doing that than arguing about weirdo-alien-Mr-Newton with you nerds, but Mrs Gnash confiscated the ball yesterday.'

Elemenope said, 'Well, my mum reckons he was burnt in an accident or something, and has really bad scars. He wears that mask so as not to frighten people. You know, like *The Phantom of the Opera.*' Elemenope's whispering made people focus on what she was saying.

'What about the voice thing?' I asked. 'Why does he sound like that?'

'Oh ... Mum says he probably burnt his throat and his voice box doesn't work.'

'No way,' said Michael. 'He's Darth Vader.'

That made us all laugh. Then I asked, 'Who's Darth Vader?' They all just looked at me.

Hakeem said, 'Oh come on, Martha. *Star Wars*. Darth Vader? You know.'

I said, 'I haven't seen those movies.' Then they looked at me like *I* was an alien.

* * * * *

Mrs Gnash started to ring the bell. She was waving something in her other hand. It was a football, punctured and deflated. As she rang the bell she screeched, 'Look what happens to balls that nearly hit me.'

Michael said, 'Don't look at her. She's evil. I don't like her eyes.'

I said, 'You just don't like any teachers, do you?'

He shrugged and said, 'Guess not.'

I looked around and saw Bella lining up in the reception area, holding Mum's hand. It was her first day and I had been steadfastly ignoring her. I'd been at St Finbar's for a week; I knew my way around. I had a group, even if one of them was an idiot and one of them was inaudible, so I didn't need to be saddled with a little-cry-baby-just-starting-school sister.

I avoided Mum's eyes, but then I heard her call out, 'Martha. Look out for your little sister.' I pretended not to hear.

* * * * *

It was Monday, my second week at St. Finbar's, and I was starting to feel OK, even relaxed, until Mr Newton said, 'OK ... Monday morning ... cobwebs test.' What's a cobwebs test? Were we meant to know about spiders suddenly? I don't like spiders.

'Don't worry, Martha Gibbons. It's a test to wipe away the cobwebs of the weekend.'

He meant all that stuff that doesn't involve schoolwork; all that stuff like eating and computer games and watching telly. 'All those things just fill your brains with cobwebs, and I have to wipe them away before you can start learning.'

He was seriously strange; maybe Michael was right. Maybe he *was* an alien.

We started with maths again, but I was ready. He pointed straight at me; his index finger wriggled in its glove.

'Martha Gibbons ... seven eights?'

'Fifty-six,' I shouted. I'd remembered.

He didn't waver. He pointed to Elemenope: 'Nine sevens?'

'Sixty-three,' she whispered.

Next were two boys at the back of the class. I didn't know their names; they got theirs right, and suddenly it was back to our table. He pointed at Michael: 'Seven sevens?'

'Sixty-four.'

I hung my head, embarrassed for him. I vowed to never make another mistake in Mr Newton's maths tests.

We survived the cobwebs test and it was time for English. We were supposed to look up some facts about William Shakespeare over the weekend. I had remembered at breakfast and scribbled down a few lines after Dad let me use his laptop. That was only after he made a big show of moving his coffee cup six feet away from it.

'Let's hear some information from your research.' Mr Newton looked around the room; I knew he was going to ask me first. He didn't. He asked Elemenope.

'William Shakespeare was born in Stratford-upon-Avon,' she whispered. Then she stopped. I looked at her; there was more on her page – dates and all – but she just stopped talking. She was staring at Mr Newton's vest. I could see why; it was squirming.

'Well, that's a start. How about something from ... Martha Gibbons. Have you illustrated your work?'

I blushed, and slowly opened my book. There was my comic strip. I meant to tear that page out. The next page had writing on it.

'He was born in 1564,' I said with confidence in Wikipedia. What a find that was.

'And who was on the throne at that time?'

Silence. You could hear the proverbial pin drop. Hakeem's hand shot up.

'Yes … Hakeem.'

'Queen Elizabeth the first.' There was not a hint of doubt in the answer. Hakeem knew stuff.

'Very good. That's why we say Shakespeare's language was Elizabethan.'

I stopped paying attention at that point. I saw what Elemenope claimed she had seen the other day. Mr Newton's pocket watch just appeared and popped straight back in again. His hands were nowhere near it.

In the playground later, Elemenope could barely contain herself. 'Did-you-see-that?'

I said, 'I saw something, but I don't know what happened. Did he really pull out his watch without using his hands?'

'I don't know … he couldn't have … could he?' she said. 'But now I can't seem to remember. I wonder if the boys saw anything.'

We had a kind of group now. I'm not sure how that happened. It was me, Elemenope, Hakeem and Michael, which was weird, because Michael struck me as a *boys' boy*; a boy who just wanted to play sport all the time.

Michael was kicking a ball around with two boys I

didn't like: Mark One and Mark Two. That's what I called them. They were both Marks; their surnames were Smith and Butcher, so the school had labelled them Mark S and Mark B. But to me they were like machines, so giving them numbers made them seem more like things that had come out of a mean-boy factory.

Elemenope looked up as Hakeem walked past the Marks. She was beckoning to him and he wasn't paying attention; his face was buried in *A Complete History of Elizabethan England*. Suddenly the football hit him in the side – hard. Mark One had kicked it at him deliberately and Hakeem crumpled. The Marks were laughing and pointing, but Michael went over and helped Hakeem to his feet.

'What are you doing?' Mark Two sneered. He was only small, but really mean. Most of us stayed out of his way. When Michael didn't answer, Mark Two walked up to him and said, 'He'll be all right … just can't play football. Nerd.' He put on a whimpering voice as he said, 'Ooh, look. The nerd's book's got mud on it. Let me clean it for you.' He spat on the cover and wiped it across his bottom, before dropping it at Hakeem's feet.

Michael was so much bigger than Mark Two, but he backed away, blinked and looked from Mark to Hakeem as if making up his mind about something. I was willing him to help Hakeem, who was panting and trying to get his breath as he bent over again and slowly crumpled to his knees. It seemed like the whole playground had frozen and everybody turned to watch.

Mark One walked threateningly towards Hakeem. Mark One had a reputation: he took baby birds from nests, he kicked dogs, he picked fights with smaller boys. He was someone best avoided.

The ball was tucked under Hakeem's arm; he was cradling it for support. Mark One was shaping up for a kick. He was going to kick Hakeem to get the ball back. I screwed my eyes shut.

'MARK SMITH ... STOP THAT NOW!' shouted Mr Newton.

I didn't know he could turn up his volume. The effect was electric. Mark One stopped his foot in mid-air. I hadn't seen Mr Newton come into the playground. Usually Mrs Gnash did lunchtime duty, but she was nowhere to be seen. The Marks would have kept to themselves if she had been there.

'I just wanted the ball back, sir. Stupid Hakeem's lying on it now.' Mark One's voice was whiny at best; it was worse when he was trying to weasel out of trouble.

Mr Newton reached Hakeem at last; he was a really slow walker. 'Michael – help him up. Are you OK, Hakeem?'

'My side hurts.'

'Go to the office and lie down. Michael, you go with him.' Mr Newton turned to face the two Marks and spoke quietly to them. His volume control could obviously go way down as well as up. I couldn't hear the words, but at that volume, the buzzing of his voice box was menacing. A cold shiver ran down my back.

The two Marks hung their heads and walked away. As they walked past us, Mark One glared at me and said, 'What are you staring at, fatty?' He didn't deserve an answer.

Mr Newton walked past next. He was muttering, 'Millions of years ... still bullying ... why do I bother?' I couldn't tell whether I actually heard that, or thought it. It felt like somebody made me think the words.

Chapter Five

I walked home with Mum and Bella. Mum had taken some time off work to get Bella settled in; it was like she didn't trust Dad to do it. She was paying attention to Bella's excited prattle, all about some award for sitting still or paying attention or some other stupid thing – *big deal.*

I said, 'Mum, there was nearly a fight today, and Mr Newton stopped it with his creepy voice and …'

'Shush, Martha. Bella's telling me something very interesting. Go on, sweetheart.'

I held my tongue. I decided to wait and tell Dad. Maybe he'd show some interest in his first-born child.

* * * * *

'How was school, pumpkin?' Dad had started using food names for me. He thought it was funny. It wasn't.

'Oh … the usual … you know.' I was hungry, and food was suddenly more important than any news of my day.

'No, I don't. That's why I asked.'

I shot him the new look I'd been working on. It was meant to be a 'please shut-up' look, mixed with an 'Oh, Dad' kind of feeling. I mustn't have had it quite right yet because he asked, 'Are you OK, sweet potato? Are you sick? Your face is all pained.'

'No. I'm not in pain … I'm OK.'

I started eating a Hobnob, hoping he'd stop talking to me and hoping that one day Dad might learn to bake or make something nice. He spent all day at home, so what did he do with his time? He put out afternoon snacks for us, which was a nice idea, but it was always the same: biscuits. I mean, *he could try a bit harder, couldn't he?*

Dad looked sad. I decided to be nicer to him. Later, after I'd eaten, and maybe after I'd watched some telly.

He said, 'Haven't you got some homework to do?'

I decided not to be nicer to him.

* * * * *

My bedroom hid a new secret: an old Jacob's cracker tin I'd found in the shed beside the house. It was a real antique, and smelled of coconut. The lid was dented, but still fitted properly. I kept it under my bed, behind a cushion.

I'd been sneaking biscuits every day and slowly building a stash. That was harder to do than I thought, because I kept eating them. Especially the chocolate digestives. With some discipline, I'd manged to nearly fill it over three weeks, and now it could get a workout.

After four jammy dodgers I needed a drink, so I wandered down to the kitchen. There was Dad, with an apron not quite covering his front, and beads of sweat on his forehead.

'Hi Martha … could you help Bella set the table, please?'

I gulped. Dad cooking? I'd wanted him to do something, but now, seeing the chaos in the kitchen I wasn't so sure. 'OK, Dad.'

I didn't need to do anything; Bella had done it already. The knives and forks were back-to-front, but when I went to move them, Bella yelled, 'Mummy, Martha's wrecking my table setting.'

Mum sat at the head of the table, looking at Bella's drawing of something-or-other and snapped at me, 'Leave it, Martha. Bella's done a lovely job.'

I sneered, *'Bella's done a lovely job'* under my breath as I sat down.

'What did you say, Martha?'

'Nothing.' Mum gave me her *I know you said something mean, but I didn't hear it clearly* look. I wasn't worried about that; I was too busy worrying about Dad's dinner.

Dad came in from the kitchen with a dish of mashed potato; that was promising. Next was a dish of Brussels sprouts: not so good. He said, 'OK, everybody, sit up. Time for the main event … ta-daa.'

He'd made meat loaf. That was why it smelled so good. I love meat loaf. Just as he was about to sit down, he said, 'Wait a minute – there's gravy too.'

He brought in a dish and inside was real gravy. I was impressed. Cleary Mum was too. She said, 'Johnny … well done. This looks amazing.' I think she meant it; she only called him 'Johnny' when she was being nice to him.

Dad served us like a waiter in a restaurant. I watched my plate fill up. The meat loaf smelled so good. I noticed there was no ketchup bottle on the table, but with gravy on offer I decided to wait and see. There was a nice pile of mashed potato and a nasty little group of sprouts; I didn't want them to touch anything else in case they contaminated it. I'd decided that Bella was right about that: some foods should not touch. I couldn't tell her that, though.

Dad was getting ready to pour on the gravy. Mum

put a hand on his arm and said, 'Not too much gravy for Martha.' She looked sideways at me, and in that instant I hated my mother. She was interfering with my meal; she was ruining my life. I felt the anger boil up inside me but I couldn't say anything. I knew the look in her eyes. If I spoke up, I'd get another lecture about my weight. And that was going nowhere.

I was already out of my seat as I said, 'May I leave the table, please?' in my best table-manners voice.

'What for?' asked Mum.

'Ketchup.'

'No. No ketchup, Martha. Your father's made this beautiful meal for you. It doesn't need ketchup. Sit back down, please.'

What Mum was really saying was, 'Ketchup is loaded with sugar, and you're a fat girl and you shouldn't be eating it.' I knew my mother.

The meat loaf was pretty tasty, I had to admit. But it was dry. It needed ketchup – or gravy. My tiny ration of gravy disappeared in two mouthfuls. I liked to get mash and meat loaf on my fork together and smoosh it around in the gravy. There was no chance of that.

Mum and Dad were talking together, not looking at me. I had a perfectly balanced forkful of meat loaf with mash on top. I swooped on Bella's plate like an eagle. The meat-loaf-mash scooped up a big swipe of gravy. It was the perfect raid. Or it would have been if Bella hadn't screamed. Dad turned around at the exact moment the eagle left Bella's plate. That gave Mum a clear view of the load disappearing into my mouth. She exploded at me.

'Martha!'

I couldn't say anything; it was a really big mouthful. Mum was staring at me, which spoiled the taste, and my victory. I'd heard people say that victory is sweet, or they could taste victory. Was this what they meant? My victory was being spoiled by that look on Mum's face. Dad was trying not to laugh.

* * * * *

After dinner, I actually did some homework. I had to look up stuff about Egypt, so Mum let me use her laptop. Mr Newton told us not to use Wikipedia, so I started cruising around other websites. I found some pretty cool stuff and Mum let me print off a picture of Tutankhamun's mask. I stared at it and wondered if the pharaohs wore masks when they were alive, like

Mr Newton. Then I did my Egyptian walk and started talking like a robot. Mum sent me to bed.

I had trouble sleeping; I kept waking up in a cold sweat and hearing Mr Newton's voice in my head. I remembered seeing his watch appear and disappear. Or I thought I did.

Chapter Six

Friday at St Finbar's was sports afternoon, so we wore our PE kit all day. I loved it because Dad had taken to doing the washing and he used way too much fabric softener; my T-shirt was really fluffy. It was so much better than my normal scratchy school shirt.

The walk to school went surprisingly well. I didn't seem to have forgotten anything and I held Dad's hand the whole way. Bella walked with Mum; it was her first sports day and she was excited / nervous. She kept asking, 'What if nobody else is wearing their PE stuff?' Like it mattered.

Everybody was wearing their PE stuff and I watched Bella physically relax, like someone had taken a ruler out of the back of her shirt. I tried to remember that for later; it might be fun.

Elemenope, Michael and Hakeem were in our usual meeting place by the run-down shed in the corner.

Hakeem kept looking over his shoulder. He said, 'When I left school yesterday, Mark S and Mark B jumped on me.' Elemenope started; her eyes widened. 'No ...' he went on, 'Not like that. They sort of jumped out at me. They said they'd beat me up if I told on them.'

'Told on them for what?'

'That's the thing,' he said. 'I don't know.' He looked really freaked out, so I reached out my hand to him. Elemenope gave me a look I didn't understand at the time. Jealousy?

I saw the Marks in the opposite corner. Mark One was kicking a football against the wall. Mark Two was just pacing around him. It looked menacing. Mark One kicked the football to Mark Two and they started zig-zagging in our direction. They had really good ball control, so when the ball flew hard off Mark Two's shoe in our direction, I knew it was deliberate.

We all ducked, except Michael who did this amazing, super-hard header straight back at Mark Two. The ball hit him in the chest and he staggered back. He didn't expect that. Bullies don't expect people to stand up to them. Mark Two looked daggers at Michael and muttered under his breath.

We were saved by Mrs Gnash who started clanging the huge hand bell. It was early, but her scratchy voice said, 'If you boys can't behave, we'll just have to get the whole school in early.' She towered over everybody and for a second I thought she might be going to hit the Marks with the bell.

I stood behind Michael, with Hakeem behind me, and then Elemenope. When the Marks came into the line everybody else moved out of their way. A small boy, Glen, with glasses even thicker than Hakeem's, stumbled past in a desperate bid to get clear of them and Mark One pushed him over. When Mark Two laughed, Mrs Gnash blew her whistle right next to his ear. I couldn't help smiling as he grabbed at his head.

I gave a little wave to Bella as we marched past the reception line. She was upright, concentrating, staring straight ahead, and I remembered what she got her award for: 'good walking in the line'. *Seriously?*

Everybody seemed excited, and why not? Only the morning to do schoolwork and then we would run around all afternoon. It would be the perfect school day, except for the running around bit. A snow day would have been better.

Mr Newton got us to calm down by raising his hand. 'Rainbow maths time ... everybody has ten minutes ... let's go.' Rainbow maths was OK; everybody had a set of fifty questions and had to do as many as possible in ten minutes. You started on 'red' and progressed through the colours of the rainbow every time you got fifty out of fifty, for five days in a row. We'd been doing it for three weeks, and I was still on red. Elemenope was on orange, and Hakeem was on his last day of yellow. I'd had four runs of fifty out of fifty, so I really wanted to get another fifty. I got 49. I looked at Mr Newton with what I thought were puppy-dog eyes. But he turned his mask-face to me and said, 'Sorry, Martha Gibbons. You know the rules; they are the same for everyone. You have to earn a promotion.'

He came to the side of my desk and put a hand on my shoulder. He didn't touch people often. When his hand, or his glove, landed on my shirt I felt wobbly. It was like I could hear his thoughts, and they didn't match his words.

His words were harsh: 'Look here ...' He pointed at the question where Elemenope had put a cross rather than a tick. A tiny drop of water fell on the paper. I didn't think I was actually crying; it seemed to come from the tip of Mr Newton's glove, but I must have been crying. I thought, Elemenope's my friend. Why couldn't she have just ticked it?

I knew the answer to that. Mr Newton had caught

the Marks giving each other fifty out of fifty when they clearly made lots of mistakes. They got kept in after school every day for a week.

The question was: 490 divided by 7. I had written 7. I heard the word 'Careless,' but I felt like he was being encouraging. I felt him say 'You've got a big brain, Martha Gibbons. Imagine what would happen if you actually used it.' He didn't exactly say that, but I couldn't be sure. It was like he made me think that last bit.

* * * * *

Mrs Gnash was in charge of sports day, with her ever-present whistle. She had traded her usual long, flowing dress for tracksuit trousers and trainers. She seemed even fiercer, somehow, wearing trousers that looked like they were covering bamboo poles.

We were sent to 'warm up' on the grassy field beside the playground. Nobody was really supervising us so kids were just running around haphazardly. Year six boys were bossing the little kids about. Us year five kids were being left alone, which was mostly a good thing.

Michael was running up and down the edge of the field, there was a group of girls skipping, and the rest of our class was just standing around in little groups. I stood with Elemenope and Hakeem. His shirt was way too big; it came down below his shorts. I was too hungry to move. Where was a Mars bar when I needed one?

The Marks had a football, but they weren't kicking it. They were throwing it as hard as they could at anyone nearby and calling out, 'Dodgeball!' *Idiots.* They hurled the ball at Hakeem's head; he ducked and it hit me right on the nose – hard. I went down, too shocked to cry. I heard them laughing, 'She's too big a target … that doesn't count!'

My face was numb; then it stung. Then the blood came, and finally the pain. That's when I started to cry. Hakeem and Elemenope hovered over me, but it was Michael who got down beside me and made me hold my nose with my hand.

I heard him say, 'It'll be OK … you need some ice.' My eyes were closed, but I sensed people crowding around. When I looked up there was a haze of blurred faces, gawking. Blood is a magnet.

I missed the rest of sports afternoon because I was lying down in the office with an ice pack the size of Scotland on my face. I got news reports from Elemenope who dropped in now and again to check I was OK.

'You'll never believe it,' she said, 'they're actually playing dodgeball, but with soft rubber balls, not footballs. Oh … and Michael's been given a detention for punching Mark Two.' I liked that she was using my name for the horrible Marks.

According to Elemenope, Michael said, 'Totally worth it … I still need to get Mark Smith.' I wondered why Michael used their proper surnames; even the school didn't use them.

Elemenope was enjoying her story: 'Apparently, Mark Two made a big song and dance about Michael hitting him "for no reason", even though everybody knew why he did it. He even said so when he did it, but Mark Two just said "Oh, no. It was an accident … I never meant to hit anyone with the ball." What a liar!'

* * * * *

I felt better after Elemenope's visit, but I was getting a headache. The secretary said she'd been trying to get hold of Mum or Dad all afternoon, but nobody was answering.

I said, 'That's OK … I'm OK.' But it sounded like, 'I'bb Otay.'

My nose had stopped bleeding, but my shirt looked terrible. It wouldn't have been so bad if we had red PE shirts like the other school in town, but we didn't. Our shirts were white. I remember Mum saying, 'Who thinks white PE shirts are a good idea?' It never occurred to me that washing them might be a problem. I only cared that it was nice and soft. Good old Dad.

I was suddenly teary again as I thought about Dad having to wash my PE shirt, all covered in blood, and I imagined him getting upset and angry. I asked the secretary to stop trying to contact my parents. I wanted to delay having to deal with that problem.

I dozed off, and woke up sometime later with a fluttery feeling in my stomach. Mr Newton was standing beside me.

'No brain damage, I hope, Martha Gibbons. You need to look after that big brain of yours – even if you don't use it all.' I wished he had a normal voice. But it was nice of him to come and see me.

Mr Newton was still in the secretary's office when Dad arrived to take me home. It was early: only two-fifteen (I had a great view of the secretary's big wall clock; it was about the only thing I could see) and school didn't finish until half past three.

Dad looked flustered, like he'd just woken up, and he asked the secretary, 'Umm … do you think I could take Isabella as well, so I don't have to make a second trip in the car?' Oh no, he'd driven. That couldn't be good. He hadn't driven the car since we moved.

The secretary said, 'Of course,' and disappeared. That was a bit weird. Dad had said 'Isabella'. She was never called that unless she was in trouble, which was never.

Mr Newton said, 'Hello, Mr Gibbons. I'm Martha's teacher. I hope she gets better over the weekend, so we can have her back to normal on Monday.'

Dad said nothing; he just stared at Mr Newton. I realised they'd not met before. *Awkward.* I wanted Dad to be more normal. I wanted Mr Newton to be more normal. I wanted my face to stop hurting.

Chapter Seven

Bella whined all the way home about missing sports day. I said, 'Sorry my face got smashed in and ruined your day.' It sounded funny because my nose was totally blocked, but I wasn't laughing.

Dad had put out biscuits again. I watched him pour two glasses of milk and wince as I reached for mine. I didn't spill it and I saw his shoulders relax. 'You OK, pumpkin pie?' *Terrific;* I'd become two types of food.

I nodded. Dad said, 'I've tried calling Mum, but there's no answer on her mobile phone.' I didn't know why he was telling me that. Maybe he was just having trouble doing things on his own. 'Why don't you get changed and have a lie down?' I nodded again.

Bella piped up, 'Well, it's not fair. I missed out on sports day; I want to watch the telly.'

I said, 'Go ahead. I don't want to watch anything. I've got a headache.'

Dad came into my room and picked up my PE shirt. It was like he noticed the blood for the first time. I saw his shoulders sag and it occurred to me that his body language had become really just shoulder language. There were three stages: tense (she's near milk), relaxed (hey … nothing bad happened), and drooping (now I've got to deal with this).

I wondered when my Dad became so miserable. I must have missed it. One day we were living in London with big, bouncy, happy Dad, and the next we were living in this tiny chocolate-box town with droopy, sad Dad. I wanted my proper Dad back.

I sat up and patted the empty spot beside me. Dad sat down heavily and I put my arm around his waist. He kissed the top of my head, then said, 'Poor poppet.' I wanted to say it back to him, but it wouldn't have come out right.

We sat for a while, not talking, which was nice. I heard his tummy rumbling. He cleared his throat, then said, 'That teacher … your teacher … Mr Newton. He's an interesting fellow.' *That's putting it mildly!*

'Yeah … but I think he's nice.'

'Oh, I'm sure he is, moon-pie.' *Moon-pie? Really?*

He gave me a little squeeze, and started to cough. He did that when he wasn't sure what to say next. I decided to make it easy for him.

I said, 'Some of the kids think he's an alien, but I don't. I think he was burnt, or something. That's why he wears a mask.'

'Oh … that would make sense.'

'And he wears gloves and a hat, too.'

Dad said, 'Yes. I noticed that.' There was a long pause, then: 'Um … his voice … that's a machine, right?'

'Uh-huh.' I was beginning to wonder if Dad had even answered Mr Newton when they spoke. I don't think he did. That was a bit rude. Mum and Dad were always telling me to speak to people when they spoke to me. Rules should be the same for adults. But then I guess Mr Newton gave me the creeps when I first met him, but I'd got used to him. I didn't tell Dad about the strange feeling in my stomach when Mr Newton was nearby.

'You said there was something weird about your teacher a few weeks ago, but I didn't pay any attention … sorry.' Wow, I didn't get that often. Mum or Dad saying they weren't paying attention, even though I *knew* they didn't pay attention. They always said they did. But they didn't. *Gotcha.*

I said, 'I guess I've stopped thinking he's weird, although he is … totally … right?'

'Right.'

Our chat petered out. Dad gave me another cuddle and slumped out of the room, my blood-stained PE shirt limp at his side.

* * * * *

I must have fallen asleep, because I didn't hear Mum come in. I woke up to find her poking at my forehead. My pillow was all wet; I'd left an ice pack on my face and it had melted all over the place. I grimaced, ready to get in trouble, but she didn't seem to notice.

She said, 'What a day! Poor thing. I'm sure it looks worse than it is.'

I wanted to say it felt worse than it looked, but I didn't. I didn't feel like dinner, and I didn't feel like fighting with Mum. I got a book out of my bookcase and propped myself up on the head of my bed.

Mum said, 'You sure you want to read? It might give you a headache.'

I shrugged. I was holding my favourite book, *The Velveteen Rabbit*, and I noticed how the cover was all soft and bendy; I'd read it so many times. It felt nice just to hold it, but I wanted to show Mum I was all right, so I switched on my lamp and started reading.

She said, 'OK, Martha, suit yourself. What would I know? I've only been a doctor half my life.'

As soon as she was out the door, I put the book down.

She was right.

Chapter Eight

What a wash-out of a weekend. I missed dance, and swimming. When I woke up on Monday, I felt normal, until I looked in the mirror. It looked like someone had drawn big black circles around my eyes. My nose was still swollen, but it hadn't bled since Friday. Mum and Dad said I was fine to go to school, but I was worried what everybody would say.

Dad said, 'Oh, everyone loves seeing a good bruise … you'll be OK. Just don't go heading any footballs.'

Why did nobody believe the story about the stupid Marks and their vicious game of 'dodgeball'? I couldn't let it rest.

'It was the stupid Marks' fault; they're mean and stupid!'

Dad said, 'Come on, my little panda (I had to accept that one), I'm sure they didn't mean to hurt you.'

'No, they meant to hurt Hakeem. But it's OK they hit me instead, isn't it?'

Mum and Dad and Bella just stared at me. Nobody

said anything more. If they wouldn't believe me, they could at least be quiet.

* * * * *

I could feel everybody's eyes on me as I walked into the schoolyard. The boys were playing football, and I instinctively ducked for cover behind Dad.

Elemenope came over and whispered, 'Wow … are you OK?'

'Yeah. I'm fine. It looks worse than it is,' I said, parroting Mum. It seemed easier to say what people expected me to say.

Hakeem was next. 'Hey, Martha, that looks horrible.' He blushed; I didn't think he meant it to sound the way it did.

I thought, *This could have been you,* but I didn't say it.

When Michael came up to us he just said, 'That Mark … I hate him.'

I waited for him to say something to me. When nothing came, I said, 'Oh … I'm fine … thanks for asking.' He gave me a blank look; I shouldn't have wasted sarcasm on Michael.

* * * * *

For all I had dreaded the week at school, it wasn't so bad. I actually cracked five consecutive fifty-out-of-fifties for rainbow maths.

Mr Newton said, 'Well done, Martha Gibbons. See what you can do when you start to use your brain? Good thing it wasn't damaged by that football.'

It was a good week for Hakeem; he moved up to blue. That was the highest anybody had got so far. And Michael moved to orange with me. I was not-too-secretly delighted to discover the Marks were both still on red. I couldn't avoid a smug little smile at that.

Friday came around again really quickly. It was the day I got promoted, but it was also sports day again. My shirt was lovely and soft (thanks, Dad), but there was a big stain halfway down the front that reminded me of the time I spilled most of a margarita pizza down my front and the tomato stain hung around for a couple of months.

Mum said, 'I might be late to pick you up.'

'Why can't Dad get us? He usually does.' I didn't really want to sound mean, but I was used to Dad being there when we got out of school.

'Dad can't get you,' she snapped, 'because he has to go to an appointment ... and I'm going with him. OK, Miss Busy-body? You'll need to keep an eye on Bella too.'

It was surprisingly OK. Hakeem and Elemenope often had to wait, so we weren't alone. There was a kind of after-school club where some kids – I suppose the ones with both parents working, or something like that – had supervised activities, but we weren't in that. We just hung around.

Hakeem found an old Frisbee and we flung it around all over the playground. Even Bella was having fun and not being too annoying. She was way better than me at catching it. Probably because she didn't get breathless when she ran.

She was so much better at catching the Frisbee that it started to get on my nerves. Why couldn't she even be annoying properly? I started to throw it really hard when it was Bella's turn to catch it, but she still managed to grab it.

I tried being sneaky and flicking it sideways, and then really high. That's what brought the game to an end. Elemenope watched as I threw the Frisbee out of the school grounds, around the branches of the big pine tree that hung over the fence, and onto the roof of the spooky house next door.

I stood, staring at the house; I'd never really paid any attention to it before. It was run-down and kind of mouldy. The roof tiles were all loose and covered in moss and it looked like waterfalls had flowed down the walls in places.

Elemenope said, 'That place is haunted … Michael told me.'

Hakeem said, 'Well, Martha, you know the rule.'

What rule? My face was asking the question.

Hakeem continued, 'You know: if it goes over the fence, whoever threw it has to go and get it.'

I said, 'That's not a rule.'

'Sure, it is. Isn't it, Elemenope?'

Elemenope whispered, 'Yep … afraid so.' She was giggling and nodding her head. I really didn't want to go to the creepy house just to get the Frisbee, but Hakeem and Elemenope were standing there, hands on their hips, looking like nothing was ever going to happen unless I got on with it. Hakeem wore a broad smile as he raised his hand and pointed to the roof of the house.

I stood my ground: 'Well, it's a stupid rule.' I hadn't appreciated that Bella and I had been allowed into a kind of club: the club-of-Hakeem-and-Elemenope-after-school. This was a different social order than the usual school-hours system. We were their guests.

Hakeem said, 'Why don't we all go? I've been keen to have a look at that place for ages.' After-hours Hakeem was a different person. He was bold.

'Won't we get in trouble?' I asked nobody in particular.

Elemenope answered, 'They don't keep a register of us – the spares. Only the kids who are in the after-school club. Our parents never enrolled us. We just hang out here sometimes. Nobody cares.'

So, we climbed the fence. Elemenope was right; nobody stopped us.

* * * * *

It was not elegant. I got stuck on top of the fence for a bit, half over one side, half wobbling in mid-air. Elemenope and Hakeem pulled me over. I landed with a thump on the other side. It was really dark – like the sun had never got to shine there.

We were in an odd space, between the fence and the side of the old stone building, in the dense shade of the pine tree. The ground was soft and slippery, damp and earthy-smelling. There was no path that we could see.

The Frisbee was somewhere on the roof above us, but we couldn't see it. The tree on this side of the fence had no useful branches; we needed a ladder.

'What now, fearless leader?' I asked Hakeem.

'He's not the leader. I am,' said Elemenope. That, at least, was the same after hours. And she still whispered. She headed off along the side of the building, slipping on the rotting pine needles. Hakeem and I went to ground a couple of times. The smell of mouldy vegetation made me feel sick.

We finally reached the back of the house and looked around the garden. The grass was stupidly long and full of weeds that seemed to be in charge. They were really bushes, and some of them had thorns. My skin was starting to itch. I looked at the front of my white PE shirt and groaned; the old blood stain was hidden by fresh mud. I mumbled, 'Sorry, Dad.'

The door looked like it hadn't been opened in a hundred years; ivy had grown all over it and stuck out sideways in patches. The handle was covered in cobwebs. I wasn't going anywhere near that.

Hakeem repositioned his glasses and said, 'There might be a ladder inside.'

'Or a ghost,' whispered Elemenope.

'You're not helping,' I said. 'Why don't we just forget about the Frisbee and go back. Our parents might be here soon.'

Hakeem said, 'Come on ... let's try the door. We've come this far.' And with that, he wiped away a fistful of cobwebs and grabbed the door handle. Something didn't fit. Where were the spiders?

The door was stuck – or locked, more likely. We all put our shoulders to it, but there was no way we were ever going to move it. It didn't help that there was a slimy puddle under the door, making it hard to get any grip with our shoes. I was panting and ready to give up again, but Hakeem and Elemenope wandered among the intertwined weeds, hunting for a window. They really wanted to get inside.

They did it. There was a small window to the right of the never-going-to-open-in-a-million-years door. The woodwork was rotten and the old glass just fell through when Hakeem pushed on it.

We looked at each other. I suddenly wished Michael was with us. Hakeem got a leg over the windowsill, but hesitated as he lifted himself up. He turned back to us and said, 'It's really dark; I can't see a thing.'

I didn't want to go inside at all. I tried again, 'I think

our parents are going to be here any minute. We should go back.'

Elemenope pushed her head through the window beside Hakeem's knee. 'I think there's some light coming from over there.'

I couldn't see where she was pointing; her head and Hakeem's bottom were blocking the window. I still thought we should go, but when Hakeem jumped back down, I felt drawn to look inside. It suddenly seemed silly to have come this far and just turn back. I didn't understand why, but my nervousness had been replaced with curiosity.

I heaved myself up – feet scrabbling for purchase on the stone wall. I stuck my head and shoulders through the window and took a breath of the stale air in the house. I didn't exactly want to be sick, but I felt off-balance.

That was the problem; I lost my balance and tipped forwards. With absolutely no control, I landed on the floor of whatever room this was. It was soft; that was a surprise. I'd expected a hard stone floor but I landed, crumpled, on something that felt like soft carpet. It was squishy and musty-smelling.

Hakeem came through next, then Elemenope. We were all standing in a dark room, but Elemenope was right: there was a faint light coming from somewhere towards the front of the house.

Just then I thought I heard Mum's voice calling. It was muffled and far away.

Elemenope said, 'Hey, Martha … your Mum's calling. We'd better go.'

I didn't understand. Seconds before I really wanted to get away, but then, inside a really spooky old house, I wanted to stay. My stomach was still wobbling and my head was starting to spin. I felt a hand on my shoulder; it made me jump.

Hakeem said, 'Steady, Martha … it's only me. Elemenope's right. We need to go.'

It wasn't easy to pull myself over the window ledge again; Elemenope helped me down. We found a path on the other side of the house that led to the front garden and out a rusty steel gate on to the street.

There was Mum, wandering about the schoolyard, calling my name. There was Elemenope's mum, too, and a man I'd never seen before.

Hakeem called out, 'Hi, Dad … sorry. We're coming now.'

Mum seemed angry and relieved all at once. 'Where have you been?'

Hakeem started, 'Well, there was this Frisbee … and Martha threw it over the fence. And …'

I remembered that was why we went over the fence in the first place.

'Where's Bella?' I asked.

Mum was really impatient with me. 'She's here. Like a good girl.'

Bella poked her head out from behind Mum's skirt and gave me that 'Got-you-in-trouble' look of hers as she said, 'Yes, Martha, where have you been?'

'We went to get the Frisbee. The one *you* missed.'

'You mean the one *you* threw so badly I couldn't catch.'

Mum said, 'Bella said you climbed over the fence after something.'

'We did. It went on the roof of that house.' I pointed at the place next door.

Mum was fuming. 'Well-I-can-believe-there-was-a-Frisbee-and-I-can-see-a-very-dirty-shirt-but-I'm-listening-to-a-story-I-*don't*-believe-we-looked-in-the-garden-of-that-old-house-and-we-called-out-but-you-weren't-there-and-I-have-to-say-I'm-glad-you-weren't-there-because-it-isn't-safe-it's-derelict.' She took a deliberate breath. 'Just tell me where you kids were. Please.'

'Seriously, Mum, we were in the back of that house. We didn't hear you.'

'Well, why were you in the house if the Frisbee's on the roof?'

I had to admit that seemed like a fair question. All I could say was, 'I told you … we went looking for a ladder … really.'

Elemenope's mum said, 'Well, if you're telling us the truth, that's OK.'

'There's no harm done, is there?' said Hakeem's dad, looking at Mum. I think he was wondering how my mum could speak without taking a breath.

I gulped. At least the weird wobbling in my stomach had stopped, but I was feeling really confused.

When I looked again, I could see why Mum didn't believe us. From where we stood, the Frisbee looked really close to the edge; we could have reached it with any number of sticks that were lying around. Why, exactly, *did* we go inside?

* * * * *

That night Dad sat on my bed and put his arm around me. 'Do you know what a parent's main job is?' he asked.

He had the shadow of a smile on his face.

'Embarrassing their kids?'

He chuckled; it was a nice sound I hadn't heard in a while. 'Well, that *is* important, but we try to keep you safe. You know, out of harm's way.'

'Is this about the old house next to the school?'

'Yes, it is.'

I said, 'Well you don't have to worry. I'm never going in there again.'

'Good. It really isn't safe.'

'Why hasn't someone fixed it up?' I asked.

'No idea. Maybe it's just too hard. Maybe it needs to be knocked down. Who knows? The important thing is you stay away from it, OK?'

'OK, Dad.'

* * * * *

I tossed and turned all night. I dreamed I was back in the old house, standing in that room again, but with water up to my knees. The awful stomach-wobbling sensation kept coming, but I didn't want to leave. When I woke up, I felt really hot and sweaty.

Mum said, 'You've obviously caught something from

that terrible house.' She gave me some medicine and I missed dance class.

Dad let me call Elemenope in the afternoon, and her mum answered. She said, 'Elemenope's sick in bed, but maybe you can cheer her up.'

I was not prepared for how difficult it was to have a phone conversation with someone who whispered. Even concentrating really hard I missed every second or third word. From what I could make out, Hakeem was sick too. Maybe we really did catch something in that house.

Chapter Nine

Monday morning brought a new girl to our class: Jemima Waddington-Clarke. She thought she was a celebrity. The first thing she did was ask everybody when their birthday was. I thought, 'Oh, that's nice; she must keep a birthday list.' *Wrong!* She discovered that she was the oldest girl in the class, and from that moment, in *her* mind, being the oldest meant she was the boss.

We learned very quickly that Jemima Waddington-Clarke had horses. Jemima Waddington-Clarke had staff (well, her parents did). Jemima Waddington-Clarke lived in a mansion. Jemima Waddington-Clarke was a huge pain.

At break time, Hakeem was giggling about something. He whispered in Michael's ear and Michael burst out laughing. I needed to know what was so funny, but when I gave Hakeem a quizzical look, he went bright red.

Elemenope looked at the boys and shook her head. She leaned in to me and whispered, 'Boys. Toilet humour.' I must have been looking blank because she needed to explain, 'Don't you get it? Her initials are WC. As in *water closet*. You know: toilet.'

I tried not to smile so Elemenope didn't think I had toilet humour too.

Jemima Waddington-Clarke had taken command of a skipping game in the centre of the playground. Two girls were twirling the rope and calling out the rhyme. They sang about a hippo; they looked at me while they sang it, but I just smiled back.

Jemima stamped her foot and said, 'You're doing it the wrong way.'

The girls stopped and let her barge in. It turned out that the only thing they were doing wrong was not giving in to her. When I next looked over, I saw the same girls swinging the rope so Jemima was in the middle, doing all the jumping.

* * * * *

Mr Newton did his best to introduce Jemima to the class. We had to read out our work on William Shakespeare. I'd actually tried to read some of *A Midsummer Night's Dream*, but it was too weird.

Mr Newton pointed at Jemima, 'Have you read any

of Shakespeare's plays, Jemima?'

She gave him an odd look. It was a cross between her usual look of superiority, and one of poorly hidden revulsion. I got the feeling she didn't like Mr Newton, and that made me dislike her even more.

'Of course. My family has an extensive library.'

'And what have you read? Can you share it with us, please?'

It was Jemima's turn to go red. For once she was silent. She obviously hadn't read anything, or she would have said. She was a liar. The Marks were sniggering. Mr Newton didn't continue with her; instead he pointed at me. 'Martha Gibbons, I know you've tried some. Please tell the class what you think of Shakespeare's language.'

I knew enough of Mr Newton's tricks. He wanted us to be honest, so I didn't mince my words. 'I don't like it; it's hard to understand. It's like treacle.'

Horrible Jemima sniggered and said not-quite-softly-enough, 'Well, you'd know about that, fatty.' I didn't react; I'd been called worse. I didn't actually care about being called names.

Mr Newton must have heard her, but he kept looking at me as he said, 'It's because it was Elizabethan

English. It sounds strange to us, but back then it's how the language was spoken.'

I couldn't see how that was an excuse. I thought Shakespeare was just being a smart alec. Hakeem, of course, had read it. He said, 'No, it's really funny, Martha. Did you know Shakespeare made up lots of words?'

I said, 'That's not right. You can't go around making up words.'

Mr Newton chimed in, 'Actually, Martha Gibbons, Shakespeare had to make up words, because there weren't enough to describe what he wanted to say.'

Hakeem gave me a superior smile. I stuck my tongue out at him.

Chapter Ten

I couldn't stop thinking about *that house*. I rang Elemenope again, and we hatched a plan. I called out to Mum, 'Can I go to Elemenope's this afternoon ... please? It's only two streets away. Please, Mum?'

The plan was for me to walk to Elemenope's for a Sunday afternoon play date. Then we'd ask her mum, who was a lot less strict than mine, if we could go to the shop on the high street, and from there to the recreation ground. We knew she'd say 'yes,' and then we'd go to *the house* instead. It was a perfect plan. What could go wrong?

Mum was looking lovingly at something Bella had drawn. She looked at me and said, 'Only if you promise to behave. And don't eat too much.'

I nodded furiously and lowered my voice into the phone again: 'She said yes. Should we take Hakeem?'

Elemenope said, 'He's still in trouble for disappearing on Friday afternoon.'

I asked, 'How about taking Michael? He's big and strong.'

Elemenope said, 'Let's make it just us two. Who needs boys?'

I would feel a lot braver if we took Michael, but Elemenope had her 'I'm-the-boss' tone coming down the phone, so I went along with her plan. Just the two of us, then.

It was surprisingly easy. Mrs Miller (Miller was Elemenope's last name) even gave us five pounds to spend. That was just too tempting, so we actually went to the shop.

Elemenope said, 'It's good to have an alibi anyway.'

'What's that? Do they sell them at the Co-op?'

She explained, 'If Mum asks any questions, there will be someone to say they saw us in the shop.'

'Oh … I get it.' I thought Elemenope might have done this sort of thing before.

We bought two rolls of Fruit Tingles, two Mars Bars and a huge jelly snake. The chocolate didn't last long, and we shared the snake walking along the high street to the school entrance. We couldn't get through the gate so we walked all the way around to the back street. It was really quiet.

I said, 'Where is everybody? They must be indoors.'

Elemenope said, 'There's a big football match on the telly.'

As we walked past the school fence, we could see the dishevelled front garden of the old house. I stopped; I suddenly didn't want to go any further.

Elemenope asked, 'What's the matter?'

'My tummy feels weird.'

'You're not used to so many sweets … that's all.' How could she think that? I mean: just look at me. Elemenope took the elbow of my coat and pulled me forwards. I didn't want to go on; then I did want to go on. Why couldn't I make up my mind?

The gate creaked open like in a scary movie. The front of the house was just as overgrown as the back, and the grass had never been cut, at least not any time this century. There was half a FOR SALE sign lying by the fence. It was mouldy and grubby; it looked like it had been on the ground for ever.

'Should we knock?' That was me still being nervous.

'Don't be silly, Martha. Nobody lives here.' Elemenope's whispering made it seem like we were doing something wrong. I reasoned that we were: trespassing. We didn't own this place, and whoever did hadn't invited us to visit. And we were about to break in. I was pretty sure that was illegal.

We walked up to the front door. There was something

squishy underfoot, just like at the back. I knocked anyway; Elemenope huffed. There was no answer.

The door was stuck, or locked, and we couldn't budge it. The windows were really dirty. Elemenope wiped one of the panes with her hand, making a circle of less-dirty glass we could peer though. There was just enough light to see into a small front room. It was too dark to see much detail, but it looked like a library, with bookcases going right up to the ceiling.

'Come on,' said Elemenope, and she pulled my sleeve again. We stumbled around the side and stood outside the place where we made our entry on Friday. The door was still closed, but the window Hakeem pushed in had been put back. There were boards nailed over the edges, holding it in place, but it didn't look very sturdy.

Elemenope started pulling at the boards and the bottom one came away.

'What are you doing?' I said. My heart was pounding. 'Somebody obviously does live here. They've repaired the window, and now you've gone and damaged it again. Let's just go.'

'No way. I want a proper look … come on.' And with that she pulled the rest of the boards off and pushed the old window glass back inside. It landed with a squelch on the soggy carpet. She pulled a torch out of her jacket pocket, gave me a grin over her shoulder and pulled herself up and through the window space.

I had to follow. When I landed inside my stomach did that wobbly thing again. I wondered if it was the smell.

Elemenope said, 'Nobody could live here. It's way too smelly and damp.'

I had a sense that we were being watched: that creepy feeling that crawls up the back of your neck and makes you keep turning around. Elemenope obviously didn't have it because she charged straight ahead, her torch beam bouncing all over.

I saw bits of walls, bits of old carpet and cobwebs. There were lots of cobwebs, but no spiders, which was strange but good. I don't like spiders. The floor was damp everywhere, and my trainers were letting water in. I also don't like wet socks.

We squelched along the hallway, heading for the front of the house. I could see where the water got in. There was a crack in the ceiling with big dark patches around it. I made Elemenope shine her torch on it and I remembered why I knew about ceiling stains.

Our old house leaked and Dad was forever trying to fix broken tiles. The ceilings were stained just like this, but not as badly. We had someone come and paint over the stains before we left. I remembered thinking that was odd, because Dad always did that sort of thing.

Elemenope was huffing again, so we headed for the front room. It *was* a library. There were books on shelves that went right up to the ceiling. They were on every wall, only leaving room for the door and the windows.

I had never seen shelves over window frames before; I didn't know that was even possible. I made a mental note to ask Dad to build me some.

I took down a really old brown book, with words on the spine that didn't make any sense. Even though the rest of the house was damp, the books were dry, so someone had been looking after them. I presumed it was the same someone who did such a pathetic job of repairing the window.

I grabbed Elemenope's torch and shone its beam on the cover of the book. I couldn't make out the writing; the letters weren't right. I couldn't even be sure if it was a foreign language – it just looked wrong. I took down another, and it made more sense. The title was at least written using letters of the alphabet, but I didn't know any of the words.

The feeling that we were being watched got suddenly

worse. So much so, I actually called out, 'Who's there?'

I shone Elemenope's torch all around and saw nobody, except Elemenope, who wasn't interested in the books at all. She was sitting in an ancient leather chair with her feet up on a stool, pretending to have a drink. 'I wonder what they were like?' she said.

'Who?'

'The people who lived here. You know … what were they like?'

I shrugged; I wasn't sure we should be using the past tense.

Elemenope said, 'I can see the man sitting here, reading his books and Mrs Whoever bringing him cups of tea and cakes.'

I said, 'How do you know that's how it was? Maybe she had this library and he wasn't allowed in.'

We both laughed as we tried to imagine a couple living in this little run-down cottage with its library of strange books. I had a sudden thought as I looked again at the letters on the book I was holding. 'What if they were witches? Maybe these are spell books.'

'Don't be so silly, Martha Gibbons.' The voice sent an icy shiver down my spine. Elemenope spun around and came face to face with Mr Newton. He seemed smaller than usual. His trousers were dragging on the floor and he didn't seem much taller than Elemenope. Maybe it was the light – or the lack of it.

Elemenope, usually so quick with words, just stood there.

I mumbled, 'Sorry, Mr Newton. We didn't think anybody lived here. We were just having a look …'

'Well, you're welcome to visit, but maybe next time you knock on my door you could wait for me to answer it. I'll have to repair my back window again.'

I said, 'I'm really sorry, Mr Newton. We're really sorry. We really didn't think anybody lived here. We should go.'

'You don't have to, Martha Gibbons … and Elemenope Miller. I don't bite.' There was a pause; I wondered what was coming next. 'It's just that we're … I'm not very good with tools.'

'No, it's OK. We really should go. Our parents will wonder where we are.'

'You didn't tell them you were going housebreaking? It's OK, Martha Gibbons; that's a joke. At least I hope it is.'

The wobbly feeling had come back again; I felt dizzy. I got the feeling that Mr Newton had somehow read my mind. I thought he knew that I wished I could tell if he was being serious or joking. Why else would he say he was joking? I had to sit down.

Mr Newton said, 'You'd better sit down before you fall down, Martha Gibbons.'

Elemenope still hadn't said anything. She looked like she was in a daze. Mr Newton pointed to her, 'Does your friend often impersonate goldfish?'

That made me laugh; Elemenope was standing quite still, her mouth opening and closing, like she was trying to say something, but the words were stuck.

I wanted to say, 'It was her idea,' but I didn't. Elemenope hadn't made me come. She encouraged me when I was nervous, but it was really me who wanted to see more of the strange house. I was happy knowing it belonged to Mr Newton. He seemed to be welcoming me; I got the feeling he was lonely.

Elemenope, and her fish impression, wasn't adding much to the conversation. I was still holding the second book I took down from the shelf. Mr Newton turned his face (well, his mask) to look at it.

'You're struggling to understand the title because it's in Latin. And the other one you looked at is Greek – ancient Greek. You could learn to read them if you wanted to.'

Suddenly I wanted to. I wanted to learn. I'd never really felt like that before. I got the sense that there was a whole lot more knowledge and information all around me. I thought, 'Yes … I want to learn more.'

Mr Newton turned his gaze back to Elemenope. 'I don't think she does. Come alone next time, so we can talk. But ask your parents' permission; don't do things that might frighten them.'

That seemed like an odd thing to say. Why would it frighten Mum and Dad for me to visit a teacher? Maybe he was talking about sneaking off and not telling them where I was going. That would make sense.

'Both, Martha Gibbons … both reasons.'

OK, he was *definitely* reading my mind. I could have been a bit freaked out, but I was actually calming down, and the tummy wobbles were settling too.

'I am happy to expand your learning, but these are strange times, Martha Gibbons. There are people who hurt children and the world has become a suspicious place. So if you want to visit me, your parents have to agree. OK?'

'What do you mean: "people who hurt children"?'

'You know. We do those things on "stranger-danger": not getting into cars you don't know, not sharing personal stuff on the internet. We teach you all that to keep you safe.'

'Yes … OK. But safe from what?'

'From people who might do you harm … and I don't want to burden you with it yet. You're too young.'

I thought, I'm too young? I get that all the time. I'm ten years old. Why won't grown-ups tell me about this stuff. It's all well and good to say they're protecting me, BUT FROM WHAT?

'No need to shout, Martha Gibbons.'

OK, he really was reading my mind.

'What we try to do is protect you until you can protect yourself. I'm not trying to scare you … that's the whole problem. The world is a wonderful place, but, sadly, there are some not-so-wonderful people in it. We need to protect children without scaring them. Is that such a hard thing to understand?'

'I guess not.' I said it, but I didn't really believe it. People were trying to protect me from other people who might want to hurt me. The 'not-so-wonderful people' were in disguise and nobody knew who they were, so nobody trusted anybody and the people who might want to protect you were treated like they're the bad guys and nobody said what the bad guys did, who they were, or what they wanted. Simple. *Clear as mud.*

My head was reeling. I looked at Mr Newton, smiled, and said, 'I think we should go.' I took Elemenope by the sleeve. She seemed rooted to the spot.

'Let me open the door for you; it's easier than the window.'

Elemenope didn't speak until we were out on the street. We looked back at Mr Newton's house; it was all dark inside. Finally she said, 'Wow … that was freaky. I think I fell asleep standing up.'

'No, you were doing a goldfish impersonation. That's what Mr Newton said.'

'Mr Newton? Was he there?'

I said, 'Yes. It's his house. Don't you remember. He spoke to us … about strangers, Latin, ancient Greek. You were there; you stood still. You looked funny.'

'No. Not true. I'd know if I saw him. You're making it up.'

'Are you OK?' I had to ask. She couldn't have forgotten already.

She said, 'Never better. I'm hungry. Oh, look, there's a packet of Fruit Tingles in my pocket. How'd they get there?'

'Are you sure you're OK?'

'Sure. But what are we doing here? What's with the creepy house?'

I was getting worried about her. I said, 'Oh, come on, Elemenope. We were just inside it. It's Mr Newton's house.'

'Wow, Martha, you've got some imagination. I remember going there the other day, but I'm never going there again. Why is there a torch in my pocket?'

Chapter Eleven

I liked Sunday night, even though it was school the next day – we always watched a movie and Dad would snuggle up with us on the sofa. It was Bella's turn to choose and she wanted some stupid baby-thing about fairies.

I didn't want to watch that but Dad said, 'Come on, Martha … it's Bella's turn. She couldn't watch that show last week that you wanted. She misses out all the time on the little-kid stuff that you used to like when you were here age. Let her be a little kid.'

I wondered if that was the same kind of thing Mr Newton was talking about: protecting kids for as long as possible. Maybe Bella really was too young for the things I liked to watch. Or maybe she was just an annoying baby.

I asked Dad, 'Do you and Mum protect me from bad, scary things … the bad people?'

Dad looked surprised. 'Yes, of course we do. Why are you asking that?'

'Oh, no reason.'

* * * * *

That night I had trouble sleeping. I tried to imagine how bad people might do bad things and I thought about shows on the telly where police arrested people, and then I got scared. I remembered a visit from the police.

It was back in London, the day I realised something was wrong. Things were weird straight away because Mrs Jarvis, our neighbour, picked me up from school. There was a police car in the driveway. When I went inside there were two policemen – well, a policeman and a policewoman – sitting at the dining room table with Mum and Dad.

Mum took one look at me and said, 'Straight to your room, Martha.' I didn't even get a 'Hello.' I hid on the landing and listened.

The policewoman said to Dad, 'The window washer won't press charges if you apologise … and buy him a new squeegee.'

Dad's voice was sort of stringy. He said, 'Of course I'm sorry. I'll buy him a new bucket, too. I don't know what came over me.' That was the first time I saw him cry.

I stuck my head around the corner and asked Mum what was going on, but she just waved a hand at me and told me to go and watch telly. Well, I would never look *that* gift horse in the mouth.

Dad didn't tuck me in that night; Mum did. I asked her if Dad was OK.

She said, 'Dad's quit his job. Goodnight, Martha.'

I smiled and said, 'That's great. He can spend more time with me. He can finish that den we've been building for ever …' I stopped because Mum was giving me a look that said this was *not* a good thing.

I didn't get any more information from Mum. Instead it came from the horrible Jessica Cowper. I called her Jessica Cow-Face because she was a terrible, mean gossip and a bully. And she looked like a cow.

Jessica said, 'So, Fatty Gibbons … your dad got out of his car and punched the window-washer person. The police had to go to your house. Did they arrest you for eating all the doughnuts, you hippobottomus?'

I wondered how Jessica Cow-Face knew about this, when I didn't? Not the doughnuts; that was just her being mean. The police. That was private, family stuff.

Jessica said, 'I heard it from my mum, and *she* heard it from somebody who'd heard it from *your* mum. So, you see, fatty … *I* know everything.'

Mum was really angry when I said I knew about Dad

punching the window-washer person. She made me tell her who'd told me. Then she rang Jessica Cow-Face's mother and tore strips off her over the phone. It was much scarier than when Mum was angry with me.

In my bed, thinking about all those changes, I started to wonder if Mum and Dad's 'appointment' last Friday had something to do with it. I decided to ask Mum in the morning. I needed to know, because it seemed to be the reason we left London, but nobody ever talked about it.

I still couldn't get to sleep because I started reliving the move. The car trip dragged on, and on, and on. I wanted to read my book, but Dad said, 'Remember what happened last time.' Nobody wanted that. If I got down on the floor, I could still smell it. I got carsick if I read in the car, but I was so bored. I poked my tongue out at Bella.

I decided to hibernate; I read about animals doing that. Everybody knows about bears, but lots of animals do it, even ladybirds. I had a pet ladybird, and I was convinced it was hibernating. Dad said it was dead, but I knew it was just asleep. It slept right through winter and I checked on it every day. Then I forgot about it. I found the box when we were packing to move, so I opened it, but my ladybird really was dead.

My hibernation didn't go so well. Every time we hit

a bump I banged my head. I growled at Mum to stop hitting bumps, but she said, 'I can't sweetheart … these country lanes are a bit rugged.'

Country lanes? I had to ask, 'Are we there?' I didn't say 'yet.' That was the last car trip, too, and I really didn't want to be put out of the car.

We stopped outside a ragged stone building; it was falling down. I said, 'Please tell me this isn't our house.' Mum gave a nervous little laugh, and I swallowed hard.

'No, sweetie,' she said (which was even worse). 'Our house is the one next door. Look … isn't it lovely?'

I followed Mum's hand. A moan escaped my throat all by itself. The house was awful. I wanted the falling down one instead. I asked Dad, 'Is it going to fall down?'

He said, 'Of course not. A lot of these old places look wonky. The engineer said it's really stable. Look at those stones. How could it fall down?' I was not reassured; and why would I be? Dad knew nothing about buildings. He was a dentist. But, in his defence, our house hadn't fallen down yet.

Chapter Twelve

Monday morning was my least favourite part of the week. It meant getting up early for school and it was the longest possible time before the next weekend. And I had to put up with my annoying little sister being all goody-goody about being ready for school before I was.

Bella was already dressed. She was sitting at the table, colouring again, but at least she was in her own spot. I saw why. My school bag was on the table, and Dad was rifling through it.

'Why do I only find these things out when it's too late?' he squeezed out between clenched teeth.

'What's the matter, Daddy?' I went for cute because if I was a dad and my daughter called me 'Daddy' I could never get mad with her. My logic was way off.

He growled, 'Parent–teacher evening is this week, I've just discovered. Bella had a note in her school bag, so I presume you've got one too.'

Dad finished tipping everything out of my bag. I watched as my pencil case hit the floor, and Elemenope's drawing she did for me last week, and, *oh no,* the information sheet about the parent–teacher interviews we got last Thursday and were supposed to give our parents. And now it was the next week and I was in trouble.

'Well, why isn't Bella in trouble? She didn't give you her notice, did she? No. So why am I the one getting in trouble?'

'Because you should know better. You've been at school longer than she has. You know how it works. Honestly.'

Dad was looking at the two sheets of paper. I thought, *if you want to go through our bags, why don't you do it when we get home from school? It's not my fault you're disorganised. I'm a kid … what's your excuse?* I looked at his face and I was glad I hadn't said it.

Dad ranted on, 'Why do we always find these things out when it's too late?'

I tried again, 'It's not too late, Daddy.'

'OK … but it nearly is. Look. Your teacher interview is tomorrow night. We could have missed it.'

Mum chimed in, calmly for once, 'Yes, but we didn't. So … what time is it?'

Dad quietened down and I watched his shoulders

slump again in defeat. His answer was so soft, Mum had to ask again.

He said only a little bit louder, 'Four-thirty. I suppose *you* can't make that?' Dad was using his new tone. I'd only noticed it in his voice since Mum started work. It made everything he said seem like it was a nuisance.

Mum had a new tone too, but hers was mostly under her breath. She used it to say, 'For-better-or-worse-in-sickness-and-in-health … hah … nothing about go-back-to-a-job-you-hate-because-he-can't-hack-it.'

Mum was looking at the calendar. 'No,' she said. 'I have a late shift in the surgery. But you'll be OK. The girls can play in the schoolyard while you see the teachers. What time is Bella's interview?'

Dad said, 'Four-fifteen. That's surprisingly convenient. I can go from one to the other, I suppose.'

* * * * *

I don't like parent–teacher interviews. Not that I was allowed to attend, of course, but they are very worrying. I like to keep school and home completely separate. I don't like the idea of my two worlds being compared. The very idea of two adults – three if Mum and Dad both went – sitting there talking about me behind my back is totally unfair.

What would they talk about? I had a good idea, and I didn't like it. If I asked about it, I'd hear something vague about how I was good at something and had to work harder at something else. I could have told them that. I was deeply suspicious.

I was especially worried about the interview with Mr Newton. What if he told Dad I broke into his house – twice? Should I come clean beforehand and get in trouble, or wait until after and get in trouble then? But what if Mr Newton didn't tell Dad? Then I'd be confessing and getting into trouble when I didn't need to. It was a dilemma.

I decided to ask Elemenope. After all, she was there with me, and she must have been having the same thoughts.

When I met Elemenope in the playground before school, I took her by the arm and went over to our spot by the tree. I kept staring at the roof of Mr Newton's house.

I asked, 'When's your parent–teacher interview?'

'Tomorrow night. Why?'

I said, 'That's good – we've got time. What are we going to do? Mr Newton's bound to say how we broke into his house. Oh … I'm really worried. What should we do?'

Elemenope gave me a blank look and said, 'We didn't break into his house. What are you talking about?'

'Stop it. We broke into his house yesterday. And on Friday. Only we didn't know it was his house on Friday. He's going to tell our parents and we'll get in trouble because we said we were going to the park and we didn't. *We broke into his house.*'

Elemenope frowned, 'No way. We went into the old place next door on Friday. But that's never Mr Newton's house. What are you talking about? Have you gone mad?'

I just looked at Elemenope. Either she was a really good liar (which I suspected she was), or she really had forgotten. I suddenly remembered what I was thinking before Mr Newton spoke to us. I said, 'Maybe he cast a spell on you.'

She started to laugh. 'You've got some imagination, Martha.'

Hakeem and Michael joined us. Michael seemed to be keeping a protective eye out: for balls, the Marks – I wasn't sure which. He was a big boy, and gentle (except when he wasn't, like when he hit Mark two). I was learning to like him.

I spent the day looking for clues from Mr Newton, but he didn't offer any. He was just his normal self all day. When did I start thinking Mr Newton was normal?

* * * * *

By Tuesday afternoon I still hadn't made up my mind whether to confess to Dad or not. Suddenly it was too late; Dad turned up after school and Bella was all over him like a rash, telling him about some new award she'd just got. What for this time? Sitting still? Breathing?

I couldn't get a word in edgeways even if I wanted to, so the decision was taken out of my hands. I didn't tell Dad and I just had to sweat it out. It could have been worse; we spent the time between pick-up and the interviews at a really nice coffee shop. I had a hot chocolate and a chocolate cupcake with way too much icing: just how I like them.

I didn't even spill anything. It was better having this time without Mum; Dad didn't nag me about eating, and when I chose the biggest cupcake in the display he just smiled and paid for it. It was definitely not the time to mention my new hobby of housebreaking. I told myself it would be all right, but I wasn't very convincing.

We went back for the interviews and the after-school club was in full swing. Hakeem and Elemenope were throwing a ball against the wall.

Elemenope waved and Hakeem called out, 'You two can join in … but only if you don't throw the ball over the fence, Martha.'

I stuck my tongue out at him in a playful way, but Bella said, 'Don't be mean, Martha. Remember you ruined our game last time.'

Bella was annoyingly good at this game, too, so I started throwing the ball really hard and making it bounce awkwardly for her. She still got it. What was with her? I felt really clumsy as I fumbled for the ball; I was sweaty and breathless and Bella was just jumping around all over the place.

Hakeem was trying hard not to laugh. He said, 'Pity we don't still have a Frisbee. You were better with that. No, wait … you threw it over the fence. And, if memory serves, you never got it back. Do you want to hop over the fence and try again?'

I gave him my death stare. It was meant to stop people asking me things a second time. It worked.

'I was just joking, Martha. I never want to go near that place again.'

'Me neither,' whispered Elemenope.

But I had a sudden desire to go back to Mr Newton's house. It felt like there was a secret there, waiting to be discovered.

We must have been playing with that tennis ball for longer than I thought. Dad came out of the main door with a broad smile on his face. He said, 'Thank heavens that's over; let's go home'. I thought lots of things at once: *I'm not in trouble, Mr Newton didn't tell him, my marks aren't too bad.*

Bella asked, 'What did Mrs Johnson say about me, Daddy?'

Dad said, 'She was very pleased with how you pay attention. And you're so well behaved in class.'

I wanted to stick my fingers down my throat. I didn't ask about his interview with Mr Newton. He told me anyway. I had trouble hearing the first bit because my heart was pounding in my ears. I was listening for any reference to breaking in to Mr Newton's house; none came.

I started to relax, until Dad said, 'You know what Mr Newton said to me?' Oh no; I was going to be sick. 'He said he could offer you some private tutoring. He said you're very bright, but you could do better. What do you think of that?'

I was surprised. 'He said I'm bright? Are you sure you were talking about me?' I wasn't sure I knew what private tutoring was, so I asked, 'What would I have to do?'

'Oh, just stay after school … and have an hour or so, maybe once a week. He said it might make you use your full potential. How about that, Martha. He thinks you've got potential.'

I blushed with a mixture of relief and pride. Mr Newton thought I was bright.

The first thing Mum did when she got home was ask all about the parent–teacher interviews. She said they were really important. They really weren't.

Dad said, 'Mr Newton offered to give Martha some private tutoring.'

Mum said, 'Well, I think it's a great idea. It doesn't matter what you want to do, the better your school marks, the more options you'll have later. I think you should do it, Martha.'

'OK.' I was surprised by my own enthusiasm, so I decided to act cool. That worked a treat until I tripped over my own feet and spilled the glass of water I was carrying. Dad and Mum just looked at me; sometimes silence can be worse than shouting.

Chapter Thirteen

There was a buzz of excitement in the corner near the bins when we got to school. I could see Elemenope and Hakeem at the back of a group of kids all trying to see something that Mark One had in his hands.

As I got closer I heard, 'It's a big one / Where did you find it? / That's gross / Is it slimy? I bet it's slimy,' all at once from different voices.

Hakeem turned away and said, 'He's got a newt in a jar ... poor thing. I think it's a great crested newt; they're protected. He's got to put it back. Bet he doesn't.'

I'd never seen a newt up close. I was a bit interested, but Hakeem's anger made me keep quiet. I didn't have to worry; as soon as we got into class, Mark One put the jar on his desk like a trophy. I could see a grey creature with legs and fins wandering about in the water. It looked like a lizard; I didn't see the fascination.

Mr Newton stopped mid-greeting. He said, 'Good morning, children. It must be time for rainbow ...' He stood in front of Mark One's desk.

'What is this, Mark?'

'It's a newt. Isn't it a beauty?'

Mr Newton looked at Mark One. He didn't move, except I got the distinct impression that all of him was moving – sort of quivering.

'And what type of newt is it?'

'I dunno. It's just a big newt.'

'If you're going to bring a protected animal into my class, Mark, the least you can do is know what it is.'

I looked across at Hakeem. He was smiling a little smile that said, 'Idiot … he's got you now.'

'Does anybody know what this beautiful creature is?'

Hakeem's hand shot straight up, and he didn't wait to be called. 'It's a male great crested newt.'

'Good. That's exactly what it is. It's a protected species. It's not for collecting by grubby boys and putting in jars. I'll take that, thank you.'

Mr Newton's gloved hands gently lifted the jar from Mark One's desk and put it on his own.

'Now … rainbow maths. Ten minutes, as usual.'

We settled down to our maths sheets, while Mr Newton sat back at his desk. After ten minutes nothing happened. Normally we were told to stop writing, but not today. I checked the clock; it had been twelve minutes, then thirteen. Something was wrong; Mr Newton was just staring at the newt.

I coughed loudly – a dry, theatrical rasp that got everybody's attention.

'Sorry ... pens down. Swap your work for marking please. I was a bit distracted.'

There was a general twittering of laughter, but the school day got back to normal. Until after lunch; that's when I noticed there were two newts in the jar on Mr Newton's desk.

Without anybody asking, Mr Newton said, 'I found this one in a jar in your locker, Mark. I know you won't mind that I had a look there. It's just that these newts often live in colonies, and I didn't think you seemed very upset when I confiscated the big male this morning.

'What did worry me was that this female was in such a tiny jar she could barely move. Not very nice. Now, tell me, boy: are you hiding any more?'

Mark One looked sullen. Beside him, Mark Two was shuffling his feet.

'Is there something you want to say, Mark

Butcher? Are you part of this newt-smuggling gang?'

Mark Two said, 'I've got newts in my fish tank at home. I got them out of the garden last March. They were all over the grass.'

'Yes, they may well have been. Do you know why?'

Hakeem was jumping out of his skin to answer. When neither Mark offered anything useful, Mr Newton pointed a wobbly finger at Hakeem, who said, 'That's when they mate, sir. The newts all gather around so they can join up. Later the females lay their eggs in a pond or somewhere like that.'

'That's right, Hakeem. They're very vulnerable then. You really should leave them alone.'

Mr Newton stared at the two Marks. I was glad I couldn't see any emotion on his mask. I thought if I could it would be hatred. Teachers aren't supposed to hate their pupils, but at that moment, I thought those rules didn't apply.

'I have a new homework assignment for you two.' Mr Newton was pointing at both Marks. 'I could keep you in after class as a punishment, but I would prefer you to get something out of this.

'You have one week to bring me a five-hundred-word essay on the life cycle of great crested newts.

And don't use Wikipedia. I wrote most of what you'll find there, so I'll know if you're plagiarising.'

The Marks moaned.

Hakeem moaned because in his eyes that was no punishment. He said softly, 'I could do that standing on my head.'

* * * * *

That afternoon was my first tutoring session with Mr Newton, so we went back into the classroom after everyone else had left. He showed me non-verbal reasoning. I liked that; it was nothing like normal schoolwork. It was puzzles and patterns. I really liked trying to work out which cube pattern fitted where.

Mr Newton said, 'It's a subject some other schools do; it's a useful way to get you thinking faster.' When we finished, he said, 'I'll just pop into my house quickly. There's a book I want you to read.'

I hadn't realised there'd be extra reading as well as the tutorial sessions. While I waited on the squelchy doormat, he went through his strange front door, straight into what I recognised as the library. As he entered, I got the feeling that Mr Newton's whole body was wriggling;

the two newts in the jar were going berserk.

He put the jar down and ran a finger along a high bookshelf, going straight to a small, dull blue hardback. 'Have you ever read any Roald Dahl?'

I shook my head and he held out the book: *Matilda*. I'd seen the movie.

'No … read the book. You're going to be my Matilda.'

Chapter Fourteen

I loved it. What a great story. How I'd love to be able to move things just by thinking. There was even a newt; that was funny. I started to wonder again if there might be something magical going on with Mr Newton.

I couldn't wait to tell him how much I enjoyed the book. I couldn't wait so much I decided to visit him on the weekend.

When I told Mum and Dad where I was going, they gave each other an odd look.

Dad said, 'Well … don't be long. I'll come down there in half an hour if you're not home. OK?'

'OK.'

I knocked on the front door and waited an age. When Mr Newton eventually let me in, he seemed really small, disorganised – like his body didn't fit or something.

He gestured to me to come in, then his voice came from over in the corner, 'Come in, Martha Gibbons. What a surprise.'

I must have looked really confused, because I was.

My stomach was turning over. Out the corner of my eye I could see movement. There were things wriggling around on the floor, streaming towards Mr Newton. He was slowly getting bigger – like somebody was blowing up a balloon.

'I think you might have seen my secret, Martha Gibbons. I wonder if you can handle it?'

I was having trouble thinking, let alone speaking. I reached out a hand to steady myself, found the arm of the old leather chair and settled into it.

'Your friend, Elemenope, almost saw my secret, but I knew she would be trouble. So I made her forget. Do I need to make you forget, too?'

I really wanted to find some words. I wanted to say that he could trust me. I wanted to say I'd keep his secret – whatever it was. I liked Mr Newton; it would be a really good time for him to read my thoughts.

'OK, Martha Gibbons, I'll read them. You think I can trust you. But you don't know my secret yet. You're getting there, aren't you?'

'Yes.' It felt like the smallest word I'd ever said. But it was also the biggest. I thought how funny that idea was: how a tiny word could change people's destiny. I started to think lots of different things really quickly.

In my head, I saw people getting married – saying those little words that would change their lives for ever. I saw people saying an even smaller word, *'no,'* and it changing their lives because they missed out on something. It felt like a revelation: *little things matter*. I'd never thought that before.

'You're quite right, Martha Gibbons; little things DO matter. They matter a lot.'

I watched as Mr Newton's clothes crumpled to the ground, and out from the pile slid hundreds, maybe thousands of newts. *I knew it!* Actually, I didn't, but somehow it all seemed logical.

As the last of the clothes settled on the floor, his mask came to rest on top like a doll's face. I was used to seeing activity at the eyeholes; it seemed strange for it to be sitting there, lifeless. I realised it was the newts that animated the man I thought I knew.

'So ... what do you think, Martha Gibbons? Scary? Creepy?'

I shook my head. I wanted to ask all about it; I wanted to ask all about him, them, whatever.

'What you see is made up of eight thousand, seven hundred and fifty great crested newts – give or take. Sometimes the little ones are a bit wayward.

They're the days when I seem smaller.'

I still couldn't speak. I was looking for the source of his voice. There was a silver box sitting on a low table with about twenty newts swarming around it. Was that it?

The wobbly feeling was slowly settling. Then it came back with a vengeance as I heard his disembodied voice again, 'So, did you like *Matilda*? I see you've brought it back. Thank you. It's a particular favourite of mine.

'I don't suppose you saw the inscription in the front. I met Roald Dahl ... fascinating man. He used a lot of his brain. Well, when I say I met him ... I lived in his garden pond for a time.'

I could only nod. But I was starting to have multiple thoughts at once; it was confusing. I noticed the reference to using brains again.

'We'll get to that later, Martha Gibbons. For now, you have a lot to deal with. Your father's going to be here soon, looking for you. Do you want to wait for him? No? It's probably better if you head off.

'It's OK. I can trust you. But you *must* keep my secret; it's important for everybody. OK? Just leave the book on the table. I might read it again myself.'

I thought I heard a chuckle; it wasn't the machine voice, but a kind of trilling, natural sound – soft, like a tiny harmony. It was musical and calming; it made me feel relaxed, and it sent the wobbly feeling away.

The newts started to climb on one another, tails locked around heads, little newts linking into larger ones like puzzle pieces. The ones on the surface started hauling on a shirt and trousers, passing the material up in a series of ripples. It was like watching sails go up the mast of a ship. A little newt at knee level waved at me.

The voice-box machine was carried along the puzzle-piece body and fully covered by a ball of larger newts who pulled on the mask and hat to complete the picture.

I was in a daze as I walked back out onto the street. Dad was hurrying towards me; he waved and I stopped walking. I couldn't decide whether to walk forwards to Dad, or turn around and go back to Mr Newton. I had so many questions.

Dad walked up, smiling. He turned his head to look at the old run-down house as he said, 'That's where Mr Newton lives? I know teachers aren't paid very much, but that place is a dump. Is that where you went that day Mum said she couldn't find you? What's it like inside?'

'Huh? Oh … it's interesting. Mr Newton has a huge library.'

'He's an intriguing man.'

'He certainly is,' I said as I felt hackles rising on the back of my neck. I thought about telling Dad about Mr Newton. He wouldn't believe me; adults never believe things kids see. I decided not to tell him. I wouldn't tell anybody. As I decided that, the hackles subsided and I felt relaxed.

I smiled up at Dad and said, 'So, what movie will we watch tonight, Daddy? Why don't you choose for once?'

He said, 'How about *E.T.*?'

'No!'

Chapter Fifteen

I couldn't wait for my next tutoring session with Mr Newton. But the classes at school were dragging. They seemed extra boring, and a week was *so* long.

Mr Newton kept picking on me. Was he trying not to show favouritism? That was arrogant. What could suggest that I was his favourite? Just because he'd shared his secret with me? That was a burden, not a blessing.

Rainbow maths seemed to have got hard again. I was struggling to get off orange.

Hakeem asked, 'What happens after all the colours, Mr Newton?'

I wondered why Mr Newton hadn't chosen a smart kid like Hakeem to share his secret. Then I realised he didn't choose me; I had stumbled on his secret by accident.

Elemenope came up to me at lunchtime. She said, 'You've been in a daze for days. That's funny: *a daze for days*. I like that.'

It was true; I was distracted. I hadn't been very sociable.

I looked at my friends in a new way. We'd been joined

by Hakeem and Michael, and I said, 'Oh … sorry. I've been thinking about Mr Newton a lot.'

Michael said, 'What? About him being an alien?'

'He's *not* an alien,' I said, probably louder than necessary. They were all looking at me.

Hakeem said, 'Of course he's not. But there *is* something very strange going on. Have you noticed he's sort of … wriggly?'

Elemenope nodded and said, 'I've been trying to tell you, Martha. He does things that just aren't normal. Like his watch … you saw him. It comes out of his pocket by itself. Is he a magician, or a wizard?'

I thought Mr Newton was really cool, if a little creepy still. I couldn't decide whether to share my knowledge with my friends. What if they betrayed him? Would something bad happen? Mr Newton kept his true nature a secret. Why?

I said to Hakeem, 'Can you tell me more about newts?'

Elemenope said, 'Way to change the subject, Martha.'

Michael laughed while he said, 'Given up? You know I'm right.' He walked off in search of a game of football.

Hakeem barely took a breath as he went into raptures about how amazing newts were. 'Do you know,' he said, 'they can regrow limbs if they lose one.'

I said, 'What? Like lizards?'

'Yes. And no. Some lizards drop their own tail to fool a cat or something, and they regrow it. But newts can regrow all sorts of things. It's because they keep their stem cells through their whole lives.'

I *had* to ask, 'What are stem cells?'

Hakeem said, 'We all have them for a while; they're brilliant things. They can grow into anything, but most animals lose the ability to use them as they get older.

'Scientists are working on all sorts of ways to get human stem cells to work, but they're a long way from being able to do things newts can do without even thinking about it. I want to be a scientist; I want to work with stem cells.'

Hakeem *loved* newts. And, apparently, stem cells.

I decided to ask Mr Newton about this. It was funny; even though he was made up of thousands of newts, I still thought of him as Mr Newton. Like he was a normal person – which he wasn't.

* * * * *

Dad opened his laptop. He said, 'I see you've been researching newts. Is it for a school project?'

'Sort of,' I said. I didn't want to give anything away

and I resented him checking my search history. I wanted my own computer, but Mum and Dad kept saying no.

He shrugged and got onto a real-estate website. He said, 'I thought that house of Mr Newton's looked familiar; it was one of the places advertised when we were looking at properties to buy here.'

I looked over his shoulder, and there was a picture of Mr Newton's house on the screen: '"Two-bedroom cottage in prime location – needs work". I'll say.'

Underneath the ad were a whole lot of comments from people who had viewed the house. The last one said nobody could do anything without a special certificate from the environment agency, because rare newts were found breeding in a pond and in the cellar. I didn't know there was a cellar.

Dad said, 'So how come Mr Newton's living there?' I needed to think fast.

'Oh, he says he owns it, and he's trying to get all the environmental thingies sorted out.' *Genius.*

* * * * *

Wednesday afternoon couldn't come soon enough. I waited until everybody had left before I went up to Mr

Newton's desk. He looked at me and I thought he had forgotten the tutorial.

'No, Martha Gibbons, I haven't forgotten.'

I smiled at him; I wished he could smile back. In my mind, he did. Was I starting to read his mind now?

'No. It's just your imagination. But that's a good thing. Imagination is what makes children so much better than adults.'

My head was full of questions. The first one out of my mouth was, 'Why me?'

'Why not you?'

'Well … I'm not very smart. At least, not like Hakeem.'

'Do you think this is about knowing facts and figures? If it was, then, yes, someone like Hakeem would be ideal. But it isn't; it's about so much more. You have a real spark of imagination, Martha Gibbons. The world needs that more than you know.'

I wasn't sure that was a satisfactory answer, but it seemed like the only one I was going to get. At least for the time being. Mr Newton pulled out my worksheet from our last tutorial and studied it. How did he – they (I was really confused, but I decided on 'he') – how did he read?

I didn't get an answer to that thought as we started

on maths: three-column additions with decimals. I was determined to show him I was smart, even if he said it wasn't important.

'That's the spirit, Martha Gibbons. Impress me.'

We fiddled about with maths for half an hour, then Mr Newton said, 'So far, so good. I can see you're itching to ask a whole lot of questions. You've worked hard, so, as your reward, how about I tell you more about me?'

I nodded so hard it felt like my head might fall off.

'That happened to me once ... tricky situation. I soon learned to control it.'

Mr Newton was by the window. As he slowly walked back towards me, he said, 'Newts have been trying to influence human behaviour for hundreds of years.'

I was really struggling; part of me just took all this information in my stride while another huge part of me rebelled at the very thought of little creatures ganging up to impersonate a human being. It was unbelievable.

'It is an incredible story, Martha Gibbons, but if humans were not so arrogant and stubborn, we wouldn't need to do this.'

A sudden thought popped into my mind. It was too obvious, but I couldn't help asking, 'So, are you *Mr*

Newton because you're a collection of newts? Is that it? I get it now.'

'Maybe in the beginning, but that was a long time ago. I don't have generations the way you do; I update every year as our babies get big enough to take part. That way we always have a mix of experience and youth. We don't have to remember what it's like to be young, and we respect our elders. Not like humans. Have you heard of Isaac Newton?'

'Sure … the apple, gravity … all that.'

'Hmm … that's a start. We did a lot more than that. Why do you people only remember the apple?'

'Wait. That was you?'

'Yes, it was. I'm Isaac Newton. Well, an updated version of him. That was the last time we tried taking human form. It got a bit tricky after that, and we did a lot of writing under other names. We decided a few years ago to try again, but it's still clumsy: the mask, the gloves, the hat. You know, it's hard keeping it all together.'

'I had noticed. Actually, I'm not the only one. But I don't understand. If you're so smart, why would you be a primary school teacher? Why not be a politician or something like that?'

'We don't want a big profile. The new plan is to work with people who still have a chance. People who can still see things the grown-up world refuses to acknowledge. If we can influence children to grow up to be better than the previous generation of humans, then the whole world has a chance.

'Humans have wrecked the environment. Who do you think started all the environment agencies around the world? It wasn't humans. Well it was, but we had to push them into it … make them think it was their own idea. Honestly, Martha Gibbons, we need your generation to do big, bold things to fix the world before it's too late.

'In the beginning, it seemed like a good idea to let humans run the earth. Big brains … that was the idea. But it's a huge problem. We have a huge dumb problem.'

A little part of me was insulted.

'Please don't take it personally, Martha Gibbons. You're one of the few I think might have a chance. You see the problem with humans is you only use 10 per cent of your brain. Now, it's a big brain – just over a kilogram in most adults. It's about 2 per cent of body weight in a lean individual, so a fit 70-kilogram person's brain weighs about 1.2 kilograms. Got that? Hold that figure in your mind.'

I was struck by a thought: if the brain made up 2 per cent of body weight, why weren't fat people the smartest people on the planet?

'We'll get to that.' I couldn't get used to having my mind read; it was off-putting to say the least.

'Now, a fully grown great crested newt has a brain that represents a little over 3 per cent of its body weight, so a 70-kilogram newt would have a brain weighing about 2.1 kilograms. That's double the weight of a human brain. That's a good start, don't you think?'

I nodded my head. I thought I could see where this was going. 'So, with all you newts working together, you can be twice as smart as a human. Is that it?'

'It's a little more complicated than that. Like I said, it's a good start. Now, add in the fact that we use 100 per cent of our brains. That's a powerful multiplier, isn't it?'

I nodded again. Sometimes when Mr Newton spoke, there was no point in interrupting with words.

'And there's something else. We're still not really sure how it works, but when we work close together, like this pretend human you see, our brains actually magnify the effect ... so we have all sorts of abilities that don't fit in the simple physical world.'

'Like reading minds?'

'Yes ... and changing memories. That's very useful.'

My head was starting to spin; this was science fiction.

'And it takes a lot of coordination to make our composite mass stand upright and walk like a human. We sacrifice a little bit of brain power to appear more acceptable to you.'

'It's not really working.' I was kind of joking, but not a lot. Mr Newton still looked pretty weird.

'You'd be surprised, Martha Gibbons. Most people accept the narrative. They've even come up with some plausible stories to explain my appearance. Do you know, I've never given anyone an explanation of my appearance? They do that all by themselves. That's one human characteristic we encourage: imagination.

'Now think, Martha Gibbons, how wonderful it would be if you started to use more than 10 per cent of that big brain of yours. Imagine what you could achieve.'

I tried. It hurt.

'No, that's a headache. You haven't had enough water today. Water really is the elixir of life, you know.'

The tutorial hour was well and truly over. Mr Newton gave me some maths homework to do before our next session. I really wasn't focused on that, but I thanked him and walked outside. Dad was waiting for me, and I took his hand.

He asked, 'How was your session with Mr Newton?'

I shrugged, and managed, 'OK, I guess.' I couldn't say what I was really thinking because I was still struggling to take it all in. I wanted to go home, have something to eat and just think. I wanted to use some of my *big brain.* But my big brain had a big headache.

* * * * *

Dad asked, 'Why are you suddenly so interested in amphibians?'

'I'm not,' I said, out of habit; I didn't know why I was lying. There wasn't a problem with being interested in amphibians.

I got a bit snappy. 'Anyway, what are you doing spying

on my internet search history again? What business is it of yours?'

Dad had his 'you're disappointing me' face on. It was very effective. I had to apologise and cover my tracks. 'Oh … do you mean the newts and bullfrogs stuff?'

He said, 'Yes … like I said … how come you're so interested in amphibians all of a sudden?'

I liked 'all of a sudden'; it sounded old-fashioned and mysterious.

I said, 'Oh, you know, for school.' I hoped that would be enough. It was; Dad moved on to something else and I tuned out.

I'd been looking up brain sizes in different animals. I was trying to make sense of what Mr Newton told me the other day. That was a problem, because the further I was from him, the more trouble I had remembering what we'd been talking about.

I remembered him saying how newts used all their brain, and humans only used a bit of ours. What did we do with the rest of it?

The internet was amazing. I discovered that bullfrog brains were bigger than newt brains; they were actually nearly double the size. So that should make bullfrogs really smart. Well, really smart if they all got together the way Mr Newton's newts did. I wrote that down in my homework book.

Then I looked up Isaac Newton. There was a picture of him – well, a painting – and it looked exactly like Mr Newton. Except he had hair. I realised it was a wig: one of those weird old wigs people wore back then. *Clever.*

Chapter Sixteen

Mum said, 'I've been talking to the dietician in our practice.' I gulped, but said nothing. What would be the point? I knew she wasn't finished. 'We need to really sort out your diet, sweetheart.' That was ominous, because Mum only called me 'sweetheart' when there was something coming she knew I wouldn't like.

'Your weight is a problem, Martha.' *No, it really isn't.* 'You eat way too much junk food.'

What was 'too much'? I suspected any was too much in Mum's current mood. I got the feeling I wasn't being given a choice in this, so I decided to pretend to go along with her. I feigned interest. I found that word in a book last week, and asked Dad what it meant. He waffled on about pretending to do something. I didn't think he really knew, so I looked it up in my *Oxford Pocket Dictionary*. They must have had really big pockets in Oxford.

We were in the sitting room, with the TV off. I realised I didn't spend a lot of time just with Mum. That all ended when little-miss-never-in-trouble arrived five years ago, and monopolised everybody's time.

Mum said, 'I'm trying to get you to be healthier, sweetheart.'

I just nodded. I knew I couldn't fight this openly. Mum reeled off a list: ice cream, biscuits (well, blame Dad: 'Mr biscuits-every-day-for-afternoon-tea'), chocolate, sweets, crisps, sausage rolls, chips.

I tuned out. My eyes must have glazed over because Mum said, 'Are you paying attention, Martha?' I nodded again, limply. She followed up with, 'Really, Martha. I'm trying to save your life.'

It didn't feel like it – *ruin* my life, more likely. But I knew Mum; the die was cast.

* * * * *

Friday got off to a strange start, even for St Finbar's. We were in our lines, all neat and straight, with the ferocious Mrs Gnash watching us, when the unthinkable happened.

Jemima Toilet (that's what I decided to call her) dropped her bag, picked it up and dropped it again, causing a traffic jam. Mrs Gnash should have exploded, like she did with me on my first day. She didn't. She walked up to Jemima Toilet and instead of blowing her whistle in her face, she offered her a cupcake. *A cupcake!*

In class, Mr Newton couldn't get us to calm down; everybody was talking about the strange thing that had just happened.

Mr Newton asked Jemima, 'Can you tell me what happened outside, in the line this morning?'

She said, 'Mrs Gnash gave me a cupcake. What a nice lady.' That showed how little *she* knew!

'May I see the cupcake, Jemima?'

'Of course,' she said, her voice all sweetness (yuk). 'I haven't eaten it yet. I'm not a pig.' Those last words were aimed at me. I mean really aimed; she spat them in my direction.

'This looks incredibly sweet. Buttercream icing ... chocolate buttons in the middle. Could I keep this?'

Jemima Toilet looked crestfallen, but her pride was at stake. She couldn't keep up her attack on me if she asked to have the cake back. That cake was exactly how I like them. My mouth watered at the thought of biting into it. Really, I could just eat the icing – the cake was no more than a way to get the sugary goodness to my lips, but people would frown at me if I just had the icing on a spoon.

My icing-on-a-spoon fantasy was interrupted by a huge noise from next door – Mrs Gnash's room. It was a cheer; we'd never heard that before. Mr Newton was still struggling to get control, but he stood at his full height, which seemed to make him thinner, and called out, 'OK, you lot. Rainbow maths, with a twist.'

That got our attention. Hakeem asked, 'What's the twist?'

I thought, *It can't be good; it is maths, after all.*

'The person who scores the best result will go to class six to find out what all the commotion is about.'

I was conflicted. I wanted to do well for Mr Newton, and I really wanted to know what was going on next door, but I definitely didn't want to walk into Mrs Gnash's class. I decided to make a deliberate mistake.

I wasn't the only one. Hakeem made two mistakes, which was a first for him. As it turned out, Jemima Toilet was either stupid or more scared than the rest of us, because she came equal bottom with Mark One. I couldn't believe it; I'd come top. I should have made more mistakes!

I knocked on the door; my knees knocked too. There was a moment's silence, then a shrill, 'Come in.'

I opened the door as if the-most-frightening-thing-in-the-world was on the other side. It was. As I stepped into Mrs Gnash's classroom, all the kids turned to look at me. They were eating huge cupcakes with thick icing. What on earth was going on?

Mrs Gnash turned her creepy gaze on me. She was sitting down, so her great height was not so terrifying, but she was looking through thick glasses that made her eyes look huge. Maybe her eyes really were that big; they seemed too big for her face. Her voice was sharp and scratchy, 'Well, well … Martha Gibbons, isn't it? Class five, yes? What can I do for you?'

She scared me to death at the best of times, but what was going on with her now? She'd flipped. I folded my arms across my chest; then I unfolded them and held my hands where my lap would be if I were sitting down. I shifted my weight from one foot to the other. I couldn't speak.

'Come on, child, spit it out.'

'Um, Mrs Gnash … I'm sorry to trouble you. Mr Newton wanted to find out what was going on in your classroom. It's just … it's just … it was very noisy, is all.'

Mrs Gnash beckoned me to her desk. Her fingers were ridiculously long. As I approached, she opened a huge cake box on a table beside her desk. There were more cakes, all colours, with huge dollops of buttercream. My mouth was watering again.

'Help yourself, child. I made them myself.' That made me nervous, but I reached in and grabbed an enormous cupcake with blue and white icing. It was really heavy; that's a good sign. I know that unless the cake is really bad, the heavier a cupcake is, the more icing. It was too good to be true.

I was clearly looking doubtful. Mrs Gnash said, 'They're not poisonous. Take another one. Take one for Mr Newton. Go on.' I didn't need to be told twice. I took another heavy one, with yellow icing.

I regained my composure enough to say, 'Thank you,' then I realised I hadn't found out anything. Well, nothing more than Mrs Gnash had completely flipped and become really nice. But I still didn't trust her. There was a tingling feeling in the back of my neck; it felt like a warning.

I didn't ask the question I should have asked, but Mrs Gnash answered it anyway. 'It's my birthday, Martha. Where I come from, we give presents and cakes to other people on our birthdays. It's a … tradition.'

I found myself thinking about where she came from: *On your planet, you mean, you scary monster.* I managed not to say that. I was staring at the cakes and feeling unnaturally hungry. It was as though the cakes were calling to me, even more than cakes normally do.

I did manage to come out with, 'Thank you, Mrs Gnash. I'll let Mr Newton know.'

As I stepped away, I started to think more clearly. Mr Newton obviously didn't trust Mrs Gnash, or her cakes. I suspected he'd confiscated Jemima Toilet's cake to test it. He didn't know she'd given me another cake – another two cakes. I stood in the corridor and ate the cake with blue and white icing. It was delicious: everything a fat cupcake with lots of icing should be.

I thought about how Jemima Toilet nearly had one of these, and how I could give her the one in my hand. I thought I really should, but then I thought about how mean she'd been, when she hadn't even met me properly. She didn't know I had two cupcakes; she probably wouldn't appreciate its rich, sugary beauty. So I ate it. It was even better than the first one.

Chapter Seventeen

'You know, Martha, nothing tastes as good as being thin feels.' That was Mum's latest dig at me.

I didn't get it for so many reasons. First of all, Mum was not that skinny. OK, she wasn't as chunky as me, but she was no supermodel. Secondly, how could she say nothing tastes that good? Had she never had a Mars Bar? A chip sandwich? A sausage roll? Then I wondered if thinness had a taste; it probably tasted like water.

I sometimes ate a whole packet of Penguin biscuits; I like the ones with caramel centres. And what about ice cream? Last time we went to the seaside I had a salted caramel double cone. Ice cream can be tricky; there are so many choices: hard, soft-serve, with or without a Flake (actually, that's not a choice. Who would choose to not have the Flake? Mum, obviously).

I watched her sometimes, trying to understand why she did things. Like when she was offered a chocolate, and she'd say, 'No thanks.' Who does that? Most of the time I had to sneak chocolate, so when somebody offered you some, why on earth would you ever say no?

I did, sometimes, have trouble with clothes. Take tights, for example: they sagged around my ankles because I had to wear the size that went around my waist, but then they were too long. Who made these clothes? Have they never seen kids like me? And then there were the jumpers with sleeves that were too long. Either that or the sleeves fitted, but the middle bit squeezed me to death. How hard is it to make clothes that fit people?

Mum said it wasn't about the clothes. She said she was trying to 'save my life', but I was getting a bit tired of that. I said, 'I'm a kid. I'm not dying any time soon. That's not the natural order. It goes: grandparents, then parents, and then, once your parents die, then you have to think about healthy things so you don't just die.'

Mum said, 'That's not right. What you do and eat as kids has an effect on your bodies as you grow, and you can get sick if you don't eat properly.'

So, she had talked to the dietician. *Great*. They were ganging up on me.

* * * * *

Bella was spying on me. Any chance to get me in trouble, she was there. At least, having our own rooms meant I could have secret food that she didn't automatically see. Every time Mum got some biscuits, I waited until the packet had been opened, and I grabbed a couple when nobody was looking, and hid them in the tin under my bed.

I used to just eat them straight away, but with everybody on the lookout for 'evil, fat, Martha', I had to ration them. I got hungry at night, especially when Mum was being a real control-freak over dinner. My puddings were definitely shrinking. I used to get two scoops of ice cream, then just one, and it looked like a hollowed-out one at that.

So, rather than grumble – that got me nowhere – I just went up to bed, and when the lights were out I'd sneak whatever I'd managed to hide in my tin. Sometimes I couldn't wait and I'd ask to go to bed early and read. That was genius; nobody argued with me wanting to read.

I've always been a hungry reader; I love books. But I liked to eat while I read, too, and if I'd had a poor pudding I could sneak off to bed and have something good to eat while I buried my head in a book.

I nearly came unstuck once when Dad came in to

check on me and I was reaching under the bed to open my tin. 'What are you doing, honeydew melon?' It didn't help that most of his names for me were food-related.

'I dropped my bookmark,' was all I could come up with. It was rubbish, because my bookmark was still in the book – in plain sight – calling out *liar* at the top of its cardboard lungs. Fortunately, Dad didn't notice. My heart was racing so hard, that after he left my appetite took a whole ten minutes to return.

Then there was the time Dad came in to talk to me about girl scouts. He actually meant Brownies, but I think he didn't want to say that because he knows how hard it is for me to walk past a brownie.

The point of that conversation was to get me interested in physical activity. I was physically active; I walked to and from school every day, I walked up stairs, I played games with my friends. OK, I didn't go in for long-distance running or tennis, but I did ballet and swimming. That was enough, wasn't it?

I overheard Mum giving Dad a lecture about my 'eating habits'. She did sound properly worried. But if I wasn't worried, why should she be? I know she's a doctor, and doctors these days are all about healthy diets. Maybe she was embarrassed by me. Maybe she thought if lard-bottomed huge patients of hers saw me, and found out I was her daughter, they wouldn't take her seriously.

Then I thought maybe I could blackmail her with that idea. I thought better of that straight away. Dad I could blackmail, but Mum? Not a chance.

Chapter Eighteen

It was the last week before half-term; everyone was excited about what they were doing in the week off.

Hakeem said, 'I'm going to science camp.'

I said, 'Oh, are you sleeping there?'

He gave me a look and said, 'No, we're not going camping. It's a study camp; we're going to spend five days at the museum. It's going to be great.'

'So, it's not really a camp, then.'

I thought: *Fun? Not.* But I didn't say it because it was right up Hakeem's street.

Michael said, 'Well I'm going to football camp.'

I asked him, 'Will you be sleeping there?'

He said, 'No, it's at the rec. There's nowhere to sleep there.'

I couldn't help myself, 'So, it's not a camp either. Why do they call these things camps?'

When he said, 'The Marks are going too,' I felt sorry for him.

Elemenope said, 'Well, I'm going to music camp.

Before you say anything, Martha, we're going to London. Mum's going too, so it does involve sleeping somewhere else. What about you?'

'Mum's organised for Bella and me to go to ballet camp. And, no – no sleeping there either.'

We all had a chuckle at that. It wasn't that funny, but why *were* these things called camps?

It was going to be four hours a day for the weekdays of half-term. I didn't want to go. I liked ballet, but did I really have to do the camp with my little sister? It was too much. I wondered if it was too late to sign up for the science camp. What was happening to me?

* * * * *

Ballet camp was surprisingly OK. I had a kind of friend at ballet, Juliette; she was what my mum called 'lissom'. I thought she was skinny; but next to me in a leotard, everybody was skinny.

We learned some lovely moves, and even did a real dance: the *Dance of the Sugar Plum Fairy*, which was proper ballet. Mum had been promising to buy me a new leotard for ages, but she hadn't got around to it. The one I was wearing was way too tight, and I was bulging out of it in all the wrong places.

I heard one of the other mothers snigger and say, 'Oh look. It's the dance of the sugar lump fairy.'

We made a plan. As I got near that mum, Juliette called out, 'Martha, your slipper's undone.'

I bent over right in front of the rude cow, and when I stood up, I did a little shimmy for her too. Served her right!

We did craft as well. That was a very good thing because Mum hated mess. She told us she liked the things we brought home, but she never even looked at mine. She never wanted us to do craft, so it was nice to use glue sticks and sparkles and paint without getting scowled at the whole time. We were supposed to make dancers and fans and door-hangers, but I made an Egyptian sarcophagus and put a tiny mummy inside. I made it for Mr Newton.

And we got to take good lunches. I guessed it was because we were on holidays and Mum felt guilty because she was working. We had lovely, guilty, crisps and chocolate biscuits.

Dad was on driving duty; that was not so good. He pretended to be relaxed about it, but I could tell he wasn't. He was really snappy with us in the car. And one day, on the way home, he even snapped at Bella.

She shoved a fairy napkin-ring holder made out of a toilet-roll tube and plastic lace into his face. He yelled, 'Isabella! Get that stupid thing away from me. Can't you see I'm trying to drive?'

Bella was so surprised she forgot to cry and I was stunned. We just *never* heard Bella's actual name. I gloated. Just a little bit. I wanted to do the crawly thing she did and show him how much better behaved I was, but I realised I didn't even know how to do that. I just smiled to myself.

Half-term ended without me noticing that it was too long or too boring; I was actually looking forward to school. There really *was* something strange going on with me.

* * * * *

The minute we walked in the school gate, I knew something was very wrong. There was a huge digger in Mr Newton's back garden, and men were putting up scaffolding around his house. I ran out the back gate and there it was: a builder's sign.

It said, A SMITH – MASTER BUILDER. There was

a phone number and underneath a proud statement: ANOTHER BRILLIANT RESTORATION. Worse was to come.

When we went into class, we had Mrs Gnash. She looked ten feet tall, like her head and shoulders were rising out of a skyscraper. Where was Mr Newton? There was a hum of panic which stopped as soon as Mrs Gnash opened her mouth. Everyone was scared of her, even the Marks.

'Good morning children,' she rasped. If she was waiting for our chorus of greeting, it didn't happen; we were all too stunned. She didn't seem to notice, but I sensed her voice went just a touch higher. It was a harsh sound.

'As you all should know, I'm Mrs Gnash. I will be taking your class today as Mr Newton is absent.'

I waited for an explanation. None came. She didn't say why Mr Newton was away, or for how long, or if he was sick or on holidays, or anything. I wanted to know; I wanted to ask her, but she scared me.

I didn't have to wait long. Jenny Harrison piped up, 'Is Mr Newton all right, miss? Will he be away for long?' It seemed a reasonable couple of questions, but apparently not to Mrs Gnash.

'I don't know, child. He didn't show up this morning.

No explanation. And now I am in front of your class. You will have me until we can get another teacher.'

I wanted to ask about her own class, but I didn't dare. She answered me without knowing it. 'Now, work quietly in your … Egypt, I think your class is doing … in your Egypt workbooks while I go and check on my own class.' I'd brought my sarcophagus to show Mr Newton, but I left it in my desk. I wasn't about to share something special with *her*.

Mrs Gnash sighed loudly as she walked out our door. She stopped, turned her head, and hissed, 'I'm leaving the door open, so no noise. I have *very* good hearing.'

If Mrs Gnash meant 'absolutely no noise' she would be disappointed; there was quite a bit of noise. It was like a hum made up of, 'Where's Mr Newton? / Why isn't he here? / Does anybody know anything? / Bet he's gone back to his own planet / How long do we have to have Mrs Gnash?' and a lot of groaning.

The hum got gradually louder and louder until the head teacher came in. Miss Slider had been the head for ever. She was ancient. She just stood at the front of the class, waiting to be noticed. That could be difficult, because as well as being ancient, she was tiny; she was no more than a couple of inches taller than me.

Miss Slider's voice was soft and velvety as she said, 'Children, please be quiet. There are other classes trying to work. I'm sure Mrs Gnash has given you some work to do, so please get on with it – in silence.'

She was standing right in front of me. Her whole outfit looked like it came off the ark, and I was overcome by the smell of mothballs. I wondered if the mothballs were for her clothes or for her.

I was made bolder by her small size, so I asked, 'Miss Slider, will Mr Newton be away for long?' My words sounded all slow and drawn out.

'I really don't know, Martha. I haven't heard. I'm sure he'll let us know soon.'

Miss Slider just stood there, and I felt leaden – heavy. It felt like time itself had slowed down. The hum started up again but I kept quiet.

Elemenope was whispering rapidly. She dug me in the ribs and pointed at the teacher's desk. How had I not seen it before? There was a note written on the bottom of the blackboard in Mr Newton's distinctive, wobbly, handwriting: *Save the newts.*

* * * * *

At break time, we were in our usual groups. Hakeem was prattling on about the dinosaur project he'd started at camp, but Elemenope interrupted him to ask, 'What does he mean: "save the newts"?'

'What does who mean?' Hakeem had obviously not seen the blackboard message.

I said, 'I think Mr Newton left us a message on the blackboard. It says "save the newts".'

Hakeem said, 'No, I've got a sticker on my lunchbox that says that. They're endangered – newts are – we should all be saving them.'

Elemenope said, 'I don't think that's what it means. Martha, do you know?'

We didn't get to discuss it much before a football landed in the middle of us. Michael trapped it and said, 'Watch this. We did this at camp.' He got the ball onto the top of his foot and flicked it in the air, then he kicked it over his head – straight back at Mark Two.

I was impressed, even though I had no interest in football. Mark Two took the ball on his chest, let it run down to his knee, then flicked it at Mark One. He missed it completely, and I couldn't help laughing. He thought he was so cool, but he didn't look it as he stumbled after the ball.

'What are you geeks looking at?' Mark One snarled as he ran past. Hakeem reacted; he really shouldn't have. 'Didn't you go to football camp, Mark?'

Mark One stopped. He had his hands on the football at last. 'No. I spent the week working with my Dad.' We must have all looked blank; he felt the need to elaborate. 'Over there. He's going to renovate that dump next door.'

My stomach did a backflip as the meaning of the builder's sign fell into place. 'Your dad's "A Smith"?'

'What of it, fatty?'

'Your dad's a builder? And he's working on Mr Newton's house?'

'It's not Mr Newton's house. It's derelict. Dad bought it ages ago, but he wasn't allowed to do anything because of the stupid newts. So, we moved all the newts. And now Dad can rebuild it. It's going to be great.'

Hakeem said, 'You moved the newts?'

'Yeah. We put them in ponds and parks – you know, the rec ground – all over.'

Panic rose from my stomach to my throat. I said, 'Ponds and parks? Where?'

Mark One said, 'What's it to you, fatso?'

'Hey!' said Hakeem. 'She's got a name!'

I barely heard him, I needed answers. 'And what

about the books? What did you do with all his books?'

'All who's books?'

My frustration made me spit, 'Mr Newton's books. He's got a whole library in there ... all sorts of things. Where are the books?'

Mark One said, 'I dunno. I guess they'd still be there. Dad's just started working on the outside. He's got to fill in all the stinky old ponds first. He said we'll clear out the rotten insides later.'

I was fuming; I started to feel sick. Mr Newton had been scattered. I had to save him and I was going to need my friends' help.

Mark One wandered off, and I looked in turn at Elemenope, Hakeem and Michael; I took a deep breath, then another one for good measure. Before I could speak, Hakeem said, 'We've got to find those newts and protect them.'

I said, 'Guys, there's something you should know. I ... Mr Newton ... that is ...'

Hakeem laughed, 'Well, spit it out, Martha. What is it?'

'Mr Newton's not who you think he is.'

Michael said, 'I've been trying to tell you: he's an alien.' He had a look of triumph as he went on, 'He's gone back to his mothership, or his planet or something. But what does this have to do with newts?'

I said, 'Promise you won't tell anyone?'

Nobody said anything.

I said it through clenched teeth, '*Promise* me you won't tell anybody. *Please*.'

Hakeem said, 'Wow, OK, Martha.'

Elemenope crossed her heart and said, 'Promise.'

Michael nodded.

'He's not an alien. He's made of newts. Thousands and thousands of newts.'

Hakeem's eyes widened, 'No. That's not possible. Is it …?' His voice trailed off.

Elemenope was doing her goldfish impression again, and Michael said, 'Yeah, right. Alien newts.'

I said, 'No, seriously. Listen, guys; it's the truth. I've seen him. So have you, Elemenope, but you decided to forget about it for some reason.'

Hakeem looked like he was thinking – hard. He took his glasses off, polished them on his shirt tail, and put them back on. Then he did it again. Finally he said, 'He is wriggly, isn't he? And I've never actually seen his eyes behind his mask.'

I said, 'Exactly. He says all those newts working

together can make him look human, and we don't know any different so we assume he is. Human, that is.'

Hakeem was warming to the idea. He said, 'And his voice? We all know that's a machine. But how does he make it work?'

Elemenope spoke up, 'If you're right – and I'm not saying you are – but if you are, then we should talk about him as "them", shouldn't we? How many newts is he?'

'I can't remember exactly. I think he said eight thousand and something.'

Michael said, 'Why would you believe him? An alien would obviously lie. Newts? Ridiculous.'

I was getting exasperated. 'I've seen him … them. It's true.'

The bell rang. I needed to keep explaining about Mr Newton, but when we got back into class, there was Mrs Gnash, glaring at us. Was it just my anxiety, or did she always look hungry? I realised I was starting to panic, and the more I looked at her, the more I knew we had to get Mr Newton back – and soon.

* * * * *

I passed Elemenope a note. It was folded over, with Hakeem's name on it. She knew the code; she wouldn't open it. She passed it to Jenny, who passed it to Hakeem.

I couldn't concentrate until I got the return in my hand, but by then Mrs Gnash was staring at us with those horrible big eyes behind those horrible big glasses. I had to wait.

Hakeem's note said: *I have a plan. Meet me after school.*

His plan was too simple: find out where Mark One put all the newts and bring them back. 'But where to?' I asked. 'Mr Smith has started to dry out all the wet areas in the old house, and anyway, he'll stop us putting the newts back. He won't exactly let us set up a newt sanctuary.'

Hakeem said, 'And he moved the newts illegally, I'm sure. I don't think he's a nice man. I mean, just look at his son. If we put them back, he'll probably kill them.'

Then it hit me. The house next door to us had never been sold; it was run down and damp. I bet it would suit newts. I checked with Hakeem and he said, 'It sounds good, and if we get them in there, they won't be able to sell it easily. Or maybe not at all. That could be a long-term fix. Clever idea, Martha.' My head swelled; Hakeem called me clever.

In my mind the idea was rapidly taking shape. Nobody needed to know, and we could protect Mr Newton's secret. I got a little surge of excitement thinking he'd be next door. I really liked that idea.

* * * * *

Michael was the obvious choice to get information from Mark One. He wasn't very subtle but, right at that moment, any information would help. Elemenope, Hakeem and I watched from the far corner of the playground while Michael played football with the Marks.

Hakeem said, 'I don't like it when people call you names, Martha. It's not nice.'

I said, 'Thanks. But I don't care anymore. I'm not my weight problem – or my size; I'm just me.' That was the first time I'd used the 'weight problem' phrase. Was Mum getting through to me?

Michael came back to us after a few minutes and said, 'He took most of the newts to the big pond in the recreation ground. He told me it took six trips because there were so many. He says he dropped some others in garden ponds, but he doesn't remember where.'

I said, 'I bet he does remember; he's just being horrible.'

Chapter Nineteen

Friday came. Another pointless sports afternoon. Jemima Toilet was wearing a white T-shirt, but the white was not like anybody else's. It positively shone, and it had been ironed. *Who irons a T-shirt?* Dad washed our clothes, but I don't think he ever ironed anything. He did like to use a lot of fabric softener and I loved that. My shirt still had a big splodge right in the middle, a reminder of last term. It was slowly fading, but when I looked at it, I remembered being hit in the face by a football, and my heart raced.

My eyes went from my grubby but oh-so-soft shirt to Jemima's pristine, sparkling-probably-diamond-encrusted-fur-lined shirt, and all I wanted to do was push her into the mud. Mrs Gnash blew her whistle; everybody stopped what they were doing and stood still. Everybody except Jemima Toilet.

She acted like she was so much better than everybody else. She kept jogging around, lifting her knees high, and wearing a 'look-at-me' snooty face. She only stopped when Mrs Gnash walked up to her and raised her hand.

Everyone stared. It looked like Mrs Gnash was going to slap her; those big hands would hurt. Instead, Mrs Gnash pulled out a digestive biscuit from her sleeve and said, 'Here, you look hungry.' *Something was seriously wrong.*

I was standing with Elemenope and Hakeem, who was trying to tuck in his shirt. It kept falling out of his shorts and puffing up like a sail. We looked at Jemima Toilet in amazement.

Elemenope whispered, 'I don't understand. She's so mean and scary, then all of a sudden she's handing out cupcakes and biscuits. Is it just me, or does that seem a bit creepy?'

Hakeem looked thoughtful, then a smile crossed his face. I hoped it was another toilet joke; I was getting a lot of mileage from the last one.

He said, 'What if Mrs Gnash is related to Jemima? That would make sense; she's being really nice to her. Maybe she's an auntie or something.'

I shook my head. 'No, they don't look even remotely alike. There must be some other explanation.'

Elemenope said, 'Well I think it's because Jemima whatsit-hyphen-who-cares is rich. That's what it'll be, for sure. Mrs Gnash wants something.'

None of my friends' theories rang true. Mrs Gnash

blew her whistle again. 'Pair-up for three-legged races. Hurry up.' She might have been trying to be nicer, but she couldn't disguise her awful, raspy voice.

I grabbed hold of Elemenope and we stood as close together as we could. The Marks did the same, and Michael paired up with Hakeem. That wouldn't have been his first choice because Hakeem was nowhere near as fast and strong as Michael, but the Marks had pushed him away. I watched it happen; Mark one said, 'Go away, you big lump, I always team up with Mark.'

Mark Two sneered, 'Yeah, we're a team. Buzz off.'

Michael looked confused, but I could have told him: boys like the Marks only look out for themselves. There's no room in their selfish, mean lives for another friend, unless it suits them. For the Marks, Michael was a spare.

Everybody stood in pairs. Except for Jemima Toilet. She was standing in the middle of the playground, with her hands on her hips, munching her digestive. Mrs Gnash took Jemima by the hand and walked towards our group. We all stood with our heads down, being as small and invisible as possible. I wasn't very good at that.

My hand was grabbed by a hard, cold claw; she had me! I was pulled away from Elemenope, and my hand was placed in Jemima's.

Mrs Gnash looked down from her great height, her face screwed into an unnatural smile. 'I think Jemima deserves a partner, don't you?' Nobody argued with Mrs Gnash, but just this once I really wanted to.

I said, 'But what about Elemenope? Now *she* doesn't have a partner.'

'She's going to help me with the race, aren't you, Penelope?' That was another thing I really didn't like about Mrs Gnash. She refused to pronounce Elemenope's name properly. She usually called her 'Penelope', but the other day she called her 'Primrose', and once she called her 'Elementary'.

It's not nice deliberately getting peoples' names wrong, but she did it all the time. OK, this was a double standard for me, the girl who called Jemima Waddington-Clarke 'Jemima Toilet'. I let myself off, though, because 'Toilet' was a nickname. And, anyway, it was funny.

Elemenope helped Mrs Gnash hand out the ribbons we used to tie our legs together. There was a problem immediately. Whenever I did a three-legged race with Elemenope, I'd be on the right, and she'd be on the left – so my left leg got tied to her right.

Jemima Toilet said, 'You have to tie you right leg to my left one.'

I said, 'That's not going to work. I always do it the other way.' She burst into tears. Who cries over a stupid three-legged race?

Mrs Gnash came over, discovered how *very* important this issue was to Jemima Toilet, and I had to have my right leg tied to her left. I decided immediately that she was going down. It meant I had to go down too, but it was *so* going to be worth it.

The first race was hilarious; the Marks tripped on the starting line and spent the whole race wrestling and calling each other names. It ended in a fist fight which Mrs Gnash broke up with her huge hands. I was too busy trying to work with Jemima Toilet to see that Michael had carried Hakeem across the line and won by a mile.

As we shuffled up to the line, for the start of our race, I tried to teach Jemima the secret that had seen Elemenope and me actually win some races. 'It's simple,' I said. 'I call out "inside – outside – inside – outside …" so we know which leg to put forwards. It works.'

She wouldn't listen. She said, 'Oh, that's just stupid. You've never won a race in your life. Look at you!' If we were in a cartoon, steam would have come out of my ears.

The whistle blew, and Jemima started calling out 'Left – right – left – right.' Well, that was just rubbish.

Of course, it worked for her; they were her legs she was calling out. I had to reverse it in my head or we were going to fall down. I willed myself to go on, thinking, *Not yet – only when I'm good and ready.*

There was a big patch of mud at the end of the track, just off to the side. I didn't want to fall until we crossed the finish line. We came third, behind little Emma and Grace. They're tiny, and they jumped about; they'd never won anything before. Evelyn and Claire usually won everything, but they'd come second. They were busy being angry and shouting at each other. Nobody was looking at Jemima Toilet and me.

I yanked hard on the ribbon, trying to walk normally. I was pretending to be cross. Well, I was a little bit. I was still angry at being taken from Elemenope and paired with horrible Jemima, but I really just wanted her to follow me.

'What are you doing, you big lump?' That did it; I yanked even harder, but I controlled my voice.

I said, 'Just come over here, away from the track. We can untie ourselves much more easily.'

'Why not just do it here?' She was huffing.

'Here's better,' I said, just as the mud presented itself in front of me. She hadn't seen it; she was too busy arguing.

I pirouetted gracefully (in my mind, my ballet teacher, would be *so* proud), and when that didn't work, I leaned my whole bodyweight on Jemima – and down she went, face first in the mud. I had to go down too, or it wouldn't look like an accident. I belly-flopped.

I was too busy laughing to worry about my own shirt. I knew Dad wouldn't be happy, but it gave him another chance to soak my PE shirt and use too much fabric softener. I faked being annoyed. It didn't work; I couldn't stop laughing.

'It's not funny, you great elephant!' Was that the best she could do? I didn't care. I'd been called far worse, and with less provocation. I was still laughing when Mrs Gnash yelled at Elemenope to help us untie our ribbon.

Elemenope started to laugh and Jemima Toilet burst into tears again, 'Why is everybody at this school *so stupid*?' That made Elemenope and me laugh louder. I wanted to roll around, I was laughing so hard, but the thought of Dad's face when he saw the state of my shirt made me stop.

I watched Jemima Toilet storm off; she was filthy. The pristine, sparkling white shirt was no more; it was caked in nasty brown-black mud, already drying to a hard clay.

I hoped she had to do her own washing, but I realised some poor servant would do it for her, and place the immaculately washed and ironed shirt in her huge chest of drawers. Or her rich parents would probably send some staff member out to buy her a new one. No, ten new ones. And a ball gown. And a tiara.

* * * * *

When Dad came to pick us up, he took one look at my T-shirt and shook his head. I said, 'What? You and Mum want me to do more sporty stuff. Well, this is what happens with sport; I get dirty because I'm *soooo* involved. I literally throw myself into things.'

Bella got up close to Dad and held her arms up so he had to lean in. She gave him a kiss and said, 'Look at me, Daddy: clean as a whistle.' As we walked out the gate I 'accidentally' stepped on the back of Bella's shoe. As it came off, she tripped and landed in a puddle. So much for miss goody-goody-look-at-how-clean-I-am.

I got in first, 'Oh … sorry Bella. It was an accident. You stopped right in front of me. I'm *so* sorry.'

She started her angry cry: the one that normally got me in trouble. But it was too late. I knew I was safe when

Dad said, 'Come on, Isabella, Martha didn't mean it. She said she was sorry. Let it go.' My timing was perfect!

Chapter Twenty

I couldn't concentrate on my maths homework. That was nothing new, but it seemed like every time I tried to work out an answer, I heard Mr Newton's voice telling me, 'Use that big brain, Martha Gibbons.' It was no use; I had to stop. I propped my head on my arms, and let out a groan.

Dad was peeling potatoes at the kitchen sink. He looked over at me, 'What's the matter, cream puff?' I was food again. Still, he sounded more like normal Dad.

I didn't answer straight away. Should I mention the newts or Mr Newton? They were the same problem, but I couldn't draw attention to that. I was thinking about my plan.

'Dad, do you know what's happening with the house next door? You know, the falling-down one?'

'No … but it's still for sale. And it's not falling down.'

I whispered a bit too loudly, 'Could have fooled me.'

He ignored me. 'But I haven't seen anybody looking. Winter's coming and I can't imagine someone wanting to look at it then. It's cold and miserable at the best of times.'

I thought, 'Yes, perfect. Cold and damp.'

I wondered how we were going to collect the newts. I wondered how we were going to get them into the house next door. I wondered how I was going to rescue Mr Newton's library. No wonder I couldn't concentrate on my homework.

* * * * *

Dad seemed flustered as he said, 'Why do you want to be at school so early? You never want to leave this early.' Mum had already left for work and he was on his millionth cup of coffee.

'Oh, we've got a project to work on … for Halloween.' I made that last bit up. Actually, I made the whole thing up, but we did sort of have a project: getting the newts back and hoping they could settle in next door. It just wasn't for Halloween – or school.

Hakeem was really excited when we met up in the playground. 'I've got these huge plastic jars; we can shift hundreds of newts at once.'

'That's great,' I said, 'We'll need to. There are thousands of them. I don't know how many we'll have to find for Mr Newton to reconstruct himself. I just hope we can get enough.'

Hakeem said, 'And there must be a leader – a king newt or something – someone who's in charge. A boss newt.'

I had an image of a huge newt wearing a crown and directing the others. It made me snort.

'What's so funny?' asked Elemenope.

I couldn't really answer, so I changed the direction of the conversation. 'We've got to find a way into the house next to ours. I'll start looking tonight when I get home.'

I left Elemenope and Hakeem to put the elements of the plan together. I discovered that the back door of the house next to us wasn't locked, but it wouldn't move easily. It was jammed at the bottom, so when I pushed hard the top wobbled; I just couldn't force the whole thing open.

I remembered a problem like this with our old house. Dad said the wood swelled up sometimes, and I remembered him having to push it really hard. I tried hitting the door; it shuddered and I got the feeling it might fall in if I tried a bit harder.

The best thing I discovered was a path on the side farthest from our house, so if anybody was looking from the street, they wouldn't see us.

We had to endure another ten whole days of Mrs Gnash. Why couldn't the school find a substitute teacher? Any-old-teacher would have to be better than one-hundred-foot-tall Mrs I'm-looking-at-you-like-I'm-going-to-eat-you Gnash.

Chapter Twenty-one

Sunday was my favourite day because nobody expected me to do anything. Mum had been on call, which meant we'd hardly seen her all weekend, but she got home just as we were settling down to watch *Frozen* for the millionth time. It's Bella's favourite movie. If I had to sit through her 'wanting to build a snowman' one more time, I was going to scream.

Mum wore a look I'd not seen before; she beckoned Dad out of the living room, and Bella and I carried on watching the movie by ourselves. It was *so* boring; I was determined not to watch it. Before I knew it, I was singing along.

Dad came back in and snuggled between Bella and me; now *he* looked weird. When the movie ended I was sad; I loved it. I didn't know why I never chose it. I thought maybe because it was Bella's all-time favourite, I was just determined to tell her I hated it.

Normally Dad chased us up to bed straight after the movie, but he stayed sitting down. He sent Bella off with, 'Go clean your teeth and climb into bed. I'll be up to tuck you in.' He turned to me and I couldn't read his face; he looked sad. No help there.

'Martha,' (that worried me. No 'honey-bunny', no 'pumpkin-bumpkin', just plain old 'Martha'; that meant trouble), 'is there a new girl in your class?'

'Uh-huh. Jemima Toi … err … Waddington-Clarke. She's a pain.'

'Interesting you should say that. Do you not get along?'

'Get along? I *hate* her.'

'I see. Did you have a fight with her the other day?'

'No. Well, I kind of pushed her in the mud. It was really funny. She …' I stopped because Dad was not smiling. I just shut up. He had a new kind of angry-dad-face on. I got the feeling he wouldn't appreciate my hatred of Jemima's spotless overly white PE shirt.

He said, 'It's just that Mum had to see her today. And, you know she's not supposed to talk about her patients. It's just that, well … that little girl said you trod on her head.'

'I did not! OK, I pushed her over so she got muddy, but I never trod on any part of her. *I wish I had!*'

Dad looked at me, using a mixture of 'I-want-to-believe-you' and 'I'm-confused-and-angry-because-I-think-you're-lying-to-me'. I was an expert on looks.

I didn't know what was going on. Why did Mum have to see Jemima Toilet? Dad had gone quiet. What was happening?

When I went to my room, Mum sat on the bed. Normally she gave me a kiss on the cheek, told me to only read for ten minutes and I wouldn't see her again until the morning. It was *in-kiss-out,* no chit-chat. Not that night. Mum sat close and looked at me. She took my hands in hers and said, 'Now, sweetheart,' (oh dear), 'I'm going to tell you a secret, and I want you to be really honest with me. We have to keep this just between us. You can't tell anyone. Not your friends – not anyone. OK?'

It sounded serious. 'OK'. I like secrets. Well, normally I like secrets, but I hated this one.

'Sweetheart, I'm a doctor,' (it was boring so far), '… and doctors aren't allowed to talk about the private things their patients tell them or show them.'

I nodded; I already knew that. I remembered asking Mum if she ever saw anything really gross and she said she couldn't share the details. I thought she could tell me stories of nasty sicknesses, as long as she didn't tell me the people's names, but she had said she wouldn't even do that. So, I had no idea where this conversation was going. It didn't seem good.

She said, 'Well, I want to talk to you about something I did today. But you mustn't tell anyone that I told you.'

I thought, *OK. I get it. Let's get to the juicy part already.* I nodded my head. But I had a feeling I wasn't going to enjoy the next bit.

'Well, today I saw a little girl – your age – with a nasty bump on her head.' I was none the wiser. Mum went on, 'She said it happened at school. She said another girl stepped on her head. Actually, she said this girl *stomped* on her head.' There was an uncomfortable pause. Mum had stopped looking at me. 'Sweetheart, she said *you* stomped on her head.'

I was outraged. 'That stupid Jemima. It was her, wasn't it? Stupid Jemima stupid Waddington-stupid-Clarke!'

'I shouldn't say her name.'

'You don't have to, Mum.' The rage was building. I hated Jemima Toilet, but this new rage was something else. If she'd said I pushed her in the mud, well, OK; I did that. But to go around saying I stomped on her head? It was too much!

'I didn't do that, Mum. Honestly, I didn't. I mean, I pushed her in the mud to get her dirty. She's so smug – so clean. But no way did I stomp on her head, or any other part of her. You have to believe me!'

Mum gave me a hard look. I was crying; a big glob of snot ran down my lip. I wanted a tissue. I wanted my mum to hug me. I wanted my mum to believe me. I wiped my face on the sleeve of my pyjamas and Mum pulled a face.

She didn't believe me! I sobbed and spluttered. Mum put her arm around me, but it was stiff and awkward. I wanted Dad.

Chapter Twenty-two

As a rule, I don't like Mondays, but I decided to hate that Monday more than usual. I would hate everything about it. I was not going to school. Then I decided I would; I was going to go, and shout in Jemima Toilet's face that I hated her.

I was so determined about what I would do at school, I even got dressed before heading down stairs. I never did that. I stormed into the breakfast room, straight to the table. Little-miss-I'm-always-up-and-dressed-before-you took one look at me and, for once, stayed quiet. I must have perfected my 'don't talk to me' face. Good.

The silence suited me, until Dad said, 'My goodness. What's the story, morning glory?' The rhyming was getting to me. Couldn't he tell I was carrying a big load of self-righteous anger? I swung around and the edge of my jumper caught my milk; down it went.

I screamed before anyone else, 'Urghh … what's that doing there?' Nobody said anything. I stomped over to the bench and ripped some kitchen paper off the roll.

My elbow knocked Dad's coffee over. The cup rolled off the bench and smashed on the floor. Coffee went everywhere. It splashed onto my sock; I hate wet socks. At least it wasn't too hot, but I jumped around as though it was. Dad was shouting, Bella was screaming. I yelled, 'It's not my fault!'

Dad said, 'Get out of the kitchen while I clean up. I don't want you to cut your foot on broken bits of coffee mug.'

But I heard, 'You're not able to clean up your own mess and *yes, it is all your fault.*' I stormed back upstairs to my bedroom and changed my socks. It was winter and we were supposed to wear tights but mine never fitted properly, so I was wearing socks. I didn't care that my knees were cold; it was better than having rolls of sloppy tights material flopping around my ankles.

Why that went through my head when I was so angry about Dad's coffee cup and stupid Jemima Toilet was a mystery. I was too busy hating myself.

* * * * *

Mum didn't mention the coffee cup, or the milk. She stood in the doorway, looking at me, looking at the pile of clothes on the floor, and looking at her watch. I wanted to ask, 'WHAT?' but I just looked back.

I could feel the tears starting again. I needed a hug, a proper one. I knew I wouldn't get one from Mum – not with that look on her face. I was expecting a lecture about putting my clothes in the washing basket. I didn't get that either. I got, 'I hope you remember what we talked about last night. Remember, you aren't supposed to know about your school-friend's injury.'

'Jemima Waddington-Clarke is *NOT* my friend.'

'Well, OK. Whatever you say, but *I* didn't tell you about it. What are you going to say if she comes up to you today?'

'Don't worry, Mum, I won't let anybody know you told me about her. Anyway, I don't get it. Why would she tell you I hurt her?'

Mum said, 'Well, to be fair, I don't think she knows I'm your mother. You know, you and Bella have Dad's last name. I'm not Mrs Gibbons, am I?' Mum was very proud of having kept her own name when she and Dad got married. She sometimes let herself be called 'Mrs Gibbons' for convenience, like at school meetings, and when horrible Jessica Cow-Face swooned all over her at my flop of a birthday party last year.

But I heard her all the time on the phone when people called her 'Mrs Gibbons'. She usually said, 'There's nobody here by that name.' Sometimes she got really uppity and said, 'It's DOCTOR Fielding, actually.' So, lots of people didn't know she was my mum. Like it was a secret.

Mum was more concerned about her reputation than about me being slandered. Slander: that's when someone tells a big lie about you. Stupid, horrible Jemima Toilet had slandered me. *Just you wait!* was all I could think.

I asked Mum, 'What did Jemima Toi … err … Jemima *actually* say?' She flustered at that.

She said, 'Well, she didn't actually say your name, but she said a big girl in her class did it.'

'Really, Mum? She actually said "a big girl" did it? Or did she say "a *fat* girl" did it?'

She flustered again; I had her. She couldn't say exactly what stupid Jemima Toilet said because she didn't want to upset me (it was *way* too late for that), and she was embarrassed to admit out loud that I was fat.

* * * * *

I was nervous walking into the playground. I held Dad's hand; I didn't want him to go. He didn't get the message.

He flicked my hand out of his, kissed me on the forehead and said, 'Have a great day, honey-muffin.' Bella got a pick-up hug, a smoochy kiss and, 'Bye, little Bella. Learn lots.'

I looked for Elemenope; I needed support. There was some excitement, a buzz in the air.

Elemenope got to me just ahead of Hakeem. She was breathless, which made her perpetual whispering even harder to understand. It sounded like the wind in the trees: all air movement, but nothing that hung together.

Hakeem interpreted for her. He said, 'Jemima's got a black eye.' Black eyes are like blood: they make kids stare, even when they're trying not to. There was a crowd jostling around, with Jemima, the queen bee, in the middle.

I didn't want to be anywhere near Jemima Toilet, but like everybody else, I needed to see her injury. I walked past the seething crush of kids, pretending to be deep in conversation with Elemenope who, by that stage, had regained some speech, and could actually pull off the part of someone having a conversation. I wanted to see the black eye, the one I had been accused of causing.

Part of me needed to find out if she really was going to blame me for it. She wouldn't want to. There were plenty of people who'd say I didn't put my foot anywhere near her stupid head. How could I have? Our legs were tied together; I'd need to be some sort of contortionist. I could barely do the leg stretches at ballet.

My fake conversation with Elemenope was completely silent – a mime. I could hear Jemima Toilet telling a spellbinding story to her audience. I heard her say, 'I fell down the stairs at home, and hit my face on the banister. It's got a big, marble, knob. It got me right here.'

I looked straight at her. That was her chance, but she didn't change her story. She didn't point at me and accuse me. And I knew she saw me because she turned her nose up. So why was she not blaming me?

A huge part of me was relieved, and I made a note in my head to tell Jemima's story to Mum and Dad. I needed to stop them thinking I was some kind of bully. I *hate* bullies. I felt outraged all over again. Mum and Dad believed some made-up story from some brat over their own daughter. Was I so awful that my own parents could think like that?

I paced around on my own, trying to think; that was when I saw him for the first time. There was a man standing by the back gate of the school. He was shabby and half hidden in the shadows. He seemed to be just looking. I tried to work out who he was looking at. It wasn't me. I turned to follow his line of sight; he was definitely looking at the group of kids listening to Jemima. I thought he might be a private detective. I looked back to see if he had a notebook or a spy camera, but he'd disappeared.

Chapter Twenty-three

I loved Halloween. Well, I liked dressing up, but I *loved* sweets. Whenever else do you get to ask for sweets and people just hand them to you? Sadly, it wasn't going to be that kind of Halloween.

We were all set. I'd organised for Elemenope, Hakeem and Michael to meet at our place. We were a spooky team of witches and warlocks; except for Hakeem, who came as Harry Potter.

My look said *'Really?'* But out loud I said, 'That's good, Hakeem.' He meant well, but I wasn't feeling all that generous, so I said, 'I mean, we've all gone to some effort with make-up. Look …' I had a green face and a huge fake nose with a monstrous wart on the end.

Elemenope had gone for the white-out face with blotches. She looked like a zombie, with wild hair and torn jeans.

I looked at Michael and said, 'Wow. You look amazing.' He was wearing a tuxedo, a huge top hat and a cape with a dazzling red lining. He had fake blood running down his chin from vampire fangs.

He said, 'Thanks. Mum used to work in the theatre.'

And there was Hakeem, in normal clothes with just a felt-tip zig-zag drawn in the middle of his forehead. He already had the glasses, but they were the wrong shape. I couldn't be too mad with him; we needed his enthusiasm.

We were nearly ready to head off, just milling about in our front hallway. Hakeem gave us each two huge plastic containers. They were like big zippy versions of what you get given goldfish in at the fair.

I looked at him quizzically (I thought he'd said he had jars), and he said, 'These look better tonight, don't you think?'

Then I saw it. Instead of spending time on his own costume, he'd decorated each plastic bag with drawings of witches and monsters. Brilliant. They looked like big Halloween treat bags. I forgave his pathetic attempt at a costume.

As we turned to head out the door, Mum called out, 'Wait for Bella.'

What? No. She couldn't be part of this. 'Oh, Mum. Do we have to take her?'

'Yes, of course. Doesn't she look terrific?'

There was my little sister, wrapped in toilet paper. Her eyes and mouth were barely visible under swathes of the stuff. She couldn't walk properly because it had been wrapped too tightly around her hips. I burst out laughing.

Bella started to cry and the toilet paper under her eyes got wet and started to tear. She stamped her foot and said, 'I told you this was a rubbish idea. I never wanted to be a mummy.' That was directed at Mum, but somehow it felt like I was going to get the blame for it.

Elemenope was a softy. She said, 'Oh, Bella … you look very scary.'

Michael and Hakeem nodded in agreement. I wanted them to stop; I really didn't think it was a good idea to take whiny little Bella with us. She would ruin everything, but I knew I was losing.

I watched in dismay as Bella's mummy outfit was repaired and Mum gave me the look that said, 'You'll take her with you and enjoy it.'

Fortunately, when Bella was in that mood, anyone else was a better comfort option than me, so she took Hakeem's hand. Now we had to do some real trick-or-treating or we'd get found out. Snitchy little Bella would tell on us. Unless … I had a sudden stroke of genius.

'Let's start here.' I pointed at the house next door; not the one we wanted to take the newts to, but the one on the other side. It had a jack-o'-lantern outside which meant there was someone in for trick-or-treat.

The door was opened by our neighbour, wearing a barely adequate Frankenstein mask. It was barely adequate because he was pretty ugly to begin with, and the mask only covered the top half of his face. He was nice, though, and he let us shove our hands in a big bag and take as many sweets as we could grab.

I shook my head as Michael put his huge fistful of sweets in his plastic bag. 'What?' he asked from under his top hat.

'That bag is meant for other things – remember?'

'Oh, yeah. Well, I'll just have to eat this.' He stuffed a whole Mars bar in his mouth. He grinned and I could see chocolate oozing around his teeth. *Gross.*

I held out my fistful of sweets to Bella. 'Would you like some of mine?'

She smiled at me for the first time since coming down the stairs. I knew the way to her cold little heart. I swung my still empty plastic bag so the others could see what I was doing, and they all followed suit.

Naturally, we ate our favourite sweets; I couldn't pass

up a Fudge bar. Or a Curly Wurly. Or a Crunchie. But as we went from house to house, we offered most of our bounty to Bella, and her plastic pumpkin bucket filled up quickly.

Not every house had a jack-o'-lantern outside, and some that did were really stingy. At Mrs Marsh's house, we didn't even get sweets; we got apples. Who gives out apples at Halloween? *She's a real witch.*

I'd eaten a Milky Way, a Snickers and another Fudge bar by the second corner, and there was no more room in Bella's bag. She stopped caring that we seemed to be giving most of our stuff away; she was having a ball. She was giggling and doing silly mummy-walking, which was actually pretty funny. I started not to mind having her along, but I was still worried about the rest of the plan.

The recreation ground was around the corner and up the hill. We could get there still pretending to trick-or-treat. The big house at the top, just near the gate to the rec, had been decked out with lights and really detailed decorations. It looked like a haunted house, with massive cobwebs over the windows and bats on strings. There was a glowing skeleton by the door.

I said to Hakeem, 'That looks really lifelike.'

He gave me a pitying look. 'Really? A lifelike skeleton? Do you know how silly that is?' Just then the skeleton moved an arm and Hakeem screamed. I nearly wet myself.

As we approached the door, I could see the skeleton's arm was attached to the door handle by a piece of string. Hakeem was laughing to cover up his scream; he didn't fool anybody. I was too obsessed with the plan to pay much attention to the sweets on offer; I didn't even look at the fistful of things I pulled out of the bag held by the tiny vampire at the door. I shoved them in the pocket of my fleece and mumbled, 'Thank you.'

'You're welcome, Martha.' It was Miss Slider. I was startled; I didn't realise she lived in this big house. Then it occurred to me to not be startled. I'd never given any thought to where teachers might live, not even Mr Newton. We only discovered his house by accident.

I realised I didn't think about teachers having any life other than what we see of them at school. Obviously they did; they had families, and houses, and pets and even children of their own. None of that had ever occurred to me before, and it was all crashing into my head in the few seconds I stood on Miss Slider's doorstep.

I had the sense of time standing still, like each second

lasted a minute. When I stepped back, everything sped up again as Miss Slider closed her front door.

'OK. Let's get started,' said Hakeem, just above a whisper.

* * * * *

We needed our torches. The way into the rec was a smooth path, but once we moved outside the eerie cone of light from Miss Slider's house it was really dark. Hakeem was in the lead. He was so excited he was doing that fast-walking that's not-quite-running. I tried to keep up, but the cold air made it hard to catch my breath.

Bella started whining, 'I can't see. Why are we in the rec? Why don't I have a torch? I want a torch,' until she fell over. I heard the sharp breath before the scream.

I was by her side in an instant; I needed to shut her up. She said, 'I'm OK. Oh no …' Her sweets were scattered all over the path. I told the others to go on, and started to search with my torch. We scooped up what we could find and that kept her quiet.

By the time we'd filled her bucket again, the others were out of sight. I didn't want to call out, but it was really spooky in the rec at night. On our own. In the dark.

On Halloween. Bella was sniffling. I really wanted to call out, but I had to be brave or she would start to wail.

We walked along the path, hunched over, following the beam of light from my torch, and searching the shadows for clues. I tried a soft, 'Elemenope … Hakeem … where are you?' Nothing.

It seemed like an age as we crept along. After a minute I tried again, 'Hakeem … Elemenope … are you there?' I thought I heard breathing.

'BOO!' It was Michael. He jumped out in front of me and I screamed. I hit him on the arm.

Bella was whimpering, and he said, 'Sorry, but you didn't call out my name, so I thought I was in the clear.'

'Not funny, Michael. You've made Bella cry,' (*and I nearly wet myself again*). 'Not funny at all.'

'Shush, you lot.' It was Elemenope's loud whisper. 'We're over here.'

I realised why I couldn't see their torches; they were behind a bank of bushes, right next to the pond. We'd made it.

Hakeem was already wading in the pond with a tiny net, guiding it through his torch beam. It looked like he'd done this before. Elemenope crouched beside the pond, shining her torch into a patch of weeds. She already had a dozen newts in her bag. She looked up and said, 'I didn't know it was this easy.'

Bella was suddenly aware that we were no longer trick-or-treating. 'What are we doing here? What are they doing? There aren't any houses here.'

I decided to let her in on the truth, or at least a version of the truth which would be safe for her to know.

'We're rescuing all the newts that stupid Mark Smith and his father moved.' I waited for her to whine.

She said, 'Well, that's a great idea. Those nasty boys. Come on … what are you waiting for?'

I was amazed, and delighted. To my surprise, Bella started wading into the pond, into the arc of light from Elemenope's torch. I couldn't help laughing as her toilet paper mummy costume gradually dissolved. It wouldn't be long before she started crying with cold and wet, so we had to work quickly.

The newts were really easy to catch. Over the next few minutes I must have caught a hundred. Hakeem was whooping with excitement. Michael had been working around the corner and he came wading past me with his plastic bags overflowing; he was laughing.

I said, 'Do you think the newts are trying to get caught.?'

Hakeem looked up, 'It would make sense.'

I stopped wondering and realised it was true. Mr Newton's consciousness was there somewhere and he must have realised we were trying to save his collective parts.

'How many have we got?' I asked Hakeem.

'Nearly a thousand, I reckon. But there's lots more. Our bags are full. We'll have to come back.'

'I want to go home,' said Bella. She was shaking.

I said, 'How am I going to explain your frozen sogginess to Mum?'

Bella was smarter, and sneakier, than I thought. She said, 'I'll tell Mum that I tripped and fell in somebody's garden pond. Don't worry.' Why couldn't she be like that all the time?

Chapter Twenty-four

It was a slow, dripping walk home. We made a messy procession, with water slopping everywhere, but we didn't spill any newts; they were hunkered down at the bottom of the bags.

I'd imagined the newts would want to escape. Not this lot; they were content to stay out of harm's way. Bella's good humour almost made it home, too. She started to whine just as we turned the corner into our street.

'Can you hold it together? Just a bit longer?' I pleaded with her, using my whole body. I thought she understood the importance of our mission, even if she didn't know the whole truth.

'OK,' she whimpered. She was shivering violently and I was trying not to laugh; she looked so funny: all drippy, with bits of ragged toilet paper stuck to her tracksuit top and underwear in random strips and patches.

We had to walk past our front door to get to the 'newt house'. I was actually thinking of it as 'Mr Newton's new house', but I was scared to think that too hard in case anybody started reading my mind. I'd had about enough of that.

We stood by the side gate that led into next door's garden. 'Wait here, guys. I've got a plan.'

'That's good,' said Elemenope, 'because I don't know how to get in here. Does anybody know where we go now?'

'Yes.' I was getting testy. 'But you have to wait 'til I get back. I can't leave Bella here like this. And I can't just dump her. I've got to settle things with Mum and Dad. Bella, can you go along with whatever I say?'

'Sh-sh-sh-sure.'

Dad answered the door when I knocked (I wasn't trusted with a key). He was wearing a monster mask which was not at all scary; it was from a Disney movie, and it just looked furry and soft.

'What's happened?' he asked Bella, me and pretty much the whole street. It was a strangely echoey question, because the mask was still over his face. Bella dissolved into tears, and I spun a story.

'Poor little Bella tripped and fell into the pond outside the Maynard's house. Stupid pond. I mean, they don't even have fish. Anyway, she fell in and all her paper shredded and she's really cold. So I brought her home and here she is and now I'm going back to the others … bye.'

'Not so fast, Martha. Bella, is that true?'

I held my breath. I couldn't remember my sister ever actually lying. I had said lots of times that she was lying, but that was to stop me getting in trouble because she was telling on me and I had to defend myself. I didn't think she had ever told a real lie in her life. Until that moment.

'Y-y-yes, Daddy … it was horrible. All slimy and cold.' She looked out from under Dad's big floppy fleece and gave me a huge wink. *She did it.*

'Well, I can see you managed to save your haul, so that was a lucky thing. You'd better come in and get warm. How about I run you a nice warm bath?'

Bella was making all the right sucking-up-to-Dad cooing noises. She'd be fine. I saw her sweet bucket in one hand, but she had a bag with about fifty newts in the other. I grabbed it and swung it behind me before Dad could notice.

I mumbled something about her having my bag too.

'Please, Dad. The others are waiting for me. Can I go back now?'

Dad had his precious little Bella and she was cooing like a dove (laying it on a bit thick, I thought), so he dismissed me with a wave of his hand. *Yes.*

I scooted straight back to where the others were waiting, and showed them the way through the gate, down the path to the back door. We got hit in the face by dripping bushes and overgrown weeds. It was too dark and our torches were running low; the back door was stuck.

I said, 'Turn your torches off … save the batteries. Just follow my light.' It got a whole lot blacker.

I could barely hear Elemenope over my own breathing as she said, 'Are you sure this is worth it?'

I said, 'Do you really want Mrs Gnash teaching us for the rest of the year?'

Nobody answered, but Michael stepped up and pushed on the door. He really put his shoulder into it. After two hard shoves and a lot of grunting we were in some kind of tiled space, like a utility room. The floor was wet.

When I pointed that out to Hakeem, he smiled. I thought he smiled; it was hard to be sure in the dark.

'Where are we going to put the newts?' he asked. I showed him the stairs to the cellar, behind a cracked wooden door off the hall. I wished there was some proper light. All the torches were back on; there was a galaxy of shadows.

I only wanted to see down the stairs; it was getting really spooky. Something was pushing me from behind. 'Hey … don't push.' I had an image of us all sprawled on the floor of the cellar with broken bones and nobody ever finding us.

The cellar was perfect: not just damp, positively underwater. It was easily six inches deep in places and there were little mounds of earth and broken bricks sticking out like islands.

Hakeem let out a gasp. 'It's wonderful,' he said. He was a real newt enthusiast. We set to work releasing the newts; there were too many to count.

I imagined that the little group staying around my feet were trying to say 'thank-you,' but then I thought they might be saying, 'go back and get the rest of us,' so I tried to stop thinking what they might be saying.

'Can we go back for more?' The words were barely out of my mouth before Hakeem and Michael went bounding up the steps.

Elemenope stood on the bottom step looking back, shining her failing torch over the rippling water. 'This reminds me of something …' She shook her head and climbed the stairs.

By the time we were outside the torches had all died.

I said, 'We can't do another newt run in total darkness.' But I didn't want to waste precious out-of-home-with-nobody-suspecting-anything time.

I had an idea. 'What did horrible Mark One say? Something about people's garden ponds? I wonder if we can find some in the street lights?' I remembered what I told Dad about Bella getting wet – the lie that she was so good at embellishing. 'The Maynards … they've got that big pond just inside their gate. Mark's lazy; I bet he put some in there.'

The good thing was, we could get to the Maynard's house in a couple of minutes, without needing our torches. The bad thing was, we'd be in full view of everybody trick-or-treating along their street. Not to mention their house if they looked out the front window. We just had to risk it.

We were in luck; the streets were quietening down, but we slunk along anyway. Halloween was the perfect night for four kids to be out on their own, skulking around in the shadows, with big bags under their arms.

The gate to the Maynard's front path was right on the street, so it was kind of public; anybody with business at the house had to open it. We didn't exactly have business, but on Halloween, it didn't feel like we were trespassing.

I pushed the gate open and kept hold of it so it didn't bang shut. Michael, Elemenope and Hakeem shuffled in and went straight to the pond. Hakeem knelt, leaned forwards and started swishing his net around, but I focused on the front door of the house.

I decided to stand right on the doormat and shout 'trick or treat' loudly, as a warning, if anybody came to the door. It would probably have been a good idea to warn the others of this plan in order to prevent what was about to happen. But I didn't. When the door opened, I shouted, 'TRICK OR TREAT!' and Hakeem fell in the pond with a loud splash.

Mrs Maynard peered past me and called out, 'Are you all right?'

Hakeem spluttered and started apologising as he climbed out of the pond. Elemenope and Michael started laughing and I turned bright red.

Mrs Maynard looked at Hakeem and said, 'You poor thing. Come here and show me you're all right.'

Hakeem had to present himself to Mrs Maynard. He looked pathetic, standing there dripping in the weak porch light. I could see she was trying not to laugh, but there was something else in her tone as she called over her shoulder, 'George … I told you we need to get rid of that pond.'

She fussed around Hakeem, but he fended her off, repeating how he was fine, and, 'Yes, I'll go home straight away and dry off. Please don't worry.'

Mrs Maynard insisted we all dip our hands in her big bowl of treats. I was awed by how many sweets Michael could fit in one hand. Hakeem wiped his hands on his trousers, which had no effect. They were still wet, so I offered to take a couple of sweets for him. Elemenope picked through the bowl, looking for sherbets.

Back on the street, Hakeem pulled his bag from under his coat and said sadly, 'I think I only got a dozen … there must be more.' It sounded like he wanted to go back to the pond but I had to say, 'No. We've done enough for one night. And look at you … you're sopping wet.'

I took the bag from him, promising to add its newts to the new colony next door. We were a sorry sight; the excitement had worn off and we gave off an air of failure. But I thought that was wrong, because what we'd done in a single night had to be a really good start.

Hakeem had lost his spark; I needed to say something, 'Great job tonight, everyone.' I wanted it to sound like a pep talk, but I wasn't even convincing myself. Hakeem looked like he might cry. I didn't want that, so I tried to step it up. 'We've moved so many newts already. Let's meet tomorrow and plan some more.'

'Do we have to?' whispered Elemenope. 'I mean, we've moved what? A thousand? More? Can't we just leave them now? You know, let them sort themselves out?'

I didn't want to start arguing there and then. I said, 'It takes so many of them to make up Mr Newton.' I shrugged and went on, 'But, like I said: it's a good start. Let's go home and think what else we can do.'

Everybody nodded. We must have looked like the least successful trick-or-treaters of all time: no sweets, sopping wet, and altogether reeking of pond water. Not a good Halloween except, maybe, for the newts.

Chapter Twenty-five

Dad was in my face, 'Wake up, sleepyhead.' His breath smelled of coffee. I looked at my watch: ten to eight. Ten to eight? Half an hour before we had to leave for school? What was going on?

Dad's stinky breath told me, 'I felt sorry for you. You got home late from trick-or-treating, so I let you sleep in.' He was open-mouth-smiling at me. I wished he wouldn't.

I didn't need to sleep in; I needed to have breakfast. It was Friday, so lunch would be fish and chips. If I could only survive until lunchtime, I'd be OK.

Bella was already dressed, hair in bunches, coat buttoned – *of course*. She cosied up to Dad for the walk to school; she was back to normal.

Bella hung around our group in the playground, like she felt a sense of belonging after the Halloween adventure. I couldn't chase her away because I couldn't risk her changing her mind and telling our secret to Dad. Who knew where that could end?

Hakeem was worrying about collecting the rest of the newts, but I'd changed emphasis. I said, 'All Mr Newton has to do is get his team of newts to breed, and soon, maybe in a year or so, there'll be enough for him to reappear. I'm sure he will have the same idea. It's much more urgent that we rescue his library.'

Hakeem said, 'His library?'

'Uh-huh. He's got this amazing library – full of really old books. We've got to get them out of that house before Mark One's dad destroys them.'

Michael said, 'How can a newt read?'

'He's not just one newt. He's a whole lot of newts working together. I've told you.'

Elemenope added, 'He can obviously read. He marks our homework. But how *does* he do that?'

I couldn't say, and we were getting off topic. If I couldn't convince them about the library, I would have to do it myself.

* * * * *

With Halloween out of the way, the whole school was gearing up for Christmas. We were practising carols in music class and the end-of-year play was coming together: something about Robin Hood. I wasn't in it. It seemed to be mainly year six, and a few little kids from the reception class.

I had an idea. Rehearsals were on Wednesdays and Fridays after school. If I told Mum and Dad that I was in the play they wouldn't be worried if I was late home. I calculated that I could make two trips from Mr Newton's old house, to the house next door and get back to school in time for Dad to pick me up 'late' after rehearsal. *Genius.*

It took five weeks of subterfuge, but with only two fake rehearsals to go before the play, I'd done it. It was not easy. On my last trip I managed to smuggle Mr Newton's mask and what I thought was his voice box. Once, Dad nearly caught me as I scurried out of the house next door, and another time Bella nearly dropped me in it when she told Mum that only four kids from her reception class were taking part in the play.

I had a horrible, sinking feeling. Mum and Dad would be going to the play; they would expect to see me in it.

Mum asked, 'How come we haven't heard about your costume?'

I tried to hide the giant lump in my throat as I said, 'Oh … it's just normal clothes. It's a modern production.'

I was getting so tangled up in the lie I knew I'd get caught – and soon.

I couldn't manufacture a part in the school play, so I had to resort to the time-honoured get-out-of-anything fall-back. I would be sick. On the day of the school play I put my plan into action. When I got up, I splashed cold water on my face, didn't wipe it off, and staggered down stairs. I thought, *I could be in the play; I'm a great actor.*

I told Mum I felt awful. She saw the moisture on my face and said, 'Oh, dear. Are you hot?'

I had insight into this. I said, 'No. I feel really cold.' I remembered that from when I was actually sick months before.

Mum sent me back to bed and said she'd take my temperature. That was another part of my plan.

I heard Mum downstairs. 'Where is it? I always put it back in the cupboard. John, have you seen the thermometer?' I didn't hear his answer, but I could imagine Dad shrugging. I touched the thermometer, hidden safely under my pillow. There was some clunking and banging, then, 'I don't have time for this. I'm late for work now.'

With Dad in charge I knew I'd be OK. The master stroke would seal the deal. To make myself vomit I stuck my fingers down my throat. It didn't work the first time, or the second time. I was getting desperate, so I went *way* down. I've always been a noisy vomiter, and the sound brought Dad and Bella (I could have done without her right then) into the bathroom to witness my horror.

I overheard Dad ringing the school secretary, 'Martha won't be at school today.' *Yes.* I was safe.

But I wasn't off the hook yet. I was breathing hard as I waited to make sure he didn't overdo it. When Dad was stressed, he could be an over-communicator. And he was. He added, 'And I'm sure she's very sad to miss the play. Will someone be able to take her place?' *Oh no, no, no!*

It was too quiet. I could hear the hall clock ticking while I waited behind my bedroom door. I dived for bed when I heard Dad on the stairs.

'Pumpkin? You OK?' I had the duvet up over my head. 'I can't find the thermometer; let me feel your forehead.'

I couldn't ask about the school play situation; I was sweating for real. Dad felt my forehead and said, 'Well, you're clammy, but not too hot. Maybe you should just stay in bed. I've got to get Bella to school. Do you think you'll be OK?'

I mumbled, 'Uh-huh,' and ducked back under the covers.

'It's just … you're a bit young to be home alone, and Mum's already at work. I can't leave Bella to get to school on her own … so … stay in bed. Don't answer the door. Or the phone. I'll be quick. OK?'

I mumbled, 'Uh-huh,' again. There was no mention of the play. I'd got away with it – for the time being. I could only hope Mum and Dad weren't going to go, and that way nobody would say anything to them. It would not be a restful day.

I listened for the sounds of Dad and Bella leaving the house. At last I heard the door close and I bolted out of bed. I didn't take my pyjamas off; I just put my coat over them and plonked my boots on. It was my last chance to check on things next door.

A furtive glance showed Dad's back disappearing around the corner. Next door's back door was looser thanks to Michael, and the fresh batteries in my torch lit up the cellar. There were newts everywhere; I couldn't count them.

Back upstairs, in the room I set aside as Mr Newton's library, I saw a newspaper next to an old chair. I couldn't remember seeing that before. I didn't stay long; I had to get back home and back into bed.

I needed to make sure I was too sick for anybody to try to get to the play in the evening. My performance was flawless. When Mum got home from work, she checked on me and decided that we would all stay home. *Success.*

PART TWO

MRS GNASH

Chapter Twenty-six

The last week of school before Christmas was a strange mix of not-doing-much-work, watching movies in class, and excited talk in the playground. Our class had got used to Mrs Gnash. As much as anyone could ever get used to her.

We knew when she was going to leave us alone while she checked on her own class, and we let out a group sigh of relief as the clock's minute hand got near twelve. She was very predictable: every hour, on the hour, she disappeared for forty minutes, so we only had her for twenty minutes. We definitely had the better end of the deal.

Monday followed the familiar pattern, and Tuesday. But on Wednesday, we walked into class and my heart skipped a beat. A few months before, when I first saw him, I thought he was the weirdest person on the planet. Then I learned his secret and I *knew* he was the weirdest person on the planet.

But when I saw Mr Newton standing in front of our class, I let out a whoop. So did everyone. Yes, he was the weirdest person in the world (well, not really a person), but he was our Mr Newton and we were *so* glad to have him back.

I might have been the only person in the class to notice that he seemed a bit shorter than usual, but I knew the reason. Our plan had worked.

I imagined he was smiling, but of course there was no evidence of that. And it would have been very out of character for Mr Newton to make any kind of fuss. He got us to do a maths test. It was the first real work we'd done all week but nobody cared. I tried really hard; I wanted to impress him. But I had a new feeling as well: a feeling that I owed it to myself to try.

Mr Newton stood beside my desk; I got the familiar wobbly sensation. He looked over my shoulder at the mark Elemenope had given me in the test: 142 out of 144. 'Well,' he said, 'Martha Gibbons, it looks like you need to continue your tutoring. I trust you can attend after school today?'

I gulped and managed, 'Yes, Mr Newton. I'll have to check with my dad, at pick-up. Since we haven't been doing it for a while, he might have forgotten.' He nodded his head; the movement seemed more awkward than usual.

The day went in a flash. Mr Newton didn't offer any explanation for his absence. In the playground, Michael said, 'I told you he's an alien, and he got called back to his mothership.' That rumour had started up again while he'd been away.

I looked at Michael and said, 'But I told you about him. How can you say that? You helped rescue the newts. You helped put them ...' I gave up. Michael's face was set. He had his ideas and nothing anybody said was going to change that. I thought how silly some kids' ideas were, and then I thought, *If they only knew the truth?* but Michael had heard the truth; he just couldn't believe it. Or maybe Mr Newton had done his memory trick on him.

* * * * *

When Dad came to pick us up, I walked over to him with Bella. 'Mr Newton's back, Dad. Is it OK if I have my tutorial with him? I'll be an hour. Just like before.'

Dad seemed distracted, but after a few seconds while I thought he hadn't heard me he nodded and said, 'Sure.' There were no cute food-related names, just 'sure.' I started to think he wasn't really paying attention, but I didn't care. I skipped off to my session with Mr Newton. Me, skipping to extra work? What had happened to me?

I sat beside Mr Newton at his desk. We always sat that way; I enjoyed the look of the classroom from that angle. I got to see what it looked like as a teacher: a little sense of power.

Mr Newton said, 'Get your book out, so it looks like we're doing some work.' That seemed strange. 'I think we're being watched.' I felt a shiver down my spine.

'I want to thank you for what you did, Martha Gibbons. You saved me a lot of time and energy. I thought it would take years to get back together, but with your help it was only a few weeks. My work can go on.'

I just thought he meant teaching, so I nodded. I was smiling, too. It was so good to have him back. He tilted his head; the movement was unusually awkward.

'I'm still regrouping. I've only got seven thousand newts together at the moment. A few more manage to find our new home each night. But it's getting cold and we don't like travelling far when it's cold. It will be quite a few months until I'm my normal size again, but with a lot of effort we can function almost normally. That's the joy of so many brains working together; we are very adaptable.'

I had to ask, 'What was it like when Mark and his father moved you? You know? Took all your newts away?'

'I call that the abduction; it was horrible. That boy is very rough – and careless. He dropped several of us on the road. He didn't care. We were scattered far and wide. Luckily, he's lazy, so most of us were deposited in the park pond, where you and your friends found us. I want to ask: you didn't tell any of them about me ... about us, did you?'

'Oh, well, I sort of had to. They're a bit confused. I don't think they really understand. Except Hakeem – I think he gets it.'

'How many people know?'

'Just Hakeem and Elemenope. I tried to tell Michael, but he doesn't believe it. He still thinks you're an alien.' I wanted to change the subject, but not by much. 'What about bullfrogs?'

'Well, that's something of a non-sequitur. Do you know what a non-sequitur is?' I shook my head. 'It means the topic of conversation has no logical connection with what went before. What about bullfrogs, indeed?'

'As a – what do you call it – collective. You know, what about bullfrogs grouping together to make a person? I read they have really big brains. Well, big in relation to their bodies. I read they are about a quarter of a gram – like newts. So how about a group of bullfrogs working together?'

'It's hard for my voice to laugh, Martha Gibbons, but believe me, I'm laughing at that idea. Have you ever met a bullfrog? Really stupid. They hardly use any of their brain for anything other than eating. They're really rude, too. Rude to each other, I mean.

'They just sit around insulting each other. If you could speak bullfrog, like I do, you'd understand. All that croaking … it's mainly insults. I mean: when did you last see a group of bullfrogs working together to help the planet? Hmm? I think not. They'd never be able to co-operate.'

I laughed. Then I saw it. We *were* being watched. A tall shadow skulked across the door at the back of the classroom.

Mr Newton saw it too. 'Head down, Martha Gibbons. Work on these sums, while I take a look.'

I couldn't concentrate on maths while that was going

on. I kept my head down, but my eyes followed Mr Newton as he shuffled over to the door. He was moving oddly, as though his feet couldn't keep up with his legs.

How I wished I could see his face like a proper human face. When he came back, I couldn't tell whether he was happy, worried, frightened – any of the things I should be able to see. He sat beside me again; he was squirmier than usual.

'You kids and your imaginations. Fancy thinking I'm an alien! I tell you what, though, Martha Gibbons, there actually are aliens here. In fact, Mrs Gnash is one of them. Don't say I didn't warn you, but you have to keep it a secret. OK?'

I looked at Mr Newton's mask; the eyeholes were sparkling. I could see his mind, and I knew he was telling the truth.

'OK.'

Chapter Twenty-seven

I knew I was on their spaceship; I could smell it. The face in front of me kept changing from my mum to a green blob with too many eyes. When had Mum become an alien? It would explain a lot. Blob-face held a spiky hand in the air and said, 'The experiment is going to start – get ready,' then Mum-face told me to wake up and get ready for school. Sometimes I hated my dreams.

Why had Mr Newton told me that our PE teacher, Mrs Gnash, was an alien? I didn't want to be abducted by aliens. I knew all about it from a show on the telly. It was scary; they took you to their spaceship and did experiments on you and afterwards nobody believed you. Well I wasn't letting horrid Mrs Gnash do that to me, or my friends. Maybe my little sister.

Most kids in my situation would tell their parents, but Dad never listened to me, and Mum was out to get me. So the only person I could talk to about it wasn't a person at all.

When I asked Mr Newton during my tutorial, he got really serious.

'Yes, Martha Gibbons,' he said in his weird machine-voice. 'Please don't tell anyone. They'll think you're mad.'

I wished his voice had more tone. I needed to know when he was winding me up. I'd got so used to him that I often forgot he wasn't a real person, that he was a fabulous collection of newts all bunched together in the most brilliant disguise. He was still the best teacher I'd ever had.

'But I'm not mad, and neither are you. So, what do we do?'

'WE don't do anything. You concentrate on your schoolwork and I'LL keep an eye on her. I've been watching her for four years now.'

'Four years? And you haven't told anyone?'

'I've told you.'

That didn't make me feel any more comfortable. I could see Mrs Gnash in my mind's eye. I remembered seeing her on my first day at St Finbar's: ridiculously tall, with huge hands and a hungry look. She talked with a scratchy voice and was overly fond of her whistle.

'What kind of alien is she?'

'I think she's an exile.'

'An exile?'

'Oh dear, Martha Gibbons. When did you become a parrot?' He was shaking his head; it looked perilously like it might fall off.

I asked, 'Mrs Gnash is from another planet?'

'Do you think that's what "alien" means?'

'Well … doesn't it?'

He started that dodgy-looking head shake again. 'Alien just means "not from here". It can mean a person from another country, or an idea that comes from another way of thinking. There are lots of "alien" plants all over the place. You have to be careful with the words you use, Martha Gibbons. Words matter.'

I felt silly, but I was sure the way Mr Newton used 'alien' he meant she was from another planet.

* * * * *

Christmas was the last meal before Mum started her crusade in earnest. She'd kept Dad away from most of the cooking; he did things like setting the table and clearing up badly. We had turkey with stuffing (I love stuffing) and roast potatoes with really crispy skin, lots of gravy and little sausages. I watched Mum piling

Brussels sprouts on my plate.

I said, 'Seriously. It's Christmas. And you're making me eat Brussels sprouts?'

Bella said, 'Ooh, I *love* sprouts, Mummy.' I knew she didn't.

I gagged one down while Mum was staring at me, and slid the rest onto Bella's plate when her back was turned. Bella opened her mouth to complain, but I said, 'But you *love* sprouts, Isabella. Merry Christmas.'

That was when Mum said the thing about me not being a healthy weight. Well, I wasn't about to waste stomach space on stupid sprouts. Not when there was pudding to come.

* * * * *

The first day of term was surprisingly calm. Mr Newton was nearly back to his normal height, but he was skinnier than usual. Both Marks were absent, and Jemima Toilet kept to herself. I wasn't falsely accused of assault. It was a good day, until dinner time.

Dad said, 'I've made dinner tonight, girls: sausages, mashed potato and frozen peas.' I was pleased to see the peas weren't still frozen when they landed on my plate.

Dad was so flustered trying to get the whole meal on the plate at once (what was so hard about that? It came out together at Frankie & Benny's) that he asked me to pour drinks for Bella and me. I did Bella's first, like they were always telling me: *'do yourself last'*, but I put the milk bottle down on top of a place mat and knocked my glass over. I hadn't seen it. I tried to catch it and knocked over Bella's glass in the process. Dad went ballistic. That was when Mum came home, and it was World War Three.

Mum started in on me straight away, 'What did you have for lunch today, Martha?'

I knew where that was going, so I lied. 'I had roast chicken (that was safe), with vegetables. No gravy, and an apple.'

Bella looked like she was going to explode. She was going to rat on me; I really had a double helping of pasta, extra chips and two huge chocolate-chip cookies. I had to do something before she blurted out the truth. I kicked her under the table. She yelped and Mum rounded on me.

'Martha! What did you do?'

'She kicked me!' wailed Bella.

'Why did you do that? Say you're sorry. What's the matter with you?' Mum had been successfully deflected.

I said, 'Sorry, Isabella.' It didn't sound very sincere, but I did feel a tiny bit guilty. I'd just kicked my sister to stop her telling on me. But then, if she had told on me, I would have kicked her anyway, so it was the same in the end.

Bella had gone red. She wanted to get me in trouble, but she'd had a taste of what would happen if she did. I gave her my death stare for good measure.

Dad looked at the food on my plate; I hadn't eaten any peas. 'Is there something wrong with your dinner?' he asked. I knew what was coming next. Dad cooked the most basic stuff, and not very well. But if we didn't make a huge fuss about it, he got all sulky and started muttering under his breath.

He said, 'I've done everything today … what's the thanks I get? Good food going to waste on ungrateful children.'

Bella climbed on his lap and said, 'It's a beautiful meal, Daddy.'

I'd dodged the lunch question nicely, with a bit of unwitting help from Dad, but I knew I had only postponed the whole diet thing. Mum's obsession wouldn't go away that easily.

Ever since Christmas, Mum's issue with my weight

had got worse. She stopped short of saying I was fat, but she'd exhausted her list of not-quite-using-the-fat-word alternatives. She'd say, 'You're chunky,' or, 'You're not really a healthy weight.' She was frightened that if she hurt my feelings I'd eat more. Well, I ate more because she was annoying me.

Chapter Twenty-eight

At break, the cool kids sat on the wall, so we sat on the benches, eating our snacks. Even though I was having school lunches, I took a lunchbox. You can't be too careful about having enough snacks. I put a whole Jaffa Cake in my mouth. I love Jaffa Cakes. I packed five when Mum wasn't looking and Dad mumbled his usual, 'Don't take too many.' What's too many? Maybe eighteen would be too many.

Mrs Gnash's class wasn't out yet. That was odd because they were usually out first. They were out first for everything because Mrs Gnash didn't want to spend anymore time with her pupils than absolutely necessary.

The class six kids come out slowly; they were already eating. Sausage rolls! Where did they get them? I *love* sausage rolls.

I stared at Kathryn Frederics. She's not quite as chunky as me, but she's a year older, and a lot taller. She just looks big. I watched as she stuffed her mouth full of sausage-filled puff pastry, dripping with ketchup.

I could taste it: all that buttery pastry mixing with the spicy tomato sauce and sausage. I wanted it.

I forced myself to look away. It was no use; they were everywhere. So many kids eating sausage rolls. I was starving.

Kathryn saw me. She came over with a smug look on her face, and said, 'What's the matter? Hungry? Mmmmm … that was good. Sooo good. I think I'll just go and have another one.'

I was drooling; she took pity on me. 'Come on. There are plenty.'

We walked together into her class room. I could see Mrs Gnash sitting at the desk and I didn't want to go in. I said, 'I've lost my appetite.'

'Don't be silly.' Kathryn tugged at my sleeve. I could smell the sausage rolls and wanted one so badly my stomach hurt. Mrs Gnash looked up; her eyes magnified behind her huge glasses. She looked straight at me.

'Come in, girls. Help yourselves. I made these fresh this morning. Everyone should have one, or two … or *three*.' She looked at Kathryn when she said 'three'. Had she already eaten two? I would have.

I sidled up to the enormous plate that still had maybe twenty sausage rolls on it. There were paper plates and two bottles of ketchup standing on the table. The ketchup bottles had sticky sauce running down the sides, but it didn't matter. Sausage rolls demand ketchup. I slathered it on. As I turned to leave, I remembered my manners, and wrenched my mouth away from the sausage roll before taking a bite and said, 'Thank you, Mrs Gnash. This is very kind. They smell delicious.'

She made a kind of high-pitched trilling noise. I presumed it was a 'thank you' or a 'you're welcome' kind of noise. I couldn't wait any longer. My mouth was full of pastry, sausage and ketchup; it was divine. There was another sound, like the noise my stomach made when I was really hungry: a kind of growl from way down deep. But it was really loud and it wasn't coming from me, or from Kathryn. Mrs Gnash must have been about to eat a sausage roll. Who could blame her?

Kathryn was not my friend and, apart from eating, we had nothing in common. I didn't want to stand around trying to talk to her, so I edged away towards Elemenope and Hakeem.

I was completely lost in my enjoyment of the sausage roll. Mum's words came back to me: 'Nothing tastes as good as being thin feels.' I felt the pastry and the meat rolling around in my mouth and the rush of flavour. I snuck a look at Kathryn; I recognised the look on her face. I thought, *Rubbish, Mum. You have no idea!*

* * * * *

The 'great-sausage-roll-day' did a lot to soften my feelings towards Mrs Gnash. I still didn't trust her and, when she wasn't providing the *best* food I'd ever tasted, I still thought she was a total freak.

I looked at her ridiculously long legs and arms, her huge hands and her eyes that seemed even bigger behind her glasses, and I remembered Mr Newton's words: *'She's an alien.'* I really wanted to share, but I promised Mr Newton I wouldn't.

How did I know she was evil? Maybe she was a really nice alien who just looked and acted really scary. Maybe she was trying to be more friendly?

Michael came up to us with a sausage roll in each hand. Well, a sausage roll in his left hand and the crumbly remains of another in his right hand. His face was so full he couldn't speak, and he had a ketchup grin from ear to ear. Michael couldn't hide his feelings – not one little bit.

* * * * *

Monday's lunch menu was usually some kind of pasta with a cheesy sauce, and I was a big cheese sauce fan. After the sausage rolls it was tasteless, but I ate it anyway. And the biggest pudding on the tray: some sort of sponge cake with jam in the middle. I took the slice that had half the next one stuck to it.

I sat with my gang; I had a comfortable sense that we were OK, the four of us. Jemima Toilet was with a group of her own now. Two of them were 'horsey'; they were in a pony club, and there were a couple of girls who seemed to just follow whoever made the most noise. That was Jemima.

She was retelling the story of her black eye while her gang looked on adoringly. I thought, *Give it a rest; it's not that interesting. It's probably not even true.*

Mr Newton was on lunch duty. He was sitting at the teacher's table, not eating. I realised I'd never seen him eat. Why would I? But when I thought about what he must eat I realised why there were never any spiders or insects where he lived. That was off-putting.

I asked nobody in particular, 'How come Mrs Gnash is doing all this cooking and being really nice to everybody?'

Michael said, 'Does it matter? If she keeps bringing in

food like today, who cares?' We all nodded. Why worry about something so delicious. I caught Mr Newton looking in my direction; I'd forgotten he had super-hearing. With eight thousand sensitive little ears he could probably hear someone eating breakfast in Australia. Then I remembered he could read my mind. I'd find out what he made of my thoughts on Wednesday.

* * * * *

Dad's cooking was getting worse. He said he was going to make cauliflower cheese for dinner. I was hungry for cheese sauce, but what he brought to the table didn't match the picture in my mind.

I wanted the thick, gooey sauce that coats the cauliflower and gets stuck to the roof of my mouth. It should be a bit toasty on top. What was the watery stuff sliding around the bottom of the dish? It looked like runny glue, and I could actually taste the cauliflower – yuk! I didn't have seconds; I could barely choke down my first serving, and that was just to be polite.

There was no pudding. He asked us at the start of dinner what we'd had for lunch. Now, if I was telling the story I always left out the pudding because I knew what could happen. But little miss-goody-goody-I'm-going-to-ruin-your-life piped up about the cake and how she saw me take an extra big slice.

Dad said, 'Well, no need for pudding tonight, then.' I stared at Bella; she was too far away to hit without getting up so I used my 'I'm going to kill you when I catch you later' stare. I couldn't tell if it worked because Mum came in and started talking about her busy day and apologising for being late.

Mum took one look at the more-than-half-full dish of cauliflower muck on the table and said, 'I ate something in the car on the way home.' I knew she was lying. I didn't know what she did in this situation, but I'd be visiting my biscuit tin.

Maybe that was what she meant; maybe being thin tasted better than Dad's cauliflower cheese. It couldn't taste much worse.

Chapter Twenty-nine

I loved Wednesday afternoon; I loved having Mr Newton to myself. He was already sitting at his desk when I got back from saying 'Hi' to Dad and seeing Bella off. I got a sense of relief when she'd gone.

'Now, Martha Gibbons ... I suspect you are too full of questions to get straight down to non-verbal reasoning. Am I correct?'

My head nodded of its own accord. I was bursting to ask about Mrs Gnash. Mr Newton had been reading my mind for months now; I'd nearly got used to it. I wanted to see if he could tell what was bothering me.

'Yes. I know you want to ask about Mrs Gnash. We'll get to that. But there's something else bothering you. I think you should tell me about that in your own way, OK?'

He knew I was having trouble with Jemima Toilet. Did he want to help me with that pain as well? Where to start? What should I say first? It didn't seem as important as Mrs Gnash.

'In your own time, Martha Gibbons. If you're not ready, why don't we have a look at these.'

I relaxed. My thoughts cleared as we worked on some 'spot the difference' diagrams. I loved them, and I'd got a lot quicker. Mr Newton had made up some of his own. As I did the new ones, I thought they were a bit strange. I started to see a pattern in the stick drawings. There was a really skinny figure in the first few, then the stick figure got thicker, and by the final panel it was really fat. Was he trying to tell me something?

'Is this something to do with Mrs Gnash?' I asked

'Very perceptive, Martha Gibbons. Now, what is it about?'

'She's getting bigger. So … is she having a baby?'

'No, but that's a clever idea. Why else might she be getting bigger?'

'Is she eating too much?' *Oh no … not you, too?*

'Yes and no, Martha Gibbons. This is about Mrs Gnash, not you.'

I was relieved. There was only room in my life for not-very-subtle-attacks-on-my-size to come from one direction.

'Mrs Gnash is an alien. Yes, *that* type of alien. She's a Mantiform Caliopteryx.'

I stared at Mr Newton as though I had no idea what he just said. That was because I had absolutely no idea what he just said. My expression did not need a mind reader. He made a kind of gurgling sound; I knew that was him laughing.

'Mantiform Caliopteryxes live on one of Jupiter's moons. They're very peaceful, and live for hundreds of years. I think the one we know as Mrs Gnash did something bad and was punished. Do you remember learning about outlaws?'

I did, but not much. 'Wasn't Robin Hood an outlaw?' I was remembering last year's play.

'Yes, but that story's romanticised. Outlaws were people who broke laws and were sent away from their community to live in the wild. They were not good people.'

'So … you're saying Mrs Gnash was not a good Manti-whatsit-thingamajig?'

'Mantiform Caliopteryx. Yes. That's exactly what I'm saying. She did something bad and her punishment was being sent here.'

'Well, I guess school can be a punishment.'

'I don't mean St Finbar's. And, by the way, this is a good school. I mean Earth. She was banished from her own planet. You'd have to do something pretty bad for that, don't you think?'

I didn't have time to apologise for the school joke; my mind was racing. What did she do? What might she do here? Was she dangerous?

'I think she's very dangerous. I've been studying her for some time, but there's not much to go on. It seems some Mantiform Caliopteryxes have been here before. The only thing I could find was written in ancient Greek ... actually in the book you picked up when you first came to my house. They were seen at the siege of Troy, and it depends what translation of Homer you read whether they feature or not.'

I looked blank. I was beginning to wonder if I would understand anything Mr Newton was going to say.

'Ah ... sorry. We'll get to that another time. Troy has been thought of as not-historically-true, so nobody paid any attention to the Caliopteryxes. Good thing too; it's scary. Anyway, the Spartans saw them off, and as far as I can find out, they've never been back – until now.'

My mind was reeling. I decided to ask Dad about Troy, and Spartans; or maybe I could look at Wikipedia again.

I didn't want to distract Mr Newton anymore. I knew he wanted to tell me about Mrs Gnash. I was doing it; I was reading *his* mind.

'The thing about Mantiform Caliopteryxes is they only eat once every five years. Now, I started watching Mrs Gnash four years ago, and she hasn't eaten anything in that time, so I think she's getting ready to eat. After they eat – and they eat a lot – they blow up to about four times their normal size, and then they hibernate for a year. Then it all starts again.'

My stomach flopped over. 'What do they eat?'

'I've been trying to find out. I don't know if they're carnivores ... you know what that means, don't you?' I nodded. 'Or herbivores, or a bit of both: omnivores, like humans.'

I knew about this because we learned about it when we studied dinosaurs at my old school. A thought popped into my head. 'Are Manti-whatsit-thingamajigs dinosaurs?'

'No. They're much more advanced than that. They seem to be very intelligent, very highly evolved. And rather cunning from what I can make out.'

I had to ask, 'She makes me nervous – Mrs Gnash.

Would she eat children, do you think?' The long pause before Mr Newton answered was not reassuring.

'No, no, no. What an imagination, Martha Gibbons. Now, let's get back to this homework of yours.'

From my experience of Mr Newton, I knew several things: the topic of Mrs Gnash was closed, we would not get onto the subject of Jemima Toilet, and I needed to focus on my work. But I couldn't.

Chapter Thirty

Wednesday evening had become an odd time in our house. It seemed short because I got home much later from school and, in winter, it was already dark. Bella had usually done what little homework she had; probably colouring a page of some baby-story. Mum wasn't home yet, and Dad was struggling to make something in the kitchen. He called it a pie, which sounded promising. But before it went in the oven it didn't look like any kind of pie I'd ever seen.

When it came out, Bella and I looked on in amazement. Dad served it like something at a restaurant. I looked at it; I smelled it. It looked and smelled like pie. We had mashed potato and peas. I looked at Dad with a new-found respect.

Bella said, 'I don't want the peas touching the mashed potato.' Then she screamed. She also meant she didn't want any of the pie touching anything else.

Dad looked annoyed and said, 'Why not, Bella?' *She* never got any food-related-annoying-rhyming-nick-names.

Bella didn't really answer. She squirmed in her seat. I knew the look; I'd seen it before. I sided with Dad and said, 'Don't be so silly, Bella. Food is food.' I had already tasted the pie, and I knew I was speaking the truth. 'And this is good food. Try it.'

Bella pulled another face and said, 'I don't like it. And I don't want the pie touching anything I might eat.'

Dad said, 'What do you mean, "might eat"? You'll eat everything on your plate, missy.'

I was loving it; Bella *never* got in trouble. I had to hide my smile on the inside when she pushed her plate away.

'Isabella Margaret Gibbons, EAT YOUR DINNER!' Dad spat the words out, along with some crumbs and what I hoped wasn't actual spit as it landed on my plate.

Bella burst into tears and stormed out. Dad stayed put; he clenched his fists. I started coughing to hide a laugh. He looked at me and said, 'Not you too?'

'No, Daddy.' I was going to milk this. 'I think the pie is amazing.' It was the best meal of Dad's, ever. The food was pretty good, but Bella's meltdown made it all the sweeter.

Bella actually went to bed without eating anything. What a great evening.

* * * * *

Thursday was a nothing-much day for me. Just boring lessons, a not-much-on-the-menu lunch, more boring lessons and then home for, well frankly, more boring homework.

There was nothing to like about Thursdays. That's what I thought on the walk to school. Well, was I wrong! There was *another* buzz in the playground, centred on Jemima Toilet, but there was no fascinating injury or fake story. She was handing out little cards. I didn't imagine I'd get one, whatever they were. I didn't even go over to look, but she walked towards me. All I could think was, *What now?*

It was awkward. Jemima Toilet was standing in front of me, with a wooden lips-only smile on her face. She gave me a card that had my name on it and said, 'It's my birthday next week; I'm having a party.' That was it. No 'Please come', no 'Here's your invitation' – just a statement of fact. Was she inviting me to her birthday party? If she was, did she think I'd go?

There it was, in black and white, actually purple and blue (a really awful colour combination): my name, *Martha,* then 'You're invited to my party' and the usual stuff about a time and a place. I noticed it was at one of those party places. There would be horse riding. I couldn't ride a horse; I wouldn't be going. I smiled at Jemima Toilet and said, 'Thank you.' Mum would be proud.

I stuffed the invitation in my bag, determined to ignore it. Then I started thinking about the party food – my favourite food; it should be in a separate food group. It should be on that pyramid, way above all the usual boring things about protein, and carbohydrates and stuff.

Elemenope was watching me. She said, 'What are you thinking about?'

I had to drag myself away from images of chocolate biscuits, plates of crisps and cake smothered in rich, sticky icing. 'Oh … nothing,' I said.

Chapter Thirty-one

Saturday: party day! Should-be-excited-but-scared-to-death day. Why on Earth did I say I'd go to Jemima Toilet's birthday party? I had trouble concentrating at ballet because I was worried about the party. I was clumsier than usual; even Miss Louise noticed. She was normally kind and encouraging, but she was barely holding in her rage.

We had started work for the big end-of-year production. The ballet school took the productions very seriously; the head used to be a professional dancer. They only did a show every second year, and we had ten months to get ready.

Miss Louise was decidedly testy and kept standing in front of me, doing the movements like she was my mirror. Well, she would need to put on a few pounds to pull that off. I just couldn't concentrate. Every time Miss Louise bent and swayed I thought about trying to stay on a horse.

The problem was I was terrified and tired. I had hardly slept and my biscuit tin was empty. So instead of focusing on what Miss Louise was trying to show me I was fantasising about the discount packet of Penguin biscuits I saw in the Co-op window. I had pointed them out to Dad, but he shrugged and said, 'They're probably out of date.' I didn't care; sometimes when biscuits go past their use-by date they taste even better.

Miss Louise gave up. She didn't say as much, but I'd seen the look before. I remembered my old ballet school in London: they didn't take themselves as seriously as this one, but even there some of the teachers gave me the look that said, 'We don't expect much from you.' They never said it; I think ballet teachers are like school teachers. They're not allowed to insult kids.

They had to deal with another problem, too. Ballet dancers sometimes don't eat properly, so they get sick-skinny. It's called 'anorexia'; they don't have an appetite, or they think they're fat when they're not and they lose tons and tons of weight and actually look dreadful.

I talked to Mum about it once, and she said it was a really terrible problem. Then she said I'd never have to worry about it. I really needed those Penguin biscuits.

* * * * *

Dad had to drive me to the party because Mum was at work. She often took a Saturday shift at the surgery because it paid extra, and she said we could use the money. She said that while giving Dad a look.

Dad was not a great driver. Actually, he was terrible. Sometimes it felt like we were never going to get where we were going because he was really slow. Sometimes we got lost. Well, not actually lost, but Dad said we were lost because he couldn't follow the directions. We had one of those direction-telling-things in the car: GPS. I couldn't understand Dad's problem; the lady on the GPS told him where to go, when he had to turn and even if there were 'traffic disruptions ahead'.

The party day was one of those days; one of the Dad-getting-lost-because-he-couldn't-follow-the-directions days. Bella and I were laughing because Dad was talking back to the lady on the GPS. That's like talking back to the telly, or the radio. Even Bella knew there was nobody listening at the other end.

Dad was getting really angry; Bella and I were laughing louder and louder. Dad hadn't snapped yet but we both know it wouldn't be long, so we were getting in as much laughter as we could before the explosion. Poor Dad.

Bella was still in her ballet stuff; she was all pink, from head to toe. I'd changed into my party clothes. They weren't my 'going out' clothes because the party invitation said to wear clothes for horse riding. I'd never been horse riding before, so I made up an outfit. Jeans were essential, and I'd combined them with a long-sleeved top, a hoodie and my black boots. I thought I looked the part.

Dad eventually sorted himself out without shouting at either of us, which was a first. We arrived at a giant barn with faded bunting around the door and a blackboard sign that said WELCOME TO JEMIMA'S PARTY. The 'Jemima' was barely readable because it was written in chalk over a smudged section of the blackboard. The party people had just rubbed out the name of the person before and written the new name over the top. It wasn't very posh; I was surprised. The surprise didn't get rid of my nerves, though.

Dad walked beside me, looking around, lost again. He said, 'I have to find out when to come back and pick you up.'

The barn was huge, and smelly: a mix of hay, sweat and poo. Bella pinched her nose. There was a long table off to the side; I took a closer look, but there was no food laid out yet. Dad was obviously looking for someone who might greet us, but the place was empty.

We found a few people milling around out the back. Jemima Toilet was talking to half a dozen girls I didn't know; they didn't go to our school. I couldn't see any of my friends.

A lady walked over. She was wearing those riding trousers, jodhpurs, and really shiny boots. She held out her hand to Dad, but looked at me as she said, 'I'm Amanda Waddington-Clarke. This must be …' Dad stood still. He didn't say anything.

I had to say something, 'I'm Martha Gibbons.' I looked at Dad; he still had nothing ready to come out of his mouth, and he'd pushed Bella in front of him like a shield. 'This is my father, John.'

Dad took a deep breath and managed, 'Sorry … yes … John Gibbons. How do you do?'

The lady had a plastic smile. It wasn't just her smile; her whole face didn't move. There was no expression around her eyes and her skin was too smooth and shiny, like it had been pulled back tight. Mr Newton's mask had more life.

I got the feeling she had already decided we weren't worth talking to. She completely ignored Bella (couldn't blame her for that), and turned side-on as she said, 'We'll start with some riding, and have tea when we get back. I hope you can wait that long.' Wow. I didn't like her already. *Like mother, like daughter.*

Dad had to run after Mrs Toilet. 'Excuse me, err … Amanda. I just wanted to ask when I should come back to pick up Martha. When will the party finish?'

Mrs Toilet looked at Dad as though he was something that fell out of the back of a horse. 'Oh, about six I should think,' she said, walking faster.

I watched Bella put her hand in Dad's as they walked away, back to the safety of the car. I wished I was going with them. I could; they hadn't left yet. But the thought of party food kept my feet still.

Chapter Thirty-two

I was waiting for somebody I knew to turn up; Jemima Toilet had invited the whole class. Where was everybody? I stood under a tree, looking at the girls in their riding gear; they were all wearing proper riding stuff. I looked down at my invented outfit and groaned. I felt like an outlaw.

The back door of the barn opened and there was a familiar face: Hakeem! I looked behind him, but nobody else was there. Hakeem's dad got the Mrs Toilet treatment, not as badly as my dad, but she still looked right through him. I watched her sizing Hakeem up; he was dressed a bit like me: jeans, jumper and short boots. He came over to me and we both groaned.

He said, 'Hi, Martha. I'm glad you're here. I've never ridden a horse. Have you?'

I shook my head. 'Is anybody else coming? Where is everybody?'

'I know Michael couldn't come; he's got a football game. So that's the Marks out as well, and Craig, I guess. I don't know about anybody else.'

I asked, 'Is Elemenope coming?' I really hoped she'd show up.

'Don't know. I thought you'd know. You two are BFFs, aren't you?' I didn't use that silly BFF thing. Lots of girls at school said they were somebody-or-other's BFF, but it didn't mean a thing. The day after they said it, or gave each other one of those soppy half-a-heart dangly things, they were off with someone else being really nasty about yesterday's BFF. It was ridiculous. *Best Friends Forever? More like Boring Frenemies Forever.*

The riding was about to start, and nobody else I knew had turned up. Hakeem and I looked at each other like we were the only people on earth. Suddenly there were horses coming – huge great things – and they were getting closer.

Mrs Toilet was fussing over Jemima and the group of riding friends. They were putting on helmets; I hadn't seen those before. I worried about a sport that needed protective headgear.

The group of girls rode off, not even looking over their shoulders. There were no goodbyes or waves in our direction. They were just gone as if we didn't exist. I realised that, for them, we *didn't* exist.

I nudged Hakeem. He was surely feeling the same,

but he wasn't looking at them, or me. He was looking at two short, fat ponies being led around the corner of the barn. They were being led, uncomfortably, in our direction.

I saw Mrs Toilet's back, off in the distance, with the riding girls. I didn't even see her get on a horse. I supposed it was just some simple routine for her, and off she went without the outcasts.

That thought reminded me of Mrs Gnash. Was this how she felt when she was sent to live on our planet? Outcast and ignored by her own kind who just turned their backs on her and rode off? I tried to imagine a whole herd of Mantiform-thingamajigs riding horses; it looked silly, even in my mind.

Hakeem was standing right beside me, almost on top of me. We started to back away from the ponies as they got nearer. They were being led by a girl who looked about sixteen. Her overalls were a grubby green with big splotches of mud (I hoped it was mud) all over. Her brown riding boots weren't shiny like the riding girls'; they were all scuffed and grubby, and her face was flecked with mud (again, I hoped it was mud). She had brown hair, tied back under a brown/black helmet. She was basically brown from head to toe.

I don't know what it is about brown; I just don't like it. Whenever someone gives me brown clothes, I don't wear them. It's not that they're not nice clothes, it's the colour. Brown: it's nothing. Unless it's walking towards me with two ponies in tow – then it's terrifying.

Brownie spoke, 'You must be the kids who've not ridden before.' Hakeem nodded. I stood absolutely still; certain the ponies could sense fear.

'Well, come on then. Let's get some kit on you.' I didn't know what she was saying. I'd been cast out and sent to some foreign planet where they spoke a different language and wanted you to do things with giant animals.

Hakeem stood there and let Brownie strap a helmet on his head; it didn't fit. She took it off, fiddled with the insides and put it back on. It was slipping from side to side, so she yanked on the strap. Hakeem yelped; she'd caught his skin. I was watching all this and trying to figure out the quickest way back through the barn. I would just sit in the car park and wait for Dad.

She was coming at me with another helmet. I backed away. 'What's the matter, love? They don't bite. Looks more like you'd take a bite of one of the ponies, to me. Watch out, Silky … this one looks hungry.'

I presumed that last bit was directed to the chubby

pony, standing beside me. Brownie said, I think, to me, 'This is Silky; she's a darling. Let's get you up in the saddle, now.' I realised I had the helmet on my head. That must have happened while Brownie was warning Silky that I might eat her.

Brownie hoisted me by my feet and thighs. She was surprisingly strong, but she was not a clear communicator. I had no idea what I was supposed to do once I was 'up'. I went straight over the top of Silky and landed on my head on the other side. I hated horse riding.

I decided to not try again. My head hurt, my neck hurt and I just couldn't see the point of trying to get up on something that I would not be able to stay on. Hakeem said, 'I think I'll wait here with Martha … you know … keep an eye on her.'

Brownie shrugged and said, 'Suit yourselves. I've got to unsaddle the ponies whether you ride them or not. This way I get finished before dark.'

As she strolled off with the ponies slouching beside her, I strained to make out her words. It sounded like, 'Spoilt kids. Don't know why they bother. Don't you worry, Silky, you're better off without that big lump breaking your back.' That was what I thought I heard, and I didn't care.

We sat under the tree for a bit. I looked at Hakeem; my head hurt. Brownie hadn't even bothered to take our helmets off. Hakeem's helmet had rolled down at an angle and was sitting over his right eye. He looked ridiculous. We both looked ridiculous.

Laughing made the headache worse, but I keep doing it. I had to get my helmet off. There was a clasp under my chin; I couldn't work it lose. Struggling made it tighter.

Hakeem got my helmet off, then his own. He helped me to my feet and we walked into the barn. Somehow, in our inability to even get on a horse we'd both trodden in horse poo, Hakeem's jumper had expanded (were all his clothes too big?), and I felt like I'd been run over by a bus.

Chapter Thirty-three

The barn was still empty, except for the long table which I hoped would be piled high with a birthday feast. I was even hungrier than usual.

'I'm starving. Where's the food?'

Hakeem said, 'After stress, it's normal to feel relieved and even hungry.' How did he know this stuff? *Why* did he know this stuff?

We discovered a drinks machine. I was really thirsty, but I didn't have any money. Hakeem slid a one-pound coin into the slot. 'What do you want?'

I really wanted a Coke, but Mum said I was never to have it again after the time I drank a whole two-litre bottle one afternoon and threw up everywhere. I said 'Lemonade ... thanks.' It was sweet, bubbly and gone too quickly.

I asked Hakeem, 'What are you going to have?'

He said, 'I don't have any more money. But it's OK; I'm not really thirsty.' He'd used his only money, and I drank it. I felt awful; not thirsty anymore, but guilty and selfish.

I opened my mouth to apologise, but Hakeem held up a hand and said, 'No, really, it's fine. I'm OK. The party should be starting soon, I hope.'

Two people dressed like Brownie, but with less poo on them, rushed into the barn and started opening doors and pushing piles of chairs around. I could hear them muttering. Why were so many adults unhappy with their work?

We watched the party take shape. Bunting was strung around and a huge banner saying HAPPY BIRT DAY was hooked over nails along the wall. I presumed the H had fallen off some time ago, and nobody had either noticed or bothered to replace it. The dull lights were turned up over the table, casting the rest of the space in shadow and hiding the dusty emptiness.

Food! The brownies were laying the table. At last. I could see two plates full of sandwiches. There were two bowls of crisps. Only two? I'd counted at least nine kids. Each table setting had a paper plate in front of it, a paper napkin and a juice box. I was waiting to see the rest of the food, the good stuff: the sausage rolls, the party pies, the bowls of sweets. I kept waiting. Was there cake? Not that I could see. I'd only come to this party for the food. Hakeem had obviously seen the same performance, but his reaction was different; he seemed pleased.

'Hakeem, I can't see any real party food. Do you think there'll be cake?'

'Of course. Everybody has cake on their birthday. I'm sure it's the law.' He smiled at his own joke. 'This looks pretty good. I like sandwiches.'

I said, 'But there's no real party food.' He shrugged at that. 'Is it a boy thing? Do you just eat anything, you know, for fuel? Don't you care about the special stuff? I love the special stuff.'

I was still wondering about cake when the doors opened again and the riders appeared. Mrs Toilet stood in the doorway and sent the jodhpur-d girls to the table. There was a distinctive smell about them: earthy and sweaty and pooey. Jemima Toilet sat at the head of the table. She still hadn't said hello to me.

The riding girls ignored Hakeem and me. Their conversation was all about their horses and their gear. There was a lot of gossip too; I overheard stories about Jemima Toilet's old school. I'd never given that topic any thought. Of course, she'd been to another school. She didn't just come to St Finbar's from thin air. Those riding girls weren't just horsey friends, they were old school friends. The stories were about people I didn't know, so I tuned out.

I was happy talking to Hakeem; he always had interesting things to say. Well, they were interesting to him, anyway. Hakeem was worth ten times those girls to me. He was kind, and he was generous. I wanted to know if he really liked Elemenope.

'Hakeem?'

'Uh huh …?' He had a sandwich in his mouth.

'You really like Elemenope, don't you?'

He blushed; that was my answer. While I waited for him to swallow, I popped another mouthful of crisps in. They were good: salt and vinegar, tangy and crunchy.

'Why do you ask?' he said.

'Oh … it's just, you seem to like her. And I know you leave notes in her locker.'

'Ahh. Those. You think they're love letters?'

'Well, aren't they?'

He went red. 'No, they're not!'

I said, 'Then, what are they? Does she leave you notes too?'

'Sometimes.'

'Are you going to tell me about it?'

He lowered his voice and said, 'It's a secret.'

'Well, if you don't tell me, I'll just have to make it up … satisfy my curiosity … you know.'

He went red again, but a different kind of red. I thought, maybe he wasn't hiding some romantic secret. Then I thought that was a shame. Finally, Hakeem said, 'If I tell you, you can't tell anybody else. It's a secret. Elemenope might not be happy.'

I said, 'Well, she's not here. So?'

'OK. Here goes.' There was a long pause. Long enough for some more salt and vinegar crisps.

Hakeem said, 'Elemenope and I … we've been spying on Mrs Gnash. We think she's trying to poison kids at school.'

I paused, with my hand halfway to my mouth. Something about poisoning made me stop shovelling food. 'What?'

He said, 'Why else would she suddenly bring all this food to school? She's seriously mean, so why would she bring in the one thing kids can't resist: cakes and sausage rolls?' That was two things. And I'd eaten them both. Had I been poisoned?

There were no sausage rolls at the party. I tried a sandwich: brown bread, no butter, thinly sliced cheese, not even cheddar. Bland was not a good enough word.

I wanted to hear Hakeem's ideas about Mrs Gnash. I wanted to tell him I knew she was an alien. Worse than that, she was a criminal alien. How could I do that? I only had the word of Mr Newton. And I'd given him *my* word that I wouldn't tell.

Hakeem changed the topic, 'It's funny, really. We started spying on Mr Newton last year. Just because he seemed so different. A bit odd … you know.'

'Yes, I *do* know! And that's putting it mildly.'

He said, 'But now we know he's a whole pile of newts, it all makes sense, and there's no point spying on him anymore.' I really wanted to tell him what Mr Newton had said about Mrs Gnash, but I was trying to keep my face neutral, to not give anything away. I gave him an encouraging look.

'We only started spying on Mrs Gnash last week. She's really scary, despite the food. Have you noticed how long her arms and legs are?'

I decided the crisps weren't poisoned. I shovelled some more in quickly because the riding girl beside me had noticed them and grabbed the bowl.

Hakeem said, 'And they look kind of stiff, don't you think? Like her joints are in the wrong place, or something.'

I said, 'But I don't think having long arms and legs means anything. I mean, people come in all shapes and sizes.' I pointed at him and then me. Hakeem was polite, and a friend; he was allowed to laugh at that.

Chapter Thirty-four

Cake! At last! Mrs Toilet was carrying a cake in the shape of a horse. How do you do that? Not carry a cake; make a cake that looks like a horse? The horse *was* the cake. I'd seen normal cakes with things stuck on top of them, but never a whole cake that had been made to look like something else.

As the cake was put down in front of her, Jemima said 'Oh, Mummy. It looks just like Lucky Boy.' Was she crying? I overheard a couple of the riding girls say (nobody actually told me anything) that Lucky Boy was Jemima's old horse who'd died a few weeks before.

I felt bad. I'd been so busy hating Jemima Toilet it never occurred to me that she might have a whole history I didn't know about. I never asked her about where she had come from, her family, anything like that. I just took a set against her. And now I felt bad.

There she was with her old friends, and she still invited everybody from our class, and none of us had gone. None of us apart from Hakeem and me. I knew why I was there. It had finally arrived, and was sitting on the table, waiting to be cut, waiting for me to sink my teeth into it. I guessed Hakeem came because he was a nice person.

I felt bad for Jemima, too, because having your horse die must suck – a lot. It must be like the biggest pet you could ever have. I remembered feeling sad when my ladybird died. It was tiny and only lived a year. But a horse is huge, and years old, and you see it and ride it every day. So losing a horse must feel extra bad.

I didn't know how to feel. I felt really sorry for Jemima Toi … I decided to stop calling her that. I would call her Jemima Waddington-Clarke, or just Jemima. But I also wanted some cake. I needed some cake. So far, I'd only eaten crisps, and not enough of them.

I loved cake, especially ones with heaps of icing. There must have been tons of icing on the Lucky Boy cake, because you couldn't get all that shaping with cake and just put a thin layer on. All the detail had to be icing of some sort.

I watched in horror as Jemima said to her mum, 'I can't possibly cut the cake; it's too nice. It reminds me of Lucky Boy and I just can't do that to him.'

I looked at Mrs Toilet. She still deserved the name;

she was so rude to Dad. It looked like she was going to cut the cake anyway. I was conflicted; I wanted cake, but I understood how Jemima felt. I remembered one of Mum's sayings: 'You can't have your cake and eat it too.' What that meant was Jemima had her cake and I couldn't eat it. I was starving.

* * * * *

There were no games, just more gossiping around the table. That meant Hakeem and I were talking again. I wanted to go back to Mrs Gnash, but Hakeem was prattling on about some type of fly that only lives around horses and stables. He was a nice person, but sometimes I had to tune him out.

Dad and Bella arrived to take me home. At last. I could see if Dad brought any snacks. I'd settle for a nice biscuit; I'd never been so relieved to leave anywhere. As we climbed into the car, Dad asked, 'How was the party, honey bunny?'

Years of conditioning made me answer, 'Fine.' Dad was in driving mode, so he was concentrating on what he was doing and not on my conversation, not that there'd been any yet. I felt there should be.

I looked out the window and saw him again. The shabby private detective was standing on the edge of the car park, leaning on a tree. He was staring at the entrance to the party barn, like he was waiting for somebody. I decided to commit his face to memory. I didn't trust him. What was he up to?

Bella asked, 'Where's your party bag?' It was only then I realised there weren't any. I'd been to a few parties, and I expected a party bag: some sweets, maybe a toy and a piece of cake. I understood about the cake, but where was the rest of the stuff?

I didn't wait to be asked any more questions. I let fly, 'That was the worst party I've ever been to. I hated everything about it. I couldn't get on the horse – no – I fell off the horse and broke my head. The food was terrible – what there was of it. The cake was never cut, and nobody talked to me – except Hakeem – he talked to me – but that could be any day. It was rubbish.'

'That's nice, darling,' was all I got from Dad.

Bella's eyes were wide. She said, 'No cake? And no party bag?' I shook my head.

The rest of the trip home was silent. I thought about Jemima Toi… I made myself stop every time that came out. Poor girl. I thought about Jemima and her horse, and I felt strange. Maybe it was my empty stomach, but I felt like crying. I was going to try again with Jemima. We could have a start-over.

Chapter Thirty-five

When Elemenope asked about the party, I said, 'Oh, it was horrible. The food was hopeless; we didn't even have cake. The horses were huge and we couldn't ride them. Well, Hakeem and I couldn't ride them. Where were you, anyway?'

'Oh … I couldn't go. I, um, had a headache.' That was the first time my friend had lied to me.

Jemima arrived with her left arm in a sling. The crowd of interest formed and I went right to the front.

Her voice had to struggle over the clamour of questions, 'I had a bad fall off a horse at my birthday party. Stupid rental horse … should have had my own, but Mummy hasn't bought me a new one yet.'

I got how falling off a horse would be bad. Horses are big and scary. As the story went on, I started to feel uncomfortable. I was at her birthday party and, even though I wasn't on the ride, I'd seen her afterwards. She was fine; she wasn't injured. It was true she was crying, but that was over her dead horse.

It would have been obvious if she'd fallen off a horse; there would have been ice packs and concern and people offering sympathy, like now. All those old school-friends, her mother, would have been all over her. She was lying.

I caught Jemima's eye. She looked at Elemenope and back to me. She must have known I wasn't buying the story. Was she going to ask me to verify it? I took Elemenope's arm to steer her away.

Elemenope said, 'You never told me Jemima fell off her horse. That would have been way more interesting than telling me about the food. What's the matter with you?'

We had to get out of earshot before I said, 'She's lying. I was there. She never fell off her horse.' I was so confused I forgot that what Hakeem had told me was a secret. I said, 'Why don't you stop spying on teachers and see what you can find out about Jemima. There's something not right about her.'

'That's a secret! How did you find out about that?' Any other person would have shouted at me. Elemenope didn't shout, but her face was red; her fists were clenched. I was scared for Hakeem if I said he'd told me. But it was too late.

Hakeem said, 'I told her, El.' *El?* I'd never heard him call her *El* before. It was an intimate nickname. I was right; he had a crush on her. The sneak.

Elemenope turned on Hakeem. 'That's *our* secret … *our* thing!' Before Hakeem or I could say anything more, Elemenope stormed off, but she didn't get far. Mrs Gnash started to ring the bell. It seemed louder than usual and Mrs Gnash seemed taller than usual. Everything around me seemed big, and I felt really small.

* * * * *

Elemenope didn't speak to me for the rest of the day. Even Mr Newton noticed something was wrong; I could sense it. Tuesday was worse, because whenever I tried to talk to Elemenope she turned her back on me. Twice I saw her and Hakeem talking together, but if I got close they both gave me the look that yelled 'go away'. Actually, it was a different look from each of them. Hers was angry, his, apologetic.

By Wednesday I was resigned to losing my two best friends. Michael was around, but he just played football. He didn't seem to have noticed that we weren't all together. I felt lonely. I'd never had real friends before. There was another saying I'd heard for years and never understood before now: 'You don't know what you've got 'til it's gone.' I was beginning to understand and I didn't like it.

My afternoon session with Mr Newton didn't get off to a good start. I was really distracted but he tried to get me to concentrate on the maths problem he set me for homework. I'd made a mess of it when I tried to do it over the weekend, and I'd completely forgotten about it since. I looked at the sheet of paper like I'd never seen it before, and I started to cry.

'Oh dear, Martha Gibbons ... you'd better tell me what's wrong.'

'Don't you know? Aren't you reading my mind?'

'Only a little bit. It's blurry. Newts don't feel things the same way as you humans. It would be better if you explained it to me. I have noticed, if you talk about a problem, you get a clearer picture than if you just work it around inside your own head. Shall we try that?'

'OK.' My voice was croaky.

I tried to tell Mr Newton about Elemenope ignoring me and how that made me feel. I had to tell him the secret that Hakeem had leaked to me. The one I told Elemenope I knew. The one that broke our friendship. The more I said, the more I cried. There was snot running down my upper lip.

Every time I said something about Elemenope he said,

'And how does that make you feel?'

We hadn't done any maths by the end of the tutorial, but I felt a whole lot better. I said, 'Thank you, Mr Newton.'

'For what, Martha Gibbons?'

'For helping with the problem about my friends.'

'I didn't do anything. I just listened.'

I'd done all the talking, and he had done all the listening. He was right; talking about the problem did help. He was really smart, and kind. I still didn't know exactly what to do, but I felt happier. And hungry. Happy and hungry, that would have to do. I went home with Dad and Bella for afternoon tea: biscuits again.

* * * * *

Thursday started better. I was busy being miserable about my friends, but as I walked into the playground, I saw Elemenope making a beeline for me. I stood my ground.

She stood really close and took my hand. She said, 'I'm sorry. I forgive you.' I felt my heart relax, and we had a little cuddle; we'd never done that before. Hakeem came over. He had waited for Elemenope to make the first move. They seemed to have made up too. At least I think they had; they'd stopped fighting.

Hakeem said, 'El and I have been talking,' (there it was again – that 'El'), 'and we want you to help us spy on Mrs Gnash. Do you want to?'

'Sure.' I was delighted.

I didn't think following Mrs Gnash around was going to do anything more than annoy her, and that would not be good for us. I wanted to get to the bottom of why Jemima kept coming to school with black eyes and sprained wrists, making up stories about how she got them. The stories, themselves, were OK. They would explain the injuries, but they were clearly lies. She was making stuff up. At least she wasn't blaming me for the latest one.

Chapter Thirty-six

Sunday lunch was my favourite. Everybody had a job. Except Mum. Dad said, 'It's nice to let Mum just sit by the fire and read the newspapers. She's been really busy lately, because winter makes people go to the doctor more. So, I'm going to do all the cooking.' *Nooooo!*

Dad had been in the kitchen for hours, trying something new. I was nervous, but I had to say it smelled good.

I asked, 'Whatcha cooking, Daddy?' He shooed me away.

He said, 'It's a surprise.' That worried me; I hoped he wasn't making it up. I remembered a few months before, he decided he knew how to make pasta sauce. He didn't look at the recipe and put in way too much salt. He decided rosemary would be a good herb. It wasn't. And the pasta was soggy. I can eat just about anything, but that was horrible. My biscuit tin had a serious workout that night.

Bella had to set the table. That was a good job for her; she's a neat-freak, so lining everything up took a long time. She still had trouble remembering which side to put the knife and fork, so I said, 'Can I help you? Do you know which side to put the forks?'

She snapped, 'Of course I do. I don't need your help!' I watched silently as she got it wrong. I'd tried.

My job was to get drinks ready for Bella and me. Milk. How hard could that be? I poured two glasses and set them on the little coasters Bella had put to the top-right of our placemats; she got that bit right. I decided to fix the knife and fork situation while she was out of the room, to save an argument later. I was a great big sister.

Bella came back in with a handful of paper napkins. She'd been trying to fold them nicely; it was her new thing. She saw what I was doing and exploded.

'What are you doing? Setting the table is my job – you leave it alone.'

I said, 'But the knives go on the right, and the forks go on the left.'

'No … it doesn't matter … they go like I've done it. You're so bossy!'

I had a fork in my hand and she tried to grab it from me. I pulled away and her milk went flying. That was a bad time for Dad to come in. He was getting really flustered and he yelled at us, 'I'm trying to get this meal on the table with all its bits, all together, and I can't even ask you two to do a simple job like setting the table. Who spilt the milk?'

Bella and I pointed at each other. We both said, '*She* did!'

'Well, I don't care. Clean it up.'

There was a problem with our dining table; it had big planks of wood with gaps between them, so milk ran into the gaps and you couldn't get it out.

I got some kitchen roll and tried to wipe inside the gaps. The paper got stuck and little bits tore off and wound up poking out of the table. I moved my placemat to cover them. Bella started yelling, 'You're ruining my setting! You always ruin everything. Why do I have to have such a *stupid* big sister?'

Mum came in. She looked really tired and I felt bad for her. Bella didn't care; she ran up to her and said, 'I set the table, and Martha's ruined it … look!' Bella was right. It was a mess now.

Mum said, 'Oh, Bella, you've done a lovely job.' I knew she wouldn't say that to me. 'But, the knives and forks go the other way around.' Bella sullenly swapped the cutlery, all the time giving me that look. She couldn't do a death-stare like mine yet, but I got the meaning. It wasn't my fault; I tried to tell her.

Dad came in from the kitchen with a dish of roast potatoes. Next was a dish of Brussels sprouts. Not so good. Then, to my surprise: roast beef. I noticed the absence of Yorkshire pudding, but there was gravy. Dad was really trying hard. Even Mum looked impressed. She started to say, 'Where's the Yor— ?', but changed it to '… You're really working the whole roast thing, Johnny. Great job.' I didn't think she would get away with it, but Dad said nothing.

I got the gravy-rationing treatment again. I struggled to get a tiny bit of gravy with every bite of the beef, but there wasn't enough to deal with the evil sprouts. If we had a dog, I could have slipped the sprouts onto the floor when nobody was looking. I tried putting them in Bella's plate, but Mum saw me.

The gravy had gone, and I had to choke the sprouts down dry. It took forever because I had to have a drink of milk after every mouthful. And then, the greatest insult: no pudding.

Dad had put so much effort into the roast, that he didn't make any. Little-spoilt-brat Bella got a bowl of custard from a tin. I would have liked some of that, but no … the greedy girl got nothing. And then I was sent to my room. I dived for my tin. There were only two Hobnobs left; they would have to do.

I finished the biscuits and decided I would talk to Jemima Waddington-Clarke. I didn't know if I wanted to be her friend; we had nothing in common. But there was something going on in her life that was making her unhappy. I decided I could help. That occupied me for a whole afternoon. Well, that and reading *The Velveteen Rabbit* for the millionth time.

I forgot about all that again while I ate dinner: left-over roast beef, with ketchup. It would have been the perfect Sunday night except it was Bella's turn to choose the movie and we wound up watching *Frozen*. AGAIN.

Chapter Thirty-seven

I strode into the playground on Monday morning, and waved a bright 'Hi' to Elemenope. We linked arms and I steered us towards Jemima over by the low wall. She didn't have anyone around her admiring bruises or listening to stories of accidents, so it was the perfect time to approach her. The look from Jemima was hostile. It said, 'What do you want?' I ignored it.

I said, 'Hi, Jemima. I wanted to thank you for inviting me to your birthday party last weekend.'

She looked startled, and said, 'I didn't think you had a very nice time.'

I reddened; she was right, but I didn't want to get into it. 'Oh, it was fine. Did … um … did you have a good ride?'

'Actually, we did. We went to a clearing in the woods there; it was lovely.'

She was softening, but it was hard work. There was no reference to her falling off her horse. Not surprising, since I *knew* she had lied about that.

I nudged Elemenope. I wanted her to get involved in the conversation, but she stayed silent.

'The cake … did your mum make that? It looked amazing.' I was trying really hard.

'No. Mummy doesn't bake. She got someone at the market to do it. We always have a special cake for birthdays.'

I asked, 'Did you have any of it? Was it nice inside?'

'We had some later; it was OK.'

I had imagined that cake for a week. It should have been not just 'OK'; it should have been delicious: all buttercream, sweet and crumbly. But it sounded disappointing, like the rest of the party. A bit like this conversation.

* * * * *

Mr Newton started the school week with one of his cobwebs tests. That didn't go so well because I was distracted by how sad Jemima seemed. I skipped the second question, somehow, and put all the other answers in the wrong box. The result was a worrying one out of ten. It was Elemenope who saw what I'd done, and told Mr Newton.

She said, 'Martha actually got the answers right; she just put them in the wrong place.' Surely, he would understand.

Mr Newton said, 'I see the problem. Yes, you did get the answers to those questions correct, but they're out of order. If a computer had marked your paper instead of a friend, you would still only get one out of ten. You have to concentrate, Martha Gibbons. Use that big brain of yours. It's a good thing these cobwebs tests are just for our enjoyment.'

I was angry at Mr Newton for not giving me my proper mark, then I was angry with myself. That made me forget about Jemima's problems and focus on the lesson. Job done, Mr Newton; I was concentrating.

* * * * *

Was it my imagination, or were the kids in Mrs Gnash's class getting fat? They were eating treats every day. I was jealous. They ate muffins and cream buns. I hadn't had a cream bun for ever.

I kept trying to find excuses to go into Mrs Gnash's classroom, but when Mr Newton saw me sneaking in there at break, he called me over. He didn't usually walk around the school much, but lately he'd started hanging around in the corridors.

'Martha Gibbons ... I think you should stay away from Mrs Gnash.'

It was unusual for Mr Newton to say anything like that to me outside our confidential tutorial time. Was he worried? I tried not to shout, 'So she *is* going to eat the kids in her class! When were you going to tell me? We've got to warn them.' I was not whispering, but we were the only people in the corridor.

My heart raced. I wanted to ring the bell and get all the kids out of the school. This was *horrible*. I looked at Mr Newton; he was not much taller than me. I must have looked frightened, or maybe frightening, because he took a step back and stumbled.

There was a moment of physical confusion while his body reshaped itself. Because I knew what was going on under his clothes and behind his mask, I could see thousands of newts rearranging themselves into the familiar shape of Mr Newton. Somebody who didn't know his secret (like everybody else in the school) would have seen a very strange internal dance.

I had long suspected Mr Newton had super-powers. Not the usual ones like X-ray vision, or super strength, but some kind of super mind-power that made people either not see the truth of him, or forget what they'd seen. I remembered the weird wobbly feeling I used to get when I first met him, and the strange way Elemenope forgot ever being in his house.

I slunk out of the school and went hunting for my friends in the playground. It was a very clear but unfamiliar feeling: I had friends, and I had to protect them. I had to protect Bella too. For all her annoying goody-goodyness, she was my sister, and she *did* help with the 'great Halloween newt rescue' last year, so I owed her that.

Michael was easy to spot, out on the field, playing football. His size and strength made me want him with me if whatever-I-was-afraid-might-happen actually happened. I didn't have time to worry about the weird, evolving I-didn't-know-if-it-was-friendship-or-not feeling with Jemima, and I couldn't see her anyway.

My head was racing with, *Where's Elemenope? Where's Hakeem?* I couldn't see them anywhere. The bell rang, swung by Mrs Gnash's huge hand. I saw her now; I saw her for what she was, and I recognised the look on her face. I'd been right all along about that look. She was hungry. I was scared and angry all at once: 'scangry'. I was too worried to enjoy my new word.

As we lined up, I looked over at Mrs Gnash's class. They *were* getting fat. The boys all looked like their trousers were too tight. The girls' tights were starting to show rolls of fat bulging through. I knew how that felt.

I looked at my own classmates. We were OK, well, with the obvious exception of me – but I didn't look any bigger than usual. I still couldn't see Elemenope or Hakeem. I got an image of them locked up in some elaborate birdcage, with Mrs Gnash strolling by like the witch in *Hansel and Gretel*.

The pain in my chest settled when I reached our classroom. There was Hakeem, in his seat already, and Elemenope in her seat beside mine. But they didn't look right. They were staring straight ahead, like zombies. Elemenope said nothing. She just sat there with a blank look on her face. I waved my hand in front of her eyes: nothing. Not a flicker.

Mr Newton was out in front of the class. Miss Slider, the head, stood beside him. They were talking close together, and didn't seem to notice the classroom filling up.

Mr Newton was wrigglier than usual, and Miss Slider was nodding. She walked over to Hakeem's seat and said quietly, 'Come with me, Hakeem ... we'll go to the office.' Hakeem followed her without looking to the right or the left. His arms were limp by his side.

I heard Miss Slider say the same thing to Elemenope. Everything was happening in slow motion. Elemenope stood and followed Miss Slider and Hakeem. They were two zombies in a row.

The class was just not right; I couldn't concentrate, and Mr Newton knew it. He left me alone. I didn't need to be told to 'use my big brain' just then. It was full, and starting to hurt.

Chapter Thirty-eight

At lunch, I raced to talk to Michael. 'Did you see what happened to Elemenope and Hakeem?' He shook his head. 'Seriously? They were acting like zombies … you didn't notice that?' He shook his head again.

Jemima hurried over to us; that was a first. She was breathless, but bursting to speak. 'I can tell you something. I was in the office, waiting for Miss Slider; I wanted to go home.'

I stirred the air, urging her on. 'Well, she came in, with Elemenope and Hakeem in tow – they looked really strange, but the weird thing was … I don't know how to say this …' I was standing with my arms out, pleading for her to continue. '… well, it was like the clock stopped, or something. I don't know how else to describe it. Everything went into slow-motion. I thought I might be about to faint.'

I said, '*Thank you!* You too? I get that when she's really close. I thought it was the smell – you know, mothballs or something. I haven't told anybody; I was worried they'd think I was crazy.' I looked at Michael, and he was giving us both the 'you two are crazy' stare. I smiled at Jemima, 'See what I mean?'

Jemima was bursting, 'Anyway, I couldn't hear it all, because Miss Slider went into her office, and time sped up again. That's so weird. But they were sent home.'

I must have been looking stupid. Jemima felt the need to repeat, 'Hakeem and Elemenope … they were sent home.' I got that.

I said, 'What do you think is wrong with them?'

'I don't know. They looked really spaced out – like they were hypnotised or something.'

* * * * *

I couldn't settle into my Mr Newton tutorial. Elemenope and Hakeem had missed another whole day, and my brain was working overtime.

'I know, Martha Gibbons. You're worried about your friends, aren't you?'

I nodded. I seemed to do a lot of that with Mr Newton. It helped that I didn't usually have to say much.

'I'm worried too. I found Hakeem and Elemenope in a cupboard in Mrs Gnash's class. It appears they have been spying on her. The problem was, on Monday, she found them. When I got into the room, she had tied them up – I don't know why. But it didn't look good.

'When Mrs Gnash went out to ring the bell, I got Miss Slider to help me. There was just enough time to get them into the classroom. It was a mistake. We should have taken them to the office. But you saw what they were like; we had to get them out.'

'Will they be all right?'

'I hope so. I had to blank their memories for a couple of days. You know I can do that, right?' I thought of Elemenope again, and nodded. 'Otherwise they would have some very scary memories, and they don't deserve that. Mrs Gnash is very dangerous.'

'So, how can we stop her from eating her class?'

'That again?'

I said, 'Yes … that again. I've seen it. You must have seen it too. All the kids in her class are getting fat. She's feeding them, fattening them up. It's horrible. We have to do something.'

'Now, don't panic, Martha Gibbons.'

'Can't we catch her? Take her somewhere else? Get rid of her? You said yourself, her own kind got rid of her.

Can't we do the same?'

'Well, that just makes her somebody else's problem. It doesn't fix it, does it?'

I knew he was right.

* * * * *

I wasn't sure where the idea came from, but on Friday, as we were getting ready for sports day, I asked Jemima if she'd like to come to my house for a play date on the weekend. She looked really surprised. I'd surprised myself. I wondered if it was because I was a bit lonely. Hakeem and Elemenope still hadn't come back to school and I missed them. I'd never missed anybody before.

'I think I would like that. Thank you.' She had a funny way of speaking, almost as if she was speaking about herself to someone else. I half expected her to do that thing where people use their own names, like: 'Martha Gibbons will go home now,' instead of 'I'm going home.'

Jemima said, 'I'll ask Mummy at home time,' and she smiled at me. That was funny too. She called her mum 'Mummy' even when she wasn't around. I didn't know anybody else who did that. Well, I did say it to Mum when I wanted something. And 'Daddy' worked a treat.

Our parents were both in the playground for pick-up at the same time. I raced over to Dad and said, 'Daddy, can Jemima come over on the weekend? Please?'

I watched his face; he baulked. He didn't like having people over, and I knew he had a hard time with Mrs Toi— Mrs Waddington-Clarke … the first time they met, but eventually he said, 'Yes – as long as it's OK with her parents.' He was distracted by Bella running up to him and bouncing into his arms (she was *so* his favourite) and I raced over to where Jemima was talking to her mum.

Mrs Waddington-Clarke (I did it!) didn't look happy. I could hear her saying, 'But you've got horse riding on Saturday.'

I chimed in. I knew I wasn't being spoken to, but I spoke up anyway, 'That's OK, Mrs Waddington-Clarke,' (I thought it would help if I said the name out loud), 'I have ballet and swimming on Saturday. So, I was thinking Sunday would be a good day, if it's OK with you, of course.'

Jemima's mum looked at me. 'You? You do ballet?' It was not said nicely. I was not going to say anything, because I was trying to be a good friend. I could be Jemima's friend and still hate her mum. She went straight back to being Mrs Toilet.

I said, 'My dad says it's OK. So can Jemima come over?'

Mrs Toilet snorted, but she didn't say 'no'. I beckoned to Dad. He swung Bella one more time and they walked over together. When he saw who Jemima's mum was, he paused. I saw him actually take a deep breath. I guess he was trying to be nice. And calm.

Dad said, 'Hello. We have met, but you probably wouldn't remember me. I'm John Gibbons … Martha's dad.' I watched her do it again. She looked him up and down, clearly not liking what she saw. I didn't know what she expected. Dad didn't wear a suit, or a tie; his jeans could have been cleaner and I was pretty sure he'd worn that shirt all week, but so what?

Mrs Toilet took a deep breath herself, and said, 'Our daughters seem to have planned a play date. I suppose it's alright if Jemima goes to yours on Sunday. What sort of time?'

Poor Dad. I shouldn't have caught him unawares; he wasn't good at thinking on his feet. He was looking at me, so I said, 'Why not come for lunch? Come over at eleven.'

Dad was looking at me strangely. I realised I'd just dropped him in it. If Mum was at work, he'd be cooking. *Oh no.*

Mrs Toilet said, 'Eleven it is, I suppose …' I'd never heard a less enthusiastic conversation. She turned to walk away, but stopped and said over her shoulder, 'Oh, I don't have your address.' Dad stammered it out, followed by a whole lot of unnecessary directions. Seriously, once you were on our street there were only a couple of houses, and ours was the least falling-down of all of them. Not that reassuring.

* * * * *

Dad was agitated on Friday night. I realised I had upset his world; I'd invited someone to come over and there was a very real danger that Dad would not only have to talk to her but be responsible for the cooking as well. I should have felt bad. I did, a bit, but I should probably have felt worse.

When Mum got home, the first thing Dad asked was, 'Are you working on the weekend?'

She said, 'No. Why?' and I could see Dad's face and shoulders relax. He had very obvious body language; his body shouted for joy.

Dad and I both tried to explain about the play date, and Mum said, 'Oh, Martha, that's lovely. So, you've got a new friend. That's great.'

It was nice, for once, to have Mum seem pleased with me, so I didn't say any more.

Chapter Thirty-nine

Sunday did not get off to a great start. Bella had already finished breakfast when I got downstairs, and she was putting stickers in a book at *my* place at the table. I took the sheet she was using and slapped it down in *her* place, without saying anything.

Bella yelled at me, 'You've ripped my favourite page!' She burst into tears and ran off.

The next thing I knew, Mum was all over me with, 'Don't-be-so-selfish. If-you-don't-behave-I'll-cancel-the-play date.' There was more, but I tuned out. When did I become the bad guy? Bella was the one who was in my place, making a mess with her stupid sticker book. I've never really got sticker books. You just stick things in places and that's it; it's not creative. Bella loved them.

Mum was machine-gun talking at me, so I couldn't get a word in edgeways. I just had to wait until it went quiet and say, 'Sorry, Mummy.' But it didn't work; she kept talking. Oh, no. I hadn't been listening. What had she said?

'What did I just say, Martha? Were you even listening to me?'

'Of course, Mummy.' If I kept trying, she might soften up.

'Well, what did I say?'

'You said I shouldn't be selfish (I had definitely heard that bit), and I should apologise to Bella.' I hadn't heard that but, since I had to guess, I went with the most likely thing she would have said.

'Exactly. So … off you go.'

I said, 'But, I haven't had breakfast yet.'

'I'll put some Weetabix in a bowl for when you get back. Go on.'

I didn't know what was worse: having to do a fake apology for something that wasn't even my fault, or having to eat cardboard. I decided it was the Weetabix. Apologies were easy, especially when I didn't mean them. But Weetabix? Seriously? It was Sunday; I should have been having stacks of pancakes with maple syrup.

Mum had said we wouldn't have pancakes for breakfast because, 'I'll-have-to-do-a proper-lunch-because-we're-going-to-have-a-guest-and-I'm-not-going-to-spend-the-whole-day-in-the-kitchen.' That was said very pointedly in my direction.

Despite hoping she might change her mind, or forget (not likely), I knew pancakes were out. I had even offered to make them, but Mum reminded me what happened the last time I tried: it took longer to clean up the mess than to cook and eat them. And they were lumpy.

* * * * *

I watched the clock in the kitchen, waiting for eleven o'clock. Then it was five past, then quarter past. At half past, there was a knock on the door. We didn't have a doorbell, but we did have an imposing brass knocker. It was one of those hands holding a ball. I thought it was creepy when we first moved in, but I'd got used to it. It made a really solid *clunk*. You couldn't miss it.

I raced to the door and pulled it open. There was Jemima with a huge plaster on her chin.

'Hi, Jemima, come in.' She stumbled forwards as her mother pushed her into the hall. Mrs Toilet came in on Jemima's heels, and I noticed again how tall she was. Not Mrs Gnash, Empire State Building tall, but way taller than most women I knew. I did a quick calculation; if she got it just right, she should bang her head on the beam Dad had to duck under every time. She dodged it.

Mum hurried from the kitchen. I was so glad she was cooking lunch rather than Dad. She held out her hand to Mrs Toilet without really looking, and slowly dropped it when Jemima's mum failed to take it. Mum and Mrs Toilet looked at each other; they didn't actually speak. I was trying to read their body language.

Then I got it. Mum recognised Jemima and Mrs Toilet from that time she saw her with a black eye and she had blamed it on me. And Mrs Toilet hadn't known that my mum was the doctor she saw. That was why they were looking at each other strangely. Awkward.

I grabbed Jemima's sleeve and said, 'Do you want to see my room?'

She didn't answer, but we went anyway. I wanted to get away from the mothers.

I was right about Jemima; we didn't have much in common. She rode horses, I didn't. I did ballet, she didn't. I ate too much – she didn't do that either. But we both loved books. When I showed her my bookshelf, she did not look impressed.

She said, 'We have a very large library in our house.' I imagined she had one of those real libraries in her mansion, with ladders on wheels and hundreds of leather-bound books. I remembered her talking about it in class. I was jealous.

I said, 'But you have your own books in your room, right?'

'No ... all the books are in the library. I'm not allowed books in my room.'

'So, where do you go to read?'

'The library, of course.'

I said, 'Of course.' I decided not to share the secret of my biscuit tin. 'You know, Mr Newton lent me his copy of *Matilda*. It was actually signed by Roald Dahl.' I thought that might impress her.

But then she said, 'He's really weird, don't you think?'

'Who? Roald Dahl?'

'No. Mr Newton. You know, the whole mask and voice box and everything.'

I'd stopped thinking Mr Newton was weird. I just accepted him. He was a kind of friend, but different. I kept his secret, and he wanted me to keep the horrible secret about Mrs Gnash.

I said, 'Actually, I really like him. I trust him. Unlike Mrs Gnash! What about her? All skinny long legs and big hands. I think *she's* creepy.'

Jemima said, 'I hadn't really noticed.'

She hadn't noticed Mrs Gnash? How could anybody not

notice Mrs I'm-going-to-eat-everybody Gnash?

Bella knocked on my door. I said, 'Go away, Bella.'

She said, 'Mum sent me. Lunch is nearly ready, but I'll tell her you don't want any!' I burst out the door, and nearly knocked her flat. She sulked all the way down the stairs, but she paused as she opened the door to the dining room.

Bella said, 'Ta-daa!' and swept her hands to show us that she'd set the table. I looked closely; she'd put the knives and forks in the right places, and there were little coasters for drinks in the right place. I nodded my approval, but it was clearly not enough. Her face told me I was missing something.

Bella pointed at the napkins; she'd made those fortune-teller folding shapes. They looked stupid, but she was obviously proud of herself. I lied and said, 'You've done a very good job, Isabella.' I was a great sister.

Lunch was delicious. There was roast chicken and potatoes: the crispy kind, roasted in goose fat, and cauliflower cheese, and carrots (why?) and gravy. I watched Mum with the gravy. I watched as she poured it on everybody's plates. I was last, and there was plenty left. My eyes were pleading. She gave a little shrug and poured a proper amount on my plate; maybe not as much as I'd serve myself, but a good polite restaurant-amount. It was good gravy too – no lumpy bits.

I wanted Mum to stop being all friendly-but-really-nosey-at-the-same-time. She asked Jemima too many questions, like she was on trial, or a contestant on one of those quiz shows I sometimes watched with Dad. He loved them – the sillier the better.

Jemima could barely get a mouthful of food down as Mum grilled her about her family. She was an only child; I didn't know that. They lived quite a way out of town and had to drive everywhere. They had about twenty horses. I knew they had horses, but who needs twenty of them?

Jemima explained, 'Father goes hunting, and he does other things … eventing, too.' I wondered what that was. I thought it was odd the way she called her mum 'Mummy' but her dad 'Father'. She said it all so fast, like she expected us to know all about it. But we didn't – well I didn't, and I was pretty sure Mum and Dad didn't either. But nobody asked for more details.

I finished everything on my plate, even the carrots (thank you, gravy), and asked Mum for seconds. She shook her head. I only really wanted some more potatoes with gravy. Jemima took ages to finish. I watched Dad get seconds of everything, except the carrots. And Bella – brat. How come she got seconds? I glared at Mum, but she only had eyes for Jemima. I thought about making a raid on Bella's plate, but I didn't want to get caught again and be sent to my room when I had a guest.

Mum said, 'So, tell me, dear,' (she never said 'dear'; maybe it was her professional voice), 'how did you get that nasty cut on your chin?'

Jemima blushed. 'Oh … I fell off a horse yesterday.'

I looked straight at her and said, 'You seem to do that a lot.' I was sure she was lying – again.

She said, 'I don't want to talk about it.'

Mum leaned closer and said, 'Maybe you should, dear.' There it was again. Mum was sounding really serious, but she had to drop it when Jemima started to cry.

We had ice cream and caramel sauce for pudding. I love caramel, and poured over the cold ice cream it went chewy – even better. If I was crying, chewy caramel would make it stop. It seemed to work for Jemima. It could also have been that Mum stopped the inquisition.

I wanted to take Jemima back to my bedroom after lunch, but we didn't get long because her mum arrived early. She wasn't due until four o'clock but she knocked on the door just after three. I could hear bits of conversation from upstairs. Mrs Toilet (I was undecided, but 'Toilet' came more easily for Jemima's mum) was saying something about snow coming later and needing to get home. I hadn't heard anything about snow. Dad was a big snow fan; if there was even the slightest chance of snow, he'd have mentioned it.

I got a little chill down my spine when I heard Mum ask, 'That's new. Have you come off a horse since this morning?'

Mrs Toilet said, 'No. And it's none of your business.'

Jemima and I were halfway down the stairs when Mrs Toilet saw us. She called out, 'Come on, Jemima. Time to go. Don't keep your father waiting.'

My play date with Jemima ended without much play. I wanted to ask Mum what she meant when she was talking to Mrs Toilet. Something was very wrong.

I watched Mrs Toilet drive away with Jemima in the front seat. I was never allowed to sit in the front. Their Range Rover went around the corner and I saw a grubby yellow Toyota pull out from the kerb and follow. The driver was the shabby detective. Was he following Jemima, or her mum?

Chapter Forty

They were back! I hugged Elemenope and Hakeem in turn. Michael gave me a look and stayed where he was, hands in his pockets. I was desperate to know what had happened. Hakeem just shrugged and said, 'I was a bit off-colour.' I had to prod him to get more. 'Mum took me to the doctor, but she said there was nothing wrong with me. It's weird. I don't remember much about anything.'

Elemenope said, 'Me too. But I don't think I went to the doctor. It's like there are a couple of days missing.'

I remembered what Mr Newton had said – they'd had their memories cleared. I needed to know more; I needed to find out if they discovered anything about Mrs Gnash. But Jemima was coming over. It would have to wait.

Jemima said, 'Thanks for having me over yesterday. It was really nice.'

I was sure she was just being polite. The guys looked at me strangely. I could see the confusion in Elemenope's eyes. Jemima still had a plaster on her chin. And now she was limping.

I asked, 'Are you OK?' I didn't want to sound like Mum, but it came out like her. At least I didn't say 'dear'.

Jemima started to say, 'Yes …' but it faded away.

She looked like she might cry again, so I changed the subject. 'Hey, did it snow at anybody's place last night?'

There was lots of head-shaking and Hakeem piped up, 'How could it? There have to be clouds for it to snow – it doesn't just come out of thin air.' That's what I thought.

* * * * *

I couldn't concentrate in class; the smells coming from Mrs Gnash's classroom were too good. At break, I asked Katheryn, and regretted it almost straight away as she said, 'Oh, we've been eating doughnuts.' *Doughnuts!* Katheryn wore a huge grin as she said, 'We've had plain ones, iced ones and jam ones.'

I *love* jam doughnuts. I asked, 'Are there any left?'

She said, 'I think so.' I had to have one, or two or three. I didn't care how scary Mrs Gnash was, I had to get into that classroom.

Hakeem and Elemenope were comparing notes about their strange few days. I asked if they wanted to come with me to see if we could get doughnuts in the year six classroom. They looked at each other and shook their heads. I thought they were spying on Mrs Gnash. I thought they'd jump at the chance to check out what was happening, but they both looked scared at the prospect of going into her room.

Michael said, 'I'll come.' He was bored because the field was off-limits, and he would never turn down the opportunity for some food. The difference between him and me, though, was food made him grow taller; it made me grow sideways. Maybe Mum was right after all. I would worry about that after some doughnuts.

We didn't have to worry about being caught by Mrs Gnash – she was on playground duty. But I didn't want Mr Newton to see us, so we snuck past our own classroom. I poked my head up to look through the glass panel in the door and I could see Mr Newton and Miss Slider together again. They were deep in conversation. I wondered if Mr Newton felt that odd time-slowing-down thing when he was near Miss Slider.

The class six door was ajar; I could see a plate of doughnuts on the table beside Mrs Gnash's desk, so I went first. Michael was still scouting around the corridor to make sure it was safe. It was the first day of a new rule:

students weren't allowed inside the school during break, unless it was raining and the teachers were inside too.

I'd been wondering about the new rule, wondering if it was somehow connected to what happened to Elemenope and Hakeem. We didn't want to get caught; Miss Slider sounded serious when she announced it. *But we were talking about jam doughnuts.*

There were only four left: two plain ones with cinnamon sugar, and two with jam oozing out the top. Michael and I each grabbed a jam doughnut and I put the plain ones in my pocket. I was thinking, *One each for Elemenope and Hakeem.* Then I remembered Jemima. It would be better if I left them, but when I put them back on the plate they looked so lonely. We ate those too.

There was a sound at the door and a shadow crossed. We were caught! I grabbed Michael's sleeve and pulled him into the huge cupboard at the side of the room. I closed the door just as I heard footsteps. In the dark I concentrated on the sound. They weren't normal footsteps; the sound was more like a scraping, then a stabbing. I was being overdramatic; they were just footsteps. I started to relax and breathe normally. Michael was right on top of me and giving off a kind of heat. It had gone quiet. I knew we'd be OK.

Wrong! The door flew open and I was looking right at Mrs Gnash's mid-section. I looked up, into her red face. Her eyes, behind those huge glasses, were darting back and forth. I didn't think; I ran. Something grabbed at my collar but I slipped under it. Then something else caught my sleeve – it felt like a hook. I was caught like a fish.

I squirmed around to look at her. How did I think I was going to get away from the ridiculously tall and sporty Mrs Gnash?

She was not just tall anymore; she was huge. Her clothes were shredded and she'd doubled in height. Her head scraped the ceiling. Her legs had unfolded somehow, like one of those ugly Transformer toys. And her arms! Where each hand used to be had turned into an elbow, so she had extra-long forearms. Her new hands had long hook-like fingers, holding on to my cardigan.

She had an extra pair of short arms sticking out from the front of her chest. They had nasty-looking claws. Her other long arm (I thought it was an arm; I didn't have a better word for it), had hold of Michael. He was swinging his fists, but she held him away so he couldn't make contact.

We were both off the floor, swinging around. I felt like a cat's toy. Mrs Gnash – or whatever she really was –

leaned down. Her mouth opened and let out a sound like a groan: low and rattly. Her breath stank. Mine was sometimes a bit off if I hadn't eaten, say, in the morning, but I guess if you hadn't eaten for four or five years it must be really bad. It smelled like old garbage.

I had nothing to lose. 'Put us down!' I said. It sounded a lot bolder than it felt.

Her voice changed; it was scratchy. 'Why would I do that?'

'Because you'll get into a lot of trouble … you know … beating up students. You're a teacher – you can't do this.'

'Who said anything about beating you? Why would I want to bruise you? It would spoil the flavour.' OK. I was right all along. I wished I'd been wrong.

Mrs Gnash took a couple of giant steps, ducked under the doorway and turned into the corridor. Michael and I were just dangling from her hands-or-whatever-they-were. I needed him to jump into action, to be my knight in shining armour and slay this dragon. But he was asleep. *How could he be asleep?*

Everything slid into slow motion. Miss Slider!

Mrs Gnash (I didn't know what else to call her – the manti-whatsit-thingamajig) slowed right down. I could see her chest; it was scaly, like a gigantic insect. She was breathing – well, her chest had been going in and out – really quickly, but it had slowed so much I could barely see it moving. Miss Slider stood in front of us. She looked scared, but there she was, standing her ground, blocking the creature's path.

Mum told me once that being brave doesn't mean you're not scared; it's the opposite. Being brave is being scared, but doing something anyway. Miss Slider was being unbelievably brave.

Where were all the kids? It was still break time but it wouldn't be long before they came back in. But if Mrs Gnash was in charge of ringing the bell they'd be much safer outside.

The floor was suddenly swarming with newts: thousands and thousands of them. They were moving in normal time. Clearly Mr Newton wasn't affected by Miss Slider's weird time-warp.

The newts seemed really angry. Could newts be angry? They were swarming up Mrs Gnash's legs; they climbed up her chest, down her arms, and reached her hands. They nibbled hard at the claws holding Michael and me.

I saw Mrs Gnash's face so-very-slowly redden again.

Her eyes got bigger and her mouth started to open as she tilted her head and her glasses fell off. That was why she wore glasses. Her bug-eyes stuck out from her face, and there was another set of tiny eyes on the bridge of her nose.

The little arms with the sharp claws turned to pick at the newts. But the newts were way too fast. Whenever a claw came near one it jumped away and then went back to gnawing at her fingers. I dropped to the floor; the newts had made her let go. Michael dropped too, but he slumped to the ground. I wanted to pick him up (fat chance), but my legs could barely move.

I collapsed against the wall and watched the newts continue their attack on the gigantic Mrs Gnash. They were moving normally, but they seemed super-fast against her slow-motion actions. They jumped all over her, swarming like big ants, biting and shaking their heads when they had a mouthful of her. It looked painful and scary and a bit funny all at once. It happened so slowly, it took me a while to realise that Mrs Gnash had turned around. If she went that way, she'd go out the front of the school, away from where everybody was. Was that the newts' plan?

Miss Slider stepped back, and everything sped up

again. The newts jumped off Mrs Gnash and reformed as Mr Newton. His mask was on backwards but it moved around to face where it should. Mrs Gnash didn't stop. She (it?) didn't look around, but let out a piercing screech as she charged down the corridor and threw open the front door.

My head was spinning; I had a terrible headache. I heard Miss Slider ask, 'Will she be all right?'

'Who? Martha Gibbons? She'll be OK. She never drinks enough water … that's her problem.'

Miss Slider said, 'That's not what I meant. And what about him?' She was pointing at Michael, still asleep and looking surprisingly peaceful.

'Don't worry … I'll take care of them. You'd better sort out the children.'

'But what about *her*?' I knew she was talking about Mrs Gnash.

'Well, you're the head. You'd better get a supply teacher.'

Miss Slider didn't look happy, but I knew Mr Newton was joking. Even without any changes in voice tone I could tell when he was being funny. I wasn't sure about his timing.

Mr Newton bent low over Michael and I watched my

friend's eyes flicker open. Michael said, 'What happened? Am I in trouble? We only wanted some doughnuts, but I don't remember what happened. Are we in trouble?'

Mr Newton said, 'Well, you disobeyed the new rule and came inside during break, but I'll let you off this time. You must have bumped your head … you'll be all right. Just don't do it again, OK?'

Michael stood up and thanked Mr Newton. It was as though none of the last few terrifying minutes ever happened for him. I was worried Mr Newton would do his memory-wiping thing on me.

'Don't worry, Martha Gibbons. I don't need to make you forget. You're my ally. I've got a feeling I'm going to need your help. I *can* still trust you, can't I?'

I couldn't speak, but I thought loudly, *More than ever. You just saved my life.*

He said, 'Now we're even.'

Chapter Forty-one

The rule with play dates is you get invited to the other person's house after they'd been to yours. 'Reciprocation,' Mum called it.

I was waiting for Jemima to reciprocate. I wanted to see her mansion, and her library, but I was not so keen on seeing her horses. I kept waiting, but after a few days – more than enough, in my opinion – with still no invitation, I asked Mum about it. I wondered if maybe she'd spoken with Mrs Toilet and they'd planned something.

Mum said 'No,' but she said it in a way that meant, 'Never.'

* * * * *

Elemenope and Hakeem seemed to have forgotten all about spying on Mrs Gnash. When I asked them what they discovered, they looked at me as if there was something wrong with me. Well, there was definitely something wrong with *them*. It was as though they never had the idea at all.

Elemenope asked, 'Why would we want to do that?'

I wanted to say, 'Because she's a giant child-eating monster from another planet who's been fattening us up for her freaky once-every-five-years-meal,' but I didn't.

I was more scared of Mrs Gnash than ever. I knew she wanted to eat us; she was definitely fattening up the kids in her class. And now she was on the run and I didn't know where she lived. Was she hiding? Had she changed into something else? I was scared just walking down the street in case she jumped out and grabbed me. I had to ask Mr Newton, but he beat me to it.

He came up to me as everyone was leaving the classroom on Friday lunchtime. 'Can I talk to you, please, Martha Gibbons?' I hung back. When the room was empty, he said, 'We have a serious problem. We need to catch the Mantiform Caliopteryx.'

I said, 'You mean Mrs Gnash?'

'You can call it that if it helps.' It did; it was like calling Jemima's mum 'Mrs Toilet'.

'What can we do?'

'Not *we*, Martha Gibbons ... *you*. I don't have the strength to get hold of it. And Miss Slider ...

well, she can only hold it in a time-lock for a short period. It's very strong.' I knew that only too well.

I didn't like where the conversation was going. I liked it less and less as Mr Newton laid out his plan.

* * * * *

There was a huge chest freezer in our utility room. It was too big, really, but we brought it with us when we moved, and everybody had just got used to squeezing past it to get to the washing machine. It had all sorts of things in it. I knew, without having to look, where the ice cream was. But I had to search hard for what I needed. I didn't even know if we had a frozen leg of lamb. And if we did, I wasn't sure I'd know it when I saw it.

I found a pile of bread. I knew Mum bought it in bulk, but there was so much we could survive a siege. There was a tower of butter, and a scattering of boxes with odd bits and pieces. Some had labels, some didn't. I thought about having a party with all the unlabelled stuff. It would be funny to open up a cheesecake for main course and some old spinach for dessert. Actually, that wouldn't be funny at all. Spinach … yuck! That made me focus again.

In the far corner, there was a heap of built-up ice, and there, in the middle of it, was an obvious bone, in a thick plastic bag. I hoped that was it. I couldn't get it out; the ice had hold of it and wouldn't let go. I tugged and tried to work it sideways, but it was no good. I needed that leg of lamb, if that's what it was. In my head, I heard, 'Use that big brain of yours, Martha Gibbons.' I turned the power off. The ice would melt, and I'd get the lamb out. Easy.

On Saturday morning, the ice had melted. It *was* lamb, according to the label. Mr Newton had said it should be fresh. By the time it thawed it would be fine.

I was supposed to meet Mr Newton in the evening. I'd already told Mum and Dad that he wanted to see me for an extra tutorial, and they both said it was OK to go to school. I hadn't told them I'd be going next door to Mr Newton's house. I didn't want to worry them. They didn't know Mr Newton lived next door, anyway, so it would have involved a long, unnecessary story. Better to just say I was going to school.

I had to hide the leg of lamb, so I snuck out the back and put it under the floor of the odd little shed where Dad kept the firewood. There were some loose boards that I discovered a few months before when I was looking for somewhere to hide another biscuit tin. It would be safe enough there. It wasn't as if we ever got the dog I was promised when we moved.

When I lifted up the boards I discovered the notebook I took from Bella when she was annoying me ages ago. She had been spying on me, so when she wasn't looking I took the notebook and hid it under the boards. She'd had a fit, but nobody ever found it. More importantly, nobody knew I took it. She'd learned her lesson; I decided to give it back to her. Some day.

* * * * *

'Your little friend … Jemima … what do you know about her?' That was an odd question coming from I'm-going-to-ask-you-as-many-questions-as-I-can Mum. I thought she'd found out everything there was to know when Jemima came over for lunch.

I said, 'What do you mean, Mummy?' I decided on the sweet-little-girl-approach. It was the safest option when I didn't know what was going on.

'Well, is she happy? Does she have lots of friends? That sort of thing.'

It was one of *those* questions, so I said, 'I don't really

know. She seems OK, I guess.' Then I started to think. I knew Jemima wasn't happy. And I was pretty sure she was lonely. Why couldn't I say it?

Mum kept on, 'Dad said you had a horrible time at her party. Did you meet any of her friends? Was her father there?'

'No. I've never met Mr Toi—' (whoops), 'Mr Waddington-Clarke.'

Mum changed her tone, and she started to involve Dad. He'd been sitting in his big chair reading a book. I thought of it as our big chair; it's where we sat together while he read to me sometimes. Lately it had been Bella's chair too, and that was just not right. I had Dad first. Sometimes I wished I was an only child, like Jemima. Then I'd have Dad all to myself.

Mum didn't just involve Dad, she poked him in the leg, like he was supposed to do or say something, and he'd forgotten. They were up to something.

Dad looked up from his book and said, 'That party was terrible, and her mother's a cold fish. I don't like her.'

Mum leaned in, like she was going to say something secret. Then she stopped, went to the door of the living room and checked Bella wasn't listening. I could have told her she wasn't because she was singing along to

'Let It Go'. She had a good voice for a little kid, but no volume control.

Mum came back and said, 'Remember when I said you couldn't say anything about when I saw Jemima as a patient?' I remembered. Mainly, I remembered thinking Mum was more worried about her reputation than my feelings. I nodded my head. She paused and then said, 'Well, those other bruises and bumps ... has she said anything about them?'

I said, 'No ... wait ... yes. She has. She's always saying she fell off her horse. Well, I think she's lying. I saw her ride; she's pretty good. And when she said she'd fallen off at her party, I know that was a lie, because she was fine. *I'm* the one who fell off a horse at her party. Not her! Why would she lie?'

Mum gave Dad a 'meaningful' look. I knew what that meant. It meant she wouldn't tell me.

Chapter Forty-two

It was already dark at half past four. That was when I told Mum and Dad I had my appointment with Mr Newton. Dad said, 'I suppose I could give you a lift, pumpkin …' It was said in that way that I wasn't meant to accept.

I said, 'It's OK – the street lights are on and I feel like a walk.'

'Oh, OK, then. If you're sure.' Dad hated driving so much he seemed relieved to leave his precious older daughter to roam the lonely streets on her own.

I was getting really nervous; I knew what was about to happen but I had to remember the plan and trust Mr Newton. I wished Michael was part of it, then I thought about how useless he was the last time we came up against Mrs Gnash, or the Manti-thingy-whatsit.

I picked up a folder and a pencil, so it actually looked like I was going to a tutorial, and walked loudly out the front door. Then I scooted down the side lane and rescued my leg of lamb from the woodshed. It was only partly thawed.

Mr Newton let me in straight away. He showed me the stairs to his cellar and said, 'Tie the lamb up here.' There was a big hook right above the doorway to the cellar; I could just reach it by standing on a chair. I wobbled about a lot.

I asked, 'Why do you need me to do this?'

'Don't you remember, Martha Gibbons? I'm not very good with tools. I can't tie knots.' But he was good with plans. I listened as he laid out the whole scheme. 'You'll lure the Mantiform Caliopteryx,' (Why can't he just call her Mrs Gnash? It's so much easier.) 'by walking around town looking delicious,' (not sure about that bit), 'and get her to follow you here.

'Hopefully she'll want to eat the lamb, because it won't put up a fight, and then we'll push her down the stairs, where Miss Slider will be waiting. She'll deal with her once we've tied her up.'

The plan seemed to involve a lot of *me,* rather than *us.*

I peered into the darkness of the cellar, where I could just make out a tiny shape moving about. Miss Slider called up, 'Hello, Martha. Thank you for doing this; you're a very brave girl.' It was true. I was terrified, but I was going to do it anyway.

I didn't much like the idea of being bait, but I

understood I was ideal for the role. If Mrs Gnash-manti-nasty-hungry-whatsit was fattening up the kids in her class, then I must be just her type. I'd never thought of myself as delicious before, but if it did the job …

The horrible part was having to walk alone along the street, being deliberately tasty. I had my super heavy coat on, and that made me look even bigger. I felt like a walking cream bun. I didn't want to walk past our house, so I crossed the street. Not such a great idea; there were lots of creepy shadows on that side – just right for a giant insect-like thing to hide.

A horrible shivery feeling slid down my back. If I saw Mrs Gnash-whatever, I was supposed to run back to Mr Newton's. I kept turning, keeping an eye on his house, so I knew where to go. I was a cream bun on a hook. I started to hope I could run faster than a Mantiform Caliopteryx (I did it).

I guessed it would depend on whether she was all folded out or in her more-human form. I laughed at the idea of ever thinking she was human. But I always knew there was something not right about her. Sometimes it's not good being right.

I thought, 'This is a silly plan.' Why would Mrs Gnash-nasty be here anyway? Why would she be on my street when she could be anywhere by now? She'd fattened up plenty of kids at school.

A fat, ginger cat rushed out of a bush up ahead. It was just old Lumpy. We called him that because he waddled from side-to-side and plopped down like a lump. Nobody knew where he lived. He was moving more quickly than I'd ever seen before. He stopped when a giant claw shot out of the bush and pinned him to the ground. It was *her* … *it* … whatever it was. Mrs Gnash had Lumpy!

I froze. Had she seen me? I turned to run, but I felt that awful claw on the back of my neck. I had to get to Mr Newton's but I could feel my feet leaving the ground. The street was deserted; there was nobody to help me. Except Jemima. *Where had she come from?*

'Drop her, you monster!' Jemima wasn't screaming, but she was wielding a riding crop. She was flailing at Mrs Gnash's arm and hitting her hard. She hit me a couple of times. It was OK on my coat, but she caught my hand with the end of the riding crop – the leathery floppy bit – and it really stung. Mrs Gnash dropped me and I ran as fast as I could. Jemima was running too. We ran like our lives depended on it. Jemima didn't know the truth of that.

She said, 'Where are we going?'

'I'll show you ... run faster.' I couldn't talk and run at the same time. Jemima was slowing down; she was carrying something. I yelled, 'Drop the bag!'

We hurtled past our house; I had a vague sense of someone looking out the window. Mr Newton's front door was open and we dived inside. He pointed to the gap behind the door, and we both squeezed in. As Mrs Gnash-horrible-thingy came up the path, Mr Newton scattered into all his newts to get out of the way, and they formed a barrier that sealed us off behind the door. They made the space look like a dense shadow. I was sweating; I was pretty sure Mrs Gnash had a good sense of smell.

The giant Manti-whatsit-Mrs-Gnash stopped in the doorway. I was right; she sniffed the air and raised her head. The lamb was just ahead of her. Surely, she could smell it. I could smell it. The Mrs Gnash-thing leaned forwards to grab the lamb, and the newts suddenly formed a solid shape like a giant fist. They pushed her down the stairs into the cellar. *It worked!*

The cellar light came on and I could see Miss Slider standing there, shaking, but the Manti-nasty-Mrs-Gnash looked quiet. She didn't look so scary from up above. It was time to be brave again.

Jemima came with me as I edged down the stairs. The problem was, as we got closer to Miss Slider, time slowed, and it felt like we were barely moving. Nobody had thought this bit through. It was like a strange old-fashioned dance, with two girls barely moving around an angry monster. Miss Slider was the tiny conductor.

Mr Newton was just about fully reformed again, and he came into the cellar too. It was not a big space. He was the only one of us not affected by whatever Miss Slider did to time, but he couldn't tie knots.

Now would be a good time for you to read my thoughts, I thought as loudly as I could. Suddenly it was like Mr Newton was inside my head; I could hear his voice in normal time, even though my own world was paralysed.

'Clever, Martha Gibbons. What do I have to do?'

I thought about tying a knot, step-by-step. Over – under – through the gap. As I thought it, I could see Mr Newton taking a piece of rope and tying the same knot. It wasn't very good, but it was a start. Then I looked around at the ropes laid out on the floor. I could see some were already run through big metal hoops. I wondered how they came to be there.

'Don't get distracted, Martha Gibbons ... we have work to do.'

I thought an apology. Then I wondered if I could do my schoolwork this way. 'Martha Gibbons! Focus!'

I watched as Mr Newton ran the ropes and tied the knots that I created in my mind. The end result was like a prickly spider's web. The knots weren't tight. He was right; he wasn't very strong. When he'd threaded the last one, I thought loudly again, *Miss Slider is going to have to go away so I can tighten the knots.*

Mr Newton said, 'I think you're right ... sorry ... you'll have to be quick.'

I'd already thought about that. I would need Jemima's help. I hoped she could just pull the knots tight and ask questions later.

As Miss Slider backed away, time started to speed up again. Just as it hit normal, I grabbed two ends of a rope with a knot in the middle. I was really glad I learned how to do that as I pulled tight and the knot held. I yelled at Jemima, 'Grab a knot – any knot – and start pulling. They've got to be tight!'

'What are we doing?'

There was no time for explanations, as Mrs Gnash-nasty-manti-thing started to gyrate, trying to undo the ropes.

I said, 'Just get the ropes tight. Pull as hard as you can. I'll explain later.'

Chapter Forty-three

Back upstairs, Jemima looked confused. That was an understatement: baffled, bemused, bewildered. My feelings were all jumbled up, too, but at least I'd had some experience of this sort of thing before.

I broke the silence with, 'What *are* you doing here?'

Jemima said, 'I'm running away.'

'From where?'

'From home.'

Who would run away from a mansion and twenty horses? Well maybe the twenty horses.

I asked, 'So, why are you *here*?'

'I think you might be my only friend – or maybe my best friend.' When did that happen?

There were strange noises coming from the cellar: a sort of strangled grunting. It was spoiling the moment.

I couldn't concentrate on what Jemima was telling me. Was she really telling me she was running away from home? Now? With Mrs Gnash grumbling and whining downstairs?

I said, 'I can't deal with this all at once. I need to help sort out the Mrs Gnash problem.'

But Jemima didn't seem to grasp the immediate danger. She said, 'I'm pouring my heart out here, Martha. I'm running away!'

I wore a new look; it was, 'Can't this wait until we're out of danger?' But it might have just been, 'What are you talking about?' It's hard to perfect a new look when an alien has spent the last half hour trying to eat you.

After a few moments, Jemima's face changed, and she said, 'What is that thing down there?' It was like someone flicked a switch, and she was back in the present.

'You mean Mrs Gnash?'

'Is that Mrs Gnash? No way.'

I said, 'Well, it is … sort of. She's a Manti-thingamajig'

'Mantiform Caliopteryx.' I hadn't seen Mr Newton come over to us. 'You know the name perfectly well, Martha Gibbons. I've heard you; it's like you refuse to use the creature's proper name.'

He was right, of course. I always did that. It made things less threatening.

'We have to deal with it. I don't think we can hold it very long. And it certainly can't stay here.'

He was right about that, too. There was no way I

wanted a Mantiform Caliopteryx (there – I did it) living next door.

I asked him, 'What are you going to do with her?' I was still thinking of it as Mrs Gnash.

'If it eats, it will go quiet again for another five years, but that's not a long-term solution.'

I gulped. Surely, he wasn't going to feed us to her.

'Don't be silly, Martha Gibbons. For one thing, it would eat a huge amount. No … not children … just meat, but we'd need a truck-load. And there's still the problem of next time. We've been talking about a permanent solution.'

That sounded gruesome.

'No, not that. I'll let Miss Slider explain.'

Why did he do that? He knew what happened when Miss Slider came near me. It would take a decade for me to hear the plan.

'You're right … sorry. I'll explain, but I don't have Miss Slider's expertise.'

I'd become a lot happier with Mr Newton inside my head lately.

'Miss Slider can take it to another time zone'

I said, 'I don't understand.'

'I do.' said Jemima. *Welcome to the conversation.* She

seemed to be taking all this in her stride. 'I've read about this. Some people think time travel is actually possible, but only to the future. So, if Mrs Gnash went to the future – even a few minutes – we'd be safe. Is that it? Does Miss Slider have a time machine?'

Mr Newton said, 'Not exactly, but you're on the right track.'

I couldn't see how that was any good. I said, 'But what about the future us? Won't we just get eaten when we get there?'

'No, because she'll always be ahead of us.'

My head was swimming; it was more a dog-paddler at that moment. The solution – straight out of science fiction – was right there with us, but I was uncomfortable because I didn't understand it.

The sound from the cellar had become a whimper.

Jemima started to go down the stairs. I wanted to stop her, but Miss Slider was standing too close and everything slowed for me. I wanted her to move away, but she couldn't read my mind like Mr Newton. By the time she took a step away from me, and I could move normally again, it was too late. Jemima was at the bottom of the stairs, right next to the Mantiform Caliopteryx (did it again).

I watched, horrified, as my friend (she *was* my friend) reached out a hand and stroked the back of the creature's head. Clever. She was nowhere near its mouth. She started talking to it: soft, gentle words. It was too whispered to hear much, but I could make out bits of it: 'Poor thing … you're just hungry, aren't you …' and some sort of mumbled nonsense-words.

Mr Newton and Miss Slider were halfway down the stairs, like heroes rushing to the rescue, not that either of them was that good at rushing, but Jemima held out her other hand to them in a 'Go-away-I've-got-this' gesture.

Jemima's crooning went on for five minutes, and the Mantiform Caliopteryx stayed calm. I was blown away. The fierce creature was just standing there, not eating Jemima. It didn't eat Jemima so successfully that it refolded its extended arms and legs and came back to Mrs Gnash size. That was a whole lot better, a whole lot less intimidating. Except Mrs Gnash didn't have any clothes on. I was never going to un-see that.

* * * * *

I climbed on a chair and undid the leg of lamb. If Jemima could get near Mrs Gnash, so could I. Jemima was casually holding one of the ropes, just like she would a horse's rein. It looked so natural, and I realised she was used to being around big, strong animals and being in charge. She was good at this; there was no way she fell off her horse!

I held the leg of lamb like an oversized chicken drumstick, poking it cautiously towards Mrs Gnash's mouth. I didn't expect her to speak, but she did, 'Honestly, Martha, I can't eat that. It's frozen.'

Hearing her say my name I saw a new problem – and it was a big one. She knew that I knew her secret. She knew a whole lot more, too: Jemima, Miss Slider and the truth about Mr Newton. Mrs Gnash was a well-informed and dangerous enemy.

I could see only two options: get rid of her, or get her on our side. I mainly liked the idea of getting rid of her, but I couldn't grasp the idea of sending her to the future. Jemima kept saying over and over, 'Poor thing … you're hungry … I know … we'll get you some oats …' It sounded automatic, soothing.

I thought out loud, 'How do we know she only eats meat? Has anyone asked her?'

When nobody answered, I said, 'Mrs Gnash, do you only eat meat?'

'Well, it's all I've ever eaten. And now I've got a terrible hunger for some. You look so delicious, Martha … why don't you come closer?' I never liked Mrs Gnash.

Chapter Forty-four

Standing in the cellar of Mr Newton's house, holding a frozen leg of lamb in front of a creature from another world – a creature that had just suggested eating me – I suddenly remembered the chest freezer. Two thoughts struck at once: 'Did I turn it back on?' and 'What else is in there?'

I dropped the leg of lamb with a thump, and said, 'I'll be back.' A very large part of me didn't want to come back at all; it felt like leaving Mrs Gnash in the cold, dark cellar, tied up and out of harm's way. Another smaller, nicer, part of me had been listening to Jemima's gentle prattle and wanted to feed the starving animal – feed it anything other than delicious, juicy me.

I snuck into our house by the back door. As I opened the chest freezer I saw a possibility, a chance we could take. I filled my arms, stacking boxes under my chin. As I closed the lid, there was Bella. 'What are you doing with all that pizza, Martha?'

I looked around in panic. Was she alone? I couldn't

see Mum or Dad. I said, 'Shh … it's a surprise.'

'A surprise? Goody. Are we having pizza for dinner? Are you going to cook pizza? Nobody said anything about pizza tonight.' *Please stop saying 'pizza'.*

I said, 'No. Can you keep a secret?'

'That depends.'

'On what?'

Bella said, 'Can I have some pizza?'

'Sure … after I do the secret thing. OK?'

'OK. What's the secret?'

I had no plan for this, but I remembered how Bella helped us rescue the newts at Halloween. It was all I could come up with.

I said, 'Do you remember saving the newts?'

I could see her thinking, then she said, 'Yes, I do. What does that have to do with pizza?' *Please, please stop saying 'pizza'.*

'Well … the newts are hungry, and Hakeem is organising a food drive to help them through the rest of winter.' *What a load of rubbish.*

'Ooh … can I come?'

I said, 'We're not doing it yet. We're just putting some stuff together.'

Bella did not look convinced. She said, 'I didn't know

newts ate pizza; I thought they ate flies and insects and stuff.'

I was struggling, 'Oh, the pizza's not for them. It's for us. We don't want to get hungry while we make our plans.' My explanation was getting worse by the minute.

'Who else is going? Can I come?'

'It's not for a couple of days. Please, can you keep the secret. Don't tell Mum and Dad … *please.*' I didn't think I'd convinced her. I certainly hadn't convinced myself, but she liked Hakeem, so I added, 'For Hakeem. OK?'

I got a very sullen, 'OK,' but it would have to do.

* * * * *

I burst in next door. 'Mr Newton … is there an oven in this house?'

'Yes. I don't know if it works. I don't have any use for it.'

Mr Newton's oven was a bit strange; the knobs were stiff and the numbers had worn off. It hadn't been used for a hundred years. It was electric, so I turned the knob to about the same place I would on ours. There was no little light inside, so I couldn't watch what was happening. I liked to see the cheese bubbling up.

While I waited, I sat at the top of the stairs and listened to Jemima, still crooning to Mrs Gnash. I looked at our tormentor; she'd gone into a kind of trance. Her eyes were shut and she was rocking gently back and forth. She didn't seem so scary now, especially since someone had draped a blanket around her.

The rich, cheesy smell of the pizzas came through. I'd cooked two: a margarita and a pepperoni. I had no idea whether this would work, but I put them both on the benchtop and cut them into pieces with an old knife. The kitchen was filthy, but at least there were no creepy-crawlies. I knew the reason for that and it still freaked me out, thinking of how and what Mr Newton ate.

As I walked down the cellar stairs, carrying a plate of pizza slices, Jemima said, 'Are those for us?'

'Not really. I want to try something. Here, Mrs Gnash?' I held out a slice of pepperoni pizza. I was pretty sure if I hadn't eaten for five years and someone offered me a slice of pepperoni pizza it wouldn't last long.

'What's that?' she asked.

'It's pizza.'

'It smells disgusting. All your human food smells disgusting.'

I said, 'Don't you know about pizza?'

'Of course I do. I learned all about the food children eat when I started my fattening-up programme. Pizza was next on the list. That big boy, Michael, would have eaten a lot of it … and you, too.' She wasn't winning me over by continually talking about my friends – and me – as food.

'Try it. I think you'll like it.'

Mrs Gnash pulled a face and said, 'If I eat that I'll get sick.' I remembered getting sick after eating pizza, but I *had* eaten two-and-a-half family-sized ones all by myself.

'Have you ever tried it?'

'Of course not. I can't eat your disgusting human food. I'm nearly sick when I have to cook the bait … I mean food.'

It was too much, holding out food for someone – something – who didn't appreciate it. I mean, we were talking pepperoni pizza here. I slid the pointy, juicy end in my mouth; it was all chewy salami and cheese. Yum.

Jemima looked up at last, 'Can I have some?'

'Help yourself; I did two.' I pointed at the plate, and Jemima chose a slice of margarita. There was no sign of Mr Newton or Miss Slider. I wanted to offer them some, even though I knew Mr Newton couldn't eat it. It just seemed like the polite thing to do.

Jemima and I sat at the feet of a tethered Mantiform Caliopteryx, eating pizza and wondering how our lives came to this. Our lip-smacking was accompanied by a low rumbling coming from somewhere inside Mrs Gnash.

Just as I was about to slide the last piece of pizza in my mouth, Mrs Gnash stirred and said, 'Maybe I could try a little bit?'

I didn't even bite the tip off; that was a first. I held the slice of pizza – margarita, because I finished the pepperoni, and Jemima only ate half the margarita (she had no appetite) – just in front of Mrs Gnash's mouth. I didn't want to get too close: she had really sharp teeth and I didn't trust her.

She wrinkled her nose. I did that when I smelled something I didn't like – like broccoli. But she opened her mouth and pushed her face forwards. It was a funny, darting action. She didn't bite down with her teeth. Two nasty-looking curved blades, like scissors, came from somewhere inside her cheeks, grabbed the pizza, and pulled it back into her mouth. She chewed the pizza like a machine.

Jemima and I both just stared. We watched Mrs Gnash swallow. She looked uncomfortable, and I had a horrible feeling she was going to throw up. I took a big step back, pulling Jemima with me; she was mesmerised. I didn't want her to get alien vomit all over her, almost as much as I didn't want to get alien vomit all over me.

We waited: for a breath, for a vomit, for any kind of reaction. Nothing happened for what seemed like hours – probably just a few seconds – and then: the loudest burp I had ever heard. Michael did some pretty big ones, and Dad could go off too, but Mrs Gnash put them both to shame. The building shook. It stank! Then another, and another – like shock waves, but they got softer and gradually stopped. I didn't know whether to laugh or cry; the air was rank.

Mrs Gnash said, 'Well … OK … I didn't die.' It smelled like she had! 'Could I have another piece, do you think?'

Jemima and I raced to the kitchen. I'd left the oven on, so it was a simple matter to put two more pizzas in. Jemima looked around the kitchen. 'This is pretty gross. Doesn't Mr Newton ever clean his house?'

I wasn't ready for questions about Mr Newton. 'Oh … I think he's really busy … you know … teaching us … and stuff.' *Hurry up, pizza.*

'Well, he could get a cleaner. It can't be hygienic living like this, surely.' If only she knew.

I felt time shifting again, slowing down as Miss Slider came into the kitchen. I tried to reach for the oven door, but every movement took an age. She saw me and backed away again. I was glad she understood the effect she had on some people, especially me. She stood an arm's length away, far enough for time to feel normal, but I still had a slight tingling feeling. She asked, 'What are you doing? Are you hungry?'

I said, 'No, Miss Slider. We're feeding Mrs Gnash.'

'You're what?'

'Feeding her … pizza. She likes it, I think.'

She said, 'Oh … I was just trying to work out how far away I should take her.'

'Maybe you won't have to. What if we can teach her not to eat kids?'

'Well, I suppose you can try. For a bit. But if she gets aggressive, she'll have to go. I won't tolerate a teacher eating pupils at my school. Whatever would Ofsted say?'

We cut the pizzas and piled them up so the plate was overflowing. I wasn't actually hungry, but the smell made me want to eat a piece. Back down in the cellar, Jemima and I took turns feeding slices of pepperoni and margarita to Mrs Gnash. Each slice was hauled into that strange mouth and chomped away. We paused after every one to let her burp.

It was a strange scene: two girls holding pizza for a giant Mantiform Caliopteryx to gobble down, being watched by a tiny woman and a man made up of thousands of newts. I started to laugh, thinking, *I never wanted to move to this town. Just imagine: I'd have missed out on all this.*

Jemima started to laugh too; it was a nice sound. I'd never heard her laugh before. She was always so serious, so posh, so unhappy. That was what it was about her. I knew why she had always been a bit off. She was unhappy.

We needed more pizza. I put the last two into Mr Newton's hard-working oven. As I did, I got a nasty thought about Bella, and I really hoped she could keep the secret. But it wasn't just her I was worrying about. How was I going to explain about the missing pizza, and the leg of lamb? Mum would go ballistic.

Chapter Forty-five

I had to go home. My tutorial with Mr Newton would have finished half an hour ago; I could get away with being a bit late, but I didn't need Mum and Dad starting to worry and finding out I wasn't at school. Jemima was looking sad again, and sort of twitchy. She said, 'Can I come too. Remember, I'm running away. Not here – to your house.'

I'd completely forgotten about that. Feeding big scary aliens could have that effect. I said, 'Sure. Come on.'

Our front door was locked and I didn't have a key (wasn't allowed one), and it might have looked a bit odd going around the back, so I swung the brass hand knocker. Dad opened the door, looked at Jemima, and then looked over us, out onto the street.

Dad said, 'Did your parents drop you, Jemima? I didn't know you were coming.'

I said, 'Oh, Jemima's running away. She's going to stay here.' I said it in that matter-of-fact way I hear adults use sometimes. The tone that says, 'Don't ask any more questions / it's all settled / the judge's decision is final / no correspondence will be entered into.' That tone.

Dad said, 'I see.' I knew he would.

As soon as we got inside, Bella was all over us. 'Hi, Jemima, are you staying for dinner?' Then she terrified me. 'Dad said as it's Saturday, and Mum's not home yet, we're going to have pizza. Isn't that great? Do you like pizza, Jemima? I do. I know Martha does. Martha likes pizza a lot.'

The little rat. I whisper-yelled at her, 'Don't you dare! What about the secret?' She shrugged. Fickle brat.

There was an explosion of groaning and grumbling coming from the back of the house. Then I heard Dad's voice. He was obviously trying to keep it down because we had a guest, but it was getting pretty bad. There were a whole lot of angry words mashed together in one long diatribe. That's a word I learned to describe how Mum talked to me without taking a breath. It's more like she's talking *at* me. Now Dad was doing it – at least he wasn't aiming it at me – yet.

Dad was ranting, 'Who turned the freezer off? No … no … no. It's all ruined. We-can't-eat-anything-from-here. I'll-have-to-throw-it-all-out. She'll blame me.'

Who was he talking about? *I* wouldn't blame Dad.

I gulped as I thought, *I-never-turned-it-back-on. He's-talking-about-Mum-and-how-she'll-blame-him-when-it-was-all-my-fault. Oh dear, now I'm doing a diatribe. Maybe it's a family trait.*

'Martha!'

'Yes, Daddy?' It was going to take more than that. I was at the door to the utility room and there were bags of sloppy food on the floor. The ice had melted and soaked into everything. I thought the bread would be OK, but the bags were wet, Dad's sleeves were wet; everything was wet.

Dad's voice was brittle, 'Do you know anything about this?' *Gulp.* Why was he asking me? Why did he think I might have done it? Why didn't anybody ever accuse little-miss-perfect-could-never-do-anything-wrong Bella?

'I didn't do it.' It was all I had. Nobody actually knew I turned it off. Bella saw me here earlier, but she couldn't know I turned the freezer off yesterday because the lamb was stuck. I wondered how I hadn't noticed the water earlier when I got the pizzas. Just as well, maybe. I thought the pizzas were easy to thaw. 'Can I help, Daddy?'

'Yes. Get some of the big bin bags from under the sink. Some of this stuff might be OK, but I can't risk it. We'll have to throw it all out. What a waste!'

Not as much a waste as it could have been. I'd fed a

whole lot of pizza to an alien next door, but it was not a good time to explain this.

Mum came home as Dad and I were carrying loads of bags to the bin. Dad explained what had happened – how the freezer was accidentally switched off – and how he was stopping us all dying from food poisoning. At least in all of this nobody noticed the absence of six family-sized pizzas. And a leg of lamb.

Dad finished carrying the bags out and Mum looked in the empty freezer. She said, 'Well … it looks like takeaway tonight.' She was surprisingly calm. I wondered if it was because Dad was so agitated, she didn't want to make him any worse. Her tone stayed calm, but developed a wooden quality when she spied Jemima standing in the hall.

'Hello, dear. Have you been over again?' She turned as if to ask Dad a question, saw his back retreating with yet another bag, and directed her questioning gaze at me.

I said, 'Jemima's running away … she can stay here …' My voice lacked the same commanding tone as before. My statement turned into a question, '… can't she?'

I couldn't tell if Mum was angry, disturbed, worried or just tired. Mr Newton's mask would have been easier to read.

PART THREE

MISS SLIDER

Chapter Forty-six

Indian takeaway was one of my favourites. I loved the rich sauces that run into the rice. Butter chicken was my all-time favourite; I always asked for it if we're given a choice. We weren't.

Dad was sent out with Bella to get the food. I thought that was odd, but Bella got all excited and dressed up in her biggest coat and furry boots. She looked like a tiny Eskimo heading out the door on a special mission with Dad. I said, 'Good luck, Bella.' Dad was an even worse driver at night.

I understood why Bella went when Mum sat down in the living room with Jemima and me. She'd made herself a cup of tea and she sat in her chair, facing us. She was kind of hunched over her tea, but leaning forwards, like she was going to confide in us; actually, she wanted us to confide in her.

'OK, you two … what's going on?'

I'd said all I knew, so I waited for Jemima to speak. It took a long time – the space of three slow breaths – but in a quiet, controlled voice she said, 'I want to live here, please.'

Mum sipped her tea, letting the words settle, 'Well, that's interesting, Jemima. Can you tell me why?' At least she didn't say, 'dear'.

'You don't fight.'

Mum said, 'Yes, we do … all the time.'

'No.' said Jemima, with surprising firmness, 'You don't. You argue. It's different.'

'What do you mean, dear?' There it was.

'My mum and dad fight – a lot. And I try to keep out of the way, but sometimes … well sometimes …' Her voice had gone soft, not Elemenope soft, but frightened. '… I get pushed out of the way – like I'm a nuisance.'

Wow. I didn't know where to look. Jemima wasn't crying; she was shaking. Mum looked furious. But it was a strange fury; there was an element of triumph in it, like she was thinking, *I told you so*. I didn't know who she would have said that to – maybe just herself.

'Who pushes you, dear?'

'Father. Actually, I call him that … Mummy makes me call him that … but he's *not* my dad.'

I was getting more confused by the minute. Mum said to me, 'Martha, could you get some water, please.'

I knew she just wanted me to leave the room, so I went, but I stood outside the door.

Jemima started to cry. She didn't cry like I did; it was a neat sound. If I had to cry, everything came out: anger, bitterness, rage and snot. Not from Jemima; she was a gentle crier. I was beginning to realise she was a gentle person.

Mum asked a bunch of questions I'd always thought we weren't supposed to ask. They were rude. But Jemima answered them all. It was difficult eavesdropping because I had my ear pressed hard against the door and I was worried that somebody might open the door and I'd fall into the room.

Jemima said, 'My mum and my *real* dad got divorced. We live with the man Mummy makes me call Father. He's rich ... really rich, but he gets really angry and impatient and I know he doesn't love me. I don't think he even likes me. He hates me. I'm a nuisance. I hear him say exactly that ... that I'm a pest. That's when he pushes me out of the way. He pushed me down the stairs.' I thought I heard a gasp from Mum. I pulled my head away in case somebody came, so I missed the next bit.

My mum and dad got angry and impatient with me, but they never pushed me. Not even close. Not even when I'd hit Bella. I couldn't imagine either of them behaving like that.

I ran to the kitchen so I could get a glass of water and get back into the living room as quickly as possible. What I found surprised me: Mum was holding Jemima and patting her gently on the back. I couldn't remember the last time she did that for me. Mum seemed surprised when I offered her a glass of water. She really had just wanted me out of the room. Well, I knew the secret now.

Mum said to Jemima mainly, but a little bit to me, 'I think you can stay here tonight … you can sleep in Martha's room. It'll be fun; let's call it a sleepover. I'll give your mother a call and see what she says. OK?' Jemima nodded.

I was excited; I'd always wanted to have a sleepover, but I'd never been allowed. It was one of Mum's rules.

Mum took a deep breath as she reached for the phone. She sent us up to my room with a dismissive wave of her hand. We started making up a bed on the floor for Jemima to use. I pulled a pile of cushions together; it looked bumpy. We'd get some blankets and other things when Mum got off the phone.

'What's that?' Jemima asked as I pushed things around under my bed, trying to find more pillows.

'Oh that? That's my secret biscuit tin. Do you want one?' I opened the tin; there were three chocolate digestives, two Penguins and a Jaffa Cake left. Odd numbers are a problem if you're sharing with one other person. She watched me pop the lonely Jaffa Cake in my mouth and said, 'No thanks … I don't want to spoil dinner.'

Spoil dinner? Adults were always saying that. I'd never met a biscuit capable of spoiling dinner. Oh well … her loss.

Mum was still on the phone as we got downstairs. She looked stiff. There was silence; I imagined Jemima's mum was speaking. Then I could hear her voice coming over the phone; she was shouting. Mum took the phone away from her ear and waved us back upstairs.

Chapter Forty-seven

Jemima sat on my bed and I sat on the pile of cushions on the floor. I was wondering how much pizza a starving Mantiform Caliopteryx could eat, and whether Dad would remember to bring home butter chicken.

I had no idea what Jemima was thinking, but based on what she had said so far, I imagined she was thinking about staying at our house. I was not good at this; I lacked Mr Newton's mind-reading power.

Jemima finally spoke, 'What was that all about next door? Is that really Mr Newton's house? It was awfully dark and cold. Was that really Mrs Gnash? I'm so confused.' That was what Jemima was thinking about: all that stuff I'd got used to since getting to know Mr Newton.

I wondered where the whole 'running-away-from-home-because-my-supposed-dad-is-horrible-to-me' problem ranked compared with the scary alien and newt-person problem. They were both pretty extreme. I couldn't begin to understand what it must be like living in a house where you're afraid of the people who were meant to take care of you.

As I thought about Jemima's situation, it made my whole 'Mum-is-a-real-cow-about-my-weight' problem seem minor.

I said, 'If I tell you about next door, will you tell me about your dad?'

'Deal.'

'OK. This is all super-duper top secret. Seriously, nobody else knows this stuff. I promised Mr Newton I'd never tell anybody. So, if I tell you, I'm breaking a promise, and you will have to promise to *never* let on. OK?'

'OK.'

I wanted to ask Mr Newton's permission to tell Jemima about Mrs Gnash, but then I realised that she'd already seen Mrs Gnash turn from one shape to the other. She fed her. She stroked her. Mr Newton couldn't expect me not to explain that to Jemima.

'Mrs Gnash is an alien – a thing called a Mantiform Caliopteryx.' I waited for a response, but Jemima's eyes looked out of focus. They looked like my brain felt when I was trying to make sense of all this myself. It was a difficult thing to understand, but it was even harder to explain.

The more I tried to make things clear, the more scared I realised I should have been, and I realised I had been truly brave. Braver than Jemima, because I knew the risk I was taking. I started to shake as I went on, 'She only eats every five years, and she was going to eat the kids in her class.'

Finally: a reaction. Jemima gasped, 'I had no idea.'

I was shaking harder. 'She's … it's … truly horrible – a horrible thing.' Did I go further and talk about Mr Newton? I'd gone this far. No. I had to keep his true identity safe. Even when I'd let my friends in on that, they had been unable to grasp it. I thought Jemima was having enough trouble. I was gabbling inside my own head, and, anyway, she hadn't asked about Mr Newton.

But he'd never asked me to keep Miss Slider's weird time-thing a secret. He'd even talked about it in front of Jemima, so that was fair game. I said, 'Should we talk about Miss Slider?'

'What about her? Is she some crazy alien too?' She seemed almost angry. I got that. Sometimes if I'm learning a whole lot of new stuff, and it's really confusing, and more new stuff keeps coming at me – like maths – my brain fills up and it can get angry, or confused. Maybe both. That was the message I was getting from Jemima.

'Did you hear Miss Slider, or maybe it was Mr Newton – now I can't remember – saying she could take Mrs Gnash into the future?' Jemima shook her head. I was sure she had been part of the conversation earlier. She'd even asked about time machines. Was she doing an Elemenope?

I felt I was repeating myself as I said, 'Well … there's something Miss Slider does with time – I have no idea – but she can apparently take someone, or something, into the future. Who knew?'

'Why would she do that?'

I said, 'I guess it somehow solves the problem of bad things happening now. But I don't see how it fixes anything.'

Jemima looked thoughtful. I was expecting a flood of questions. This stuff was seriously weird, and the time thing seemed impossible. But there were no questions from Jemima. My brain was full of questions; it went round and round with the same problem. We didn't get any further because Mum called us downstairs to set the table.

She said, 'Dad's going to be home soon with dinner, and we should be ready.' Mum was agitated, but Jemima said, 'Your mum's really nice.' I didn't ever think that.

She was just my mum, and I was mainly worried about her fat-girl lectures.

While we were putting out the cutlery and sorting some paper napkins, Jemima piped up again. 'I've been thinking about the Miss Slider time thing. Do you think it's real?'

I said, 'Well, if you'd asked me a year ago if I'd meet a child-eating creature from another planet I would have called the loony bin. But look at us now. So, why not?'

'I wonder if she could take me somewhere?'

I said, 'Where would you want to go?'

'Somewhere far away from my family.'

I thought that was really sad. My family annoyed the pants off me, but I couldn't imagine running away. Jemima was hurting badly.

Chapter Forty-eight

I had a huge plate of butter chicken (Dad remembered) and rice and two poppadums. I watched the red sauce sink into the rice.

The door sounded like a drum. Dad looked up, but Mum held out her hand and said, 'I'll get it, John.' That was a warning. She rarely ever called him by his proper name. He took it as a warning, too, but he went after her anyway. I didn't think he liked the sound of that knock; I certainly didn't.

Jemima, Bella and I were still sitting at the table. I'd slowed my chewing so I could hear better. I didn't need to.

'Come out here, Jemima!' It was Mrs Toilet's voice. Jemima started to shake; her face went pale as she lowered her head into her hands. She seemed really scared, much more scared than when we were feeding pizza to the Mantiform Caliopteryx.

I could hear Mum's voice, 'Why don't you let Jemima finish her dinner … we've only just sat down. I can bring her home afterwards. It's no bother.' I heard the door slam. Mum looked defiant, flushed, and she had that look of triumph again. Dad looked like a deer in the headlights.

Mum sat at the table, but she didn't eat. She kept looking at Jemima as she said, 'Don't worry, dear.'

I was not reassured. Something big was happening, and I needed to understand it. Bella was reaching for seconds.

Jemima suddenly brightened. 'May I use your phone, please?' She just did that: used 'may' the way Mum and Dad were always trying to get me to. I was impressed.

'Of course, dear. Who do you want to call?'

'My dad.'

Mum said, 'Are you sure that's a good idea?'

'Not the "dad" who lives with Mummy. Not "Father" … my real dad. Daddy. I was promised that I could go to his house every other weekend, but it *never* happens.' She started shaking as she went on, 'Mummy keeps coming up with excuses … like today: I was supposed to be at Daddy's, but Mummy *never* lets me go. I can't remember the last time I was allowed to even see him.'

Jemima was sobbing, now, and shaking. She looked back at Mum and said, 'I'm silly. I should have thought of this earlier. It's just … well … your family is so nice, and the last time I tried to ring Daddy I got, well, you know, punished.'

Mum said, 'How?'

'Father shut me in a cupboard.'

Mum shook her head and said, 'Do you know your dad's number?'

Jemima pulled a wallet from her jeans and unfolded a little piece of paper. She treated it like a treasure, smoothing the creases with her fingers.

The phone call didn't last long: some shaky greetings, a few tears and a mention of our address. I couldn't hear anything more because she had gone into the kitchen with the phone, and I had gone back to chewing.

I was just starting some seconds of butter chicken (nobody had felt the need to comment about my plate, or my second helping, or 'saving my life'), when there was another lot of noise outside.

It didn't sound like Jemima's mum this time. I looked out the front widow and there was Mrs Gnash – not Mrs Gnash actually, a Mantiform Caliopteryx at full height – jumping over Mr Newton's gate. I saw its long green legs pounding down the street. A tiny figure was chasing her, and – bang – they both disappeared in a brilliant flash of light.

'What was that,' asked Dad.

'A broken promise,' I muttered.

'Sorry, Martha …what did you say?'

'Oh, nothing. It's … well … hard to explain, and I don't think I'm going to.'

With the sudden lightning flash, I hadn't noticed the old yellow Toyota pull up out the front of our house.

* * * * *

I'd never known such a busy night. There was another knock at the door. A gentle one – hesitant. Mum and Dad went again and this time there was a quiet discussion, and a different person came in. It was the shabby detective. He was scruffy, crumpled. His clothes were too, and it looked like he'd never done his hair.

Jemima bolted from the table and threw her arms around him. It had to be the other 'dad' she'd been talking about. She buried her face in the front of him, as he stroked the back of her head. He looked over the top of Jemima to Mum and Dad. His face looked sad and happy at the same time. I'd stopped eating again, so I could listen.

Mum said, 'I don't know what to do now.'

The man wasn't really talking to Mum directly; he was kneeling and wiping tears from Jemima's face. She clung to him.

He said, 'When Amanda and I separated, we had an agreement that Jemima would spend half the time with me. But somehow it was never convenient, and after she married that man, well, I had to fight to see my own daughter. I knew something was wrong. Now … well, I think we'll start with Jemima coming home with me. What do you say, honey-bunny?'

He did it too! That settled it. Only a real dad would embarrass his daughter that way.

Jemima didn't say anything, but she nodded her head. She was smiling, and crying. It was proper crying: snot and all. I was still confused. I said, 'So … you're not a private detective, then? How come you've been hanging around?'

The man laughed and said, 'No. I haven't had a visit in a long time, and I just wanted to make sure everything was OK with my Jemima Puddle-Duck … that's all.'

Mum invited Jemima's dad – we learned his name was Gerald – to stay for dinner. He smiled, a lovely smile, full of eye-happiness as he looked over the remnants of the food. He said 'Mmm … butter chicken – my favourite.

But I think we should get going, don't you, butter-nut?' I really liked him.

* * * * *

We all crowded into the doorway to say goodbye to Jemima and her proper dad. I watched them cross the road. Mum, Dad and Bella turned back inside, but I stayed waving, happy for Jemima.

There was another almighty bang and flash of light. I pushed myself flat against the wall to avoid being hit by Miss Slider as she rushed past, still chasing the Mantiform Caliopteryx. Jemima and Gerald stopped in their tracks as the huge monster jumped over the Toyota.

I heard Jemima's dad say, 'What, on earth, is that?'

Jemima said, matter of fact, 'Oh, that's one of our teachers.'

There was another loud popping sound, like somebody bursting a hundred balloons at once. It was so loud I closed my eyes, the way I did in fierce lightning, or when someone banged something close to me. There was a strong smell of mothballs. When I opened my eyes, they'd all disappeared: Jemima, Gerald, Mrs Gnash and Miss Slider. They'd vanished; even Gerald's car.

I don't know how long I stood there; I was waiting for them to come back. They didn't. A dark blue Range Rover arrived and parked right where Gerald's car had been. I saw Mrs Toilet and a tall man in a tweed jacket climb out of the Range Rover and walk to our front door. I guessed the tweedy-man was Mrs Toilet's husband, Jemima's 'Father'.

Mrs Toilet looked down her nose at me and said, 'Where's Jemima?'

I was still stunned; my face felt scorched. I was sure my hair was standing on end, but I summoned all my politeness and said, 'Oh, you just missed her. She went off with her dad.'

The Toilets (I was sticking with that; it really suited them) stormed off. As they drove away I saw Mrs Toilet using her mobile phone. She was probably calling Jemima, or Gerald, or the police. I really didn't care.

I went inside and sat back at the table with my little family. I looked from one to the other and thought, 'Yes, you're annoying, but you'll do.'

Mum asked, 'Did Jemima and Gerald get off OK?'

'Oh, yes. They've gone.' I didn't know where. As I thought about it, I realised I didn't know *when*!

My face must have given me away. Dad asked, 'You

OK, pumpkin?'

I said, 'Sure. I just hope Jemima's OK.'

Mum said, 'Well, that family's got a lot to worry about.'

She didn't have a clue. She held my arm as it reached for the last poppadum. 'I think you've had enough. Remember, Martha: I'm trying to save your life.'

In that instant I saw that Mum actually believed what she said. She meant well. But *I* had actually saved the life of every kid at St Finbar's. And that had worked because I was such good bait.

There was nothing to gain from arguing with Mum; I had bigger problems. Like how to find Jemima.

Chapter Forty-nine

I ran from the gigantic green insect. It reached out its horrible, hooked fingers to catch my hair, but I was too quick for it. That was how I knew I was dreaming. Skinny kids had nightmares where they ran too slowly and the monsters caught them. When I had nightmares, I ran faster than the wind.

I was sweating when I woke up; it felt like I had been running for real. Mum said I had a temperature and she let me stay in my pyjamas. I couldn't see Bella anywhere. I didn't care; I just sat at the kitchen table with my head in my hands. It felt like snot was trying to poke my eyes out from behind.

My mind was swimming with worry about Jemima, but I didn't know where to start.

Jemima Waddington-Clarke had been at my school for only one term when she disappeared. It was a really big deal; it even made the television news. 'Manhunt for missing ten-year-old,' was the banner headline on the TV, and the police had been to our house. Twice.

They came back again, only this time there were lots of them. And they had a dog with them; a big slobbery thing with one of those sad faces – a bloodhound.

I listened to a policewoman talking to Mum and Dad. She said they had to search our house because it was where Jemima had been seen last. Mum said, 'But we told you yesterday … she left here with her father, Gerald.'

The policewoman was impatient. She said, 'Well, we're looking for *him* too, but we haven't been able to find him yet. So, we'll start the search now. If you could keep out of the way, we'd appreciate it.'

I watched Mum and Dad wander about – lost in our own house. They sat at the kitchen table with me, then Dad got up and made himself another cup of coffee. Mum stood up, then she sat down again. It was like they didn't know what to do. I sneezed.

The policewoman stopped and it was as though she saw me for the first time. 'Who is this?' she said, getting down to my eye-level. She went on in a sickly adult-who-doesn't-have-children-suddenly-having-to-talk-to-a-child voice, 'What's your name, young lady?'

'I'm Martha Gibbons.' I blew my nose loudly on a tissue. The policewoman moved a step back. She kept looking at me. I didn't know if she wanted me to say more, but I wasn't in a very conversational mood. Actually, apart from feeling sick, I was annoyed. Mum and Dad had told the police everything they knew, and instead of looking for Jemima, they were obviously looking where she wasn't.

* * * * *

I blamed the Toilets. They'd come back to our house when the police arrived the first time. Jemima's mum had a piece of paper in her hand and shoved it in Dad's face. When he read it, he gave a little nervous half-laugh. I snatched it before he could give it back to Mrs Toilet.

Jemima's handwriting was super neat. The note said, 'I'm running away to live at Martha's house.' I turned the paper over, expecting an explanation, or just more words, but there was nothing.

A policeman standing beside Mrs Toilet asked me for the note, and I handed it over. He said it was an important clue.

Mrs Toilet said, 'It took a while to work out who this "Martha" was, but of course she meant you.' The look she gave me wasn't hard to read; she hated me. She hated my whole family – and our house. 'Who could possibly want to live in this hovel?' she said as she turned her nose up at everything in her line of sight.

I said, 'I don't think it's got anything to do with the house; I think it's about the people.'

Well, that did it. Mrs Toilet started yelling, and the policeman had to take her away. That was good. What wasn't so good was Mr Toilet poking his rich finger in Dad's chest and saying, 'We'll get to the bottom of this. You mark my words.'

Dad didn't say anything. I watched his face as Mr Toilet went on, 'People like us shouldn't have to associate with the likes of you.' He walked after Mrs Toilet, and I heard him say to her, 'I don't know why you ever sent her to that dreadful school. Look what's happened to her.' He said that with the tone that meant, 'It's all your fault.'

I wasn't having that. I knew the truth. I knew that Jemima wanted to run away because her stepfather was a bully. I wanted to say that to the policeman, but when I went to walk after the Toilets, Mum put her hand on my shoulder and said, 'Stay here, Martha. Let them go. Heaven knows we don't need people who talk to us like that. "People like us … the likes of you" … spare me.'

I wanted to ask Mum what she meant – what Mr

Toilet meant, but I was getting a real feeling that nobody wanted to tell me anything.

The police needed to know about Miss Slider and what she could do with time. I just had to find a way to tell them. I decided to ignore Mum, so I went straight out the door to where the Toilets were talking to the policemen on our front path. I thought it was odd that they hadn't gone anywhere, until I heard Mrs Toilet saying, 'You go right back in there and arrest that man. No ... arrest the whole family. They're all in on it. They've done something to my daughter.'

'We have not, you cow!' That felt good. I shouldn't have said it, but I couldn't keep it in. Everybody turned and looked at me. I stood on our front path, a vision in rumpled pyjamas, streaming nose and an air of defiance.

I didn't know what I was defying: the nonsense spewing from Mrs Toilet, or the incompetence of the police. Probably all of it. I just wanted them to find Jemima. I'd seen shows about missing kids; the police always think it's the dad. Well, in this case they had two dads to think about.

We'd told them Jemima had gone off with her real dad, but the problem was the police weren't smart enough to realise she'd gone to a different time.

I looked at the policewoman standing beside Mrs Toilet and said, 'You know, I think Jemima might be in a different time by now.'

'You mean a different time zone. Did she say something about travelling?'

I said, 'No. You don't understand. Jemima and her dad,' (Mr Toilet gave me a filthy look), 'got caught up in our head teacher trying to get rid of an alien, and I think they've gone to the future.'

Silence. Mr and Mrs Toilet stared at me. The policewoman started to laugh. They didn't even have the good manners to answer me before they all turned their backs on me.

If that was how they were going to treat my friend's disappearance, I knew I would have to sort it out myself.

* * * * *

The second visit from the police was only slightly better. They made a big mess emptying cupboards (like we would have hidden her in a cupboard), opening drawers, poking about under things. They rifled through my underwear! They opened my secret biscuit tin. When I went to check later it had been moved and I was sure a couple of digestives were missing. They had no idea, and they ignored everything I tried to tell them. Idiots.

Chapter Fifty

The easy part was deciding to look for Jemima without the help of the police. The hard part was convincing my friends that they should help. Elemenope said, 'I don't know, Martha. It's not like she's been very nice, is it?'

I thought that was mean, and I said so. Elemenope just said, 'Well, OK then. Even if I wanted to help … and I'm not saying I do … how do I know she went off with Miss Slider anyway?'

I thought she was being a bit thick. I said, 'Because I say she did. Or at least she and her dad disappeared at the exact same moment Miss Slider and the Mantiform Caliopteryx disappeared – with a big explosion – right outside my house. One second they were there, crossing the road, and the next second they were gone – completely vanished. Car and all. It's not like I could have missed them driving off. Gerald's car is a real old banger; I would have heard it even if I couldn't see it.'

'Who's Gerald?' asked Hakeem.

'Jemima's real dad. Keep up. I've told you all about that.'

'All about what?' It was Michael's turn to forget what I'd already told them about Jemima running away from home, having dinner at my place and then leaving with her real father – the lovely Gerald.

I realised that maybe I hadn't told the story properly, so I went over it again.

I felt like the voice-over person on a TV series. I should have started with, 'Previously on the Jemima disappearance show …' and then run through some choice highlights. The problem was there were no choice highlights, the whole thing had to start with Mrs Gnash.

How to explain about a vicious, carnivorous, child-eating monster from another planet? I did it anyway. When I got to the part about setting a trap with a leg of lamb and teaching Mr Newton to tie knots, Michael suddenly showed interest. He said, 'Wait on … you got one alien to tie up another? How'd you do that?' Exasperating boy!

'No, Michael. I told you. Mr Newton is *not* an alien. He's a collection of newts, all working together and using their brains with some kind of telepathy.' He just looked at me.

I said, 'Mrs Gnash *is* an alien – a thing called a

Mantiform Caliopteryx – she eats meat. Only now she eats pizza too.'

Hakeem seemed to refocus his eyes behind his glasses as he asked, 'How do you know that?'

'Because Jemima and I fed her pizza while she was tied up in Mr Newton's cellar.' I looked from Michael, to Hakeem, to Elemenope and back again. I had their attention, so I went on. 'Jemima was running away from her horrible parents, and then her real dad turned up …'

Elemenope said, 'Her *real* dad?'

'Yes, her *real* dad. Like I said, she was running away, but then her real dad turned up and she went off with him.'

Michael said, 'But you said she was running away – so why did she go off with her dad?'

Elemenope came to my rescue with, 'I guess her mum's her mum, but she has a real dad and a stepdad. So, she was running away from her stepdad … right?'

I said, 'Right. Can we move on?' Three nods told me I could.

'Just as Jemima was heading off with Gerald …'

'Who's Gerald?' asked Michael.

I was about to explode. 'Jemima's *real* dad!'

'Oh, sorry. Go on, Martha.'

'I'm trying to.' I didn't really mean my death stare, but I'd had about enough interruptions. 'Anyway, just as Jemima was heading off with Gerald ...' I paused; I looked my three friends in their eyes – daring them to speak – daring them to ask a question. '... Miss Slider appeared, chasing after the Mantiform Caliopteryx, and *BANG* ... they were gone.' I paused for dramatic effect.

Michael broke the spell with, 'But you said Mrs Gnash was tied up. What happened?'

'Mrs Gnash is a Mantiform Caliopteryx ... she's hugely strong ... she obviously broke out of her ropes and escaped down the street. Anyway, Miss Slider was chasing after her, there was this huge bang and they all disappeared: Miss Slider, the Mantiform Caliopteryx, Jemima and Gerald – all just gone.'

It was an incredible story. I knew if somebody else had told it to me I probably wouldn't believe it. I just had to hope my friends could take it in.

Hakeem came to my rescue. He did that thing with his glasses – he took them off, cleaned them on his shirt tail, looked through them and put them back on. I knew that was a sign he was thinking. He did it to give himself time.

'So ... what you're saying, Martha, is Jemima and her dad accidentally went to another time. And that happened because they were close to Miss Slider when she did something to get rid of Mrs Gnash. Is that right?'

'That's what I think happened, yes.'

Hakeem took his glasses off again, and gave them another, totally unnecessary, clean before saying, 'Incredible. It's unbelievable. How could that be?'

I had to say I didn't know, but I needed his help, so I said, 'I don't understand how it happened, but it fits with what Mr Newton told me about Miss Slider. He said she can take people to other times – at least I think that's what he said.'

Michael and Elemenope stared at me as if I'd gone mad. They stared so hard I had to say, 'I'm not mad … Mr Newton definitely said something like that. And I saw them … I actually saw Jemima and Gerald disappear.' I hadn't, actually, because my eyes were shut by the noise, but they had definitely disappeared – there was not enough time for them to drive off. I knew they had gone to another time, but how was I going to prove it? I needed my friends to have faith in me. There was only one thing for it; we had to talk to Mr Newton.

Chapter Fifty-one

'This looks ominous. Martha Gibbons, Elemenope Miller, Hakeem Nasri and Michael Saddler ... all looking very serious. What can I do for you?'

We had walked in to Mr Newton's classroom – our classroom – at break time, hoping for a quiet word. The rule about children inside the school building during breaks had been relaxed after Mrs Gnash's disappearance.

I started, 'Mr Newton, um ... can you please help me explain how Miss Slider took Mrs Gnash to another time?'

Mr Newton turned to face me straight-on. Well he turned his mask to face me. There was a pause, followed by a humming from his voice machine. Michael shuffled his feet and began to sweat. Elemenope fidgeted. Hakeem tried to look interested in a mark on the floor. I looked straight into the eyeholes in Mr Newton's mask.

Finally, he spoke. 'I beg your pardon, Martha Gibbons?'

'I said, can you please help me explain how Miss Slider took Mrs Gnash to another time?'

'That's what I thought you said.'

'It's OK, Mr Newton. These guys know about you. But Jemima's missing ... she got caught up in whatever Miss Slider did with Mrs Gnash. My friends don't believe me, and I need your help.'

'Take a breath Martha Gibbons. All right, then. I probably owe you all my thanks for saving me last year. And I know I can trust Martha, so I'll have to trust you lot too.'

Michael stretched out a hand. He was going to touch Mr Newton's mask. I slapped his hand away before he could. That would have been rude. And creepy. But mostly rude.

'Where to begin? How about I show you who I am?'

Mr Newton removed his mask to show the squirming mass of newts that made up his head. Even though I knew all about him, I still felt queasy seeing him like that. Elemenope let out a squeak, Michael blinked and Hakeem took off his glasses, polished them unnecessarily, and said, 'Fascinating.'

Mr Newton replaced his face – well, his mask –

while he gave a much better description of a Mantiform Caliopteryx than I ever could. He described her (its) awesome height and strength. When he got to her face, I could see the others recognising her horrible features. He started to say, 'And her mouth …' But I stopped him at that point. It was too gruesome, even for a science nerd like Hakeem.

He even mentioned how brave I had been in helping to catch it. That was nice of him. I really needed him to get to the part about Miss Slider taking Mrs Gnash to another time, but the bell rang and everybody started piling into the classroom. It would have to wait.

* * * * *

Our topic for the new term was insect life cycles. We were supposed to be drawing the stages of a ladybird's development in our working pairs. I was with Elemenope as usual, and she was diligently sketching some eggs on a leaf. I drew a huge green praying mantis with a human face and glasses – Mrs Gnash. When Mr Newton looked over my shoulder he said quietly, 'That's a very strange ladybird, Martha Gibbons.'

I blushed and tore the paper into tiny pieces. I just

couldn't concentrate. My next effort was a bit better. I actually drew a ladybird, but it only had two legs because the other four had been eaten by another gigantic praying mantis I'd drawn beside it. I tried to rub it out, but the paper tore. I stopped even trying to draw at that stage and sat fuming for the rest of the class. Mr Newton was not impressed. I knew that because he said, 'I'm not impressed, Martha Gibbons.'

When the bell rang for lunch, Mr Newton said, 'I'd like Martha Gibbons to stay back, please.'

I was crushed. I didn't think I deserved to get in trouble for being distracted and doing rubbish drawings. It didn't help when the Marks called out in unison, 'Ha, ha. Fatty's going to starve … no lunch for you!' Mr Newton told them to be quiet or they'd be staying back as well.

When everyone else had left, Mr Newton said, 'It's OK, Martha Gibbons. You're not in trouble. I need to let you know that Miss Slider is still not back. I think there must be some trouble with Mrs Gnash.'

'Can you please help me explain to my friends what has happened. I really don't understand it myself.'

'Well, I was about to at break but we ran out of time. I'm not really sure Michael is going to understand. Or Elemenope for that matter. I think you'd better go and get Hakeem. I'll try to explain, but I'm no expert. For our kind, time just travels in a straight line – I think.'

'What will I tell the others? I mean they know about you and Mrs Gnash now. I can't expect them to just forget. I might need their help.'

'Oh, all right. Get them too.'

'Can I have lunch first? I'm starving.'

Mr Newton nodded his head. For once it didn't look like it was about to fall off.

Chapter Fifty-two

I got my wish, but it wasn't good. I finally understood what people meant when they said, 'Be careful what you wish for.'

Apart from Michael, who sat through the whole thing like a stunned mullet, my friends alternately gasped, shrieked and took sharp breaths while Mr Newton laid out the history of Mrs Gnash – our PE teacher – who was really a nasty child-eating creature from one of Jupiter's moons. Hakeem was jumping out of his skin, learning that there really were alien creatures on Earth.

The part about Miss Slider was harder for him to explain. He kept saying that he was not an expert on time travel – but who was? What worried me was that, since her disappearance outside my house that night a few weeks before, Miss Slider had not returned. Mr Newton said that was out of character.

Elemenope said, 'What I don't get in all this, Martha, is why you're friends with Jemima in the first place.'

'Well, it surprised me too, at first. But she's actually a

nice person. All that snobbishness was just her stepdad wearing off on her. That's how *he* behaves.'

While Mr Newton talked about Miss Slider, I remembered how she made me feel. How time slowed down when she was near me. I asked, 'Is Miss Slider an alien too?'

'No, Martha Gibbons. She's one of a small group of people known as time benders. One of her ancestors discovered how to reshape time so it's possible to step into the future or the past.'

Hakeem piped up with, 'No … that's not correct. The mathematics of relativity means time travel is possible, but only into the future. Not backwards. I read about it in *Scientific American*. It's all to do with Einstein's theory.'

Mr Newton said, 'I don't think maths, even Einstein's maths, can hold up in the face of experience, Hakeem. All I know is what Miss Slider has explained to me, and she says she pops in and out of the future and the past.'

I said, 'So, where is she now?'

'I don't know, and I don't like it.'

I said, 'Neither do I. And I think we should do something about it.'

'Now, Martha Gibbons, please don't go messing

about with things you don't understand. Time travel is dangerous. You should leave it to the experts.'

'Well, I don't see how that's right. My friend is missing, Miss Slider's missing – and she *is* an expert. We have to do something.'

* * * * *

I knew what to do, but I would need some moral support. After Mr Newton finished making us promise not to go playing with time travel, I organised to meet Hakeem, Elemenope and Michael after school.

Before I could get a word out, Michael said, 'That was pretty intense earlier – I mean, who would have thought Mr Newton was actually a bunch of newts.'

I said, 'But I told you that last year, don't you remember?'

'Yeah, but I thought you were just making it up.'

'Well, I wasn't, Michael. Mr Newton is a collective of Newts, Mrs Gnash in alien and Miss Slider is a time bender, whatever that means. What kind of school is this?' I suddenly felt unsure of everything.

Hakeem came to my rescue. 'I think it's great. I love this stuff. What should we do first?'

Elemenope joined in as though she had been asleep. 'What should we do first about what?'

'About finding Miss Slider, and Jemima. Where have they gone?'

Hakeem blinked hard, and said, 'Don't you mean when ...?'

Chapter Fifty-three

I couldn't concentrate over dinner. Mum had come home early and made a fantastic lasagne, but I was so unfocussed I even ate the broccoli that she'd put on the side. When I asked for seconds Mum shook her head and said, 'Only if you have more broccoli too.' That was when I noticed I'd eaten the first lot. I decided against it. I'd filled my biscuit tin straight after school, so I wouldn't starve.

After dinner, I lay on my bed, ignoring Bella's invitation to watch some Barbie movie she'd found. I couldn't get interested in a doll that looked so unlike me – so unlike anybody I knew.

I thought about Miss Slider. I thought about what Mr Newton had said. I knew he'd said we weren't to play around with time travel. But what if he didn't mean it? What if we didn't play, but did it seriously? I decided he'd actually meant for me to work out how Miss Slider did it, and go after her. Suddenly I knew it.

* * * * *

'Mum … can I ring Elemenope … please?'

'You saw her all day at school today. You're seeing her again tomorrow. What's so important you have to ring her now, at bedtime?'

I said, 'It wouldn't matter if you let me have a phone. I could just call her any time I liked.'

Mum growled at me. 'No, because you'd put your phone down here at bedtime. I won't allow screens in bedrooms.'

It was a non-argument. Well, it was an argument we'd had before, and one I wasn't winning. I really wanted a phone, and Mum and Dad were dead-set against it.

I tried puppy-dog eyes. Mum just stared as if there was something wrong with me.

'I just want to ask her something.'

'Well, ask her in the morning. Now, go to bed and go to sleep.'

I sulked up to bed, but I couldn't sleep. I kept thinking about Miss Slider and the weird effect she had on me. If she was a normal person she shouldn't be able to make me feel like time was all wrong. She must have some kind of device with her. In a pocket or around her neck, maybe.

I dreamed about the big green insect-thing again. In the morning I decided that was the fault of the broccoli.

I couldn't wait to see Elemenope and Hakeem and tell them my idea. But the first person I saw was Mark One. He sidled past and said, 'Whoa, fatty! Are you getting bigger? I didn't think that was possible. You look like you're about to explode.'

Just then Michael came in the gate. He must have heard what Mark said because he ran after him. Mark was little and fast. The boys disappeared into the school corridor and I turned away. I didn't need Michael to fight my battles for me. I didn't think Mark One was worth it anyway.

Elemenope and Hakeem came through the gate together. They often did that. Hakeem had his head close to Elemenope's face. He had to do that to hear what she said. I waved and trotted over to them. Elemenope whispered, 'Hi.'

I didn't let Hakeem get any words out before I started in on my thoughts. Not the ones about broccoli – the ones about Miss Slider.

'She must use some kind of time machine that's small enough to fit in a pocket or something.'

Hakeem said, 'And good morning to you too. You're

not still on about that, are you? I read some of Stephen Hawking's stuff again last night. Going backwards and forwards in time is just not possible.' Elemenope looked at him like he was a god.

I sulked. Hakeem was really smart, but he was being so closed-minded. I knew he respected those scientists he kept mentioning, but what if they were wrong? I would have to do this myself. Maybe Michael would help me. Michael came out of the school building with a big smile on his face. He wouldn't say where he'd been or what he'd done. A minute later Mark One appeared – drenched. He looked like he'd been swimming. In his clothes.

Did I really want Michael to help me?

* * * * *

Friday just dragged. Everybody else looked forward to sports afternoon, but I dreaded it. I made it better by getting lots of energy from the chocolate éclair I'd added to my lunch. Seriously, if Mum didn't want me to eat that stuff, then she shouldn't buy it. Yes, it was hidden way up in the cupboard where she kept the odd-shaped serving dishes. And, yes, it was buried inside a tin labelled 'receipts', but I'd known about that secret spot for ages.

We played netball – what a stupid game. I was centre, which meant I stayed in the middle two zones – that was good. But it also meant people kept passing me the ball. That would be OK if they could pass to where I was, but I was supposed to move about. After five minutes I just gave up, hoping that I would be replaced. Without Mrs Gnash, sport supervision was sadly lacking. No teacher was even watching, so as my performance got (deliberately) worse and worse, all that happened was that my team kept losing the ball. In the end I gave up altogether and sat on the bench. I couldn't get my bib off – the one with the big 'C' in the middle of it – it was stuck somewhere between my stomach and my chin. I didn't care.

Hakeem had been sitting out because he had a note from his dad explaining that he had a sore knee from last week's PE class. I knew that was made up, but obviously his dad didn't. Why didn't I think of that?

Hakeem said, 'You really hate PE, don't you?'

'Is it that obvious?'

He said, 'Look at Michael. He's loving this.' It was true, Michael was on my team, and we were winning despite my efforts. All because of Michael who was our goal attack. He was really strong and fast. He could shoot the ball straight through the hoop.

I couldn't get interested in netball, even if we were winning. I was obsessed with finding Jemima and finding out about Miss Slider. Since she'd disappeared, we had an acting head – Mrs Johnson, the reception teacher. But nobody was filling in for Mrs Gnash. That's why sports afternoon was so chaotic.

I asked Hakeem if he would help me find out about Miss Slider. He gave a big sigh and said, 'If it will stop this obsession, then yes. But I think we should include El and Michael.'

I was suddenly excited. 'OK. Better than OK. Let's make plans. We have to start at Miss Slider's house … you know … the old place on the hill by the rec.'

Chapter Fifty-four

The plan was simple: break into Miss Slider's house and steal a time machine. What could possibly go wrong? The first part was easy. We gathered on Saturday afternoon – it had to be afternoon because Michael played football, Elemenope had a piano lesson, I had ballet and Hakeem had an oboe lesson. Of course he played the oboe. He told me once that it was the most important instrument in the orchestra because everybody else tuned to the oboe's A. Whatever that was.

I made a special note of the date on my calendar. I thought it would be important for future generations to know what we did on the 23rd of April – the day four kids made history. It didn't matter to me that Miss Slider maybe did this all the time. If what she did was a secret, then what we did was going to be the first time the world got to hear about time travel. We were going to be famous. And anyway, when Mr Newton was busy telling us not to play around with time travel, he hadn't said anything about keeping it secret. But I wasn't going to tell Mum or Dad – they'd only worry. Or worse, stop me going.

We met at the rec. When I told Dad I wanted to go to the park he said, 'Really?' He said it with that tone that meant, 'You're up to something!' so I went red. I kept my cool, apart from going red, by saying I was meeting the gang. He knew who that was, so he was happy to let me go. If Mum had been home she would have made some crack about getting some exercise while I was there.

It was a weird sort of day – all misty and wet, without actually raining. I couldn't see very far in front of me and walked right into Elemenope and Hakeem coming the other way – holding hands. They jumped apart when they saw me, but it was too late. I didn't care that they liked each other. Michael came sauntering over from the football field, stuffing sandwiches in his face. Why hadn't I thought to bring food?

We walked together to the front of Miss Slider's house. I hadn't given it any thought since last Halloween. It was creepy even when it wasn't decked out with skeletons and spider webs.

We stood under the little porch, all just looking at the door as though we expected it to open by magic. I knocked, waited a minute and knocked again. Nothing.

There were no sounds coming from inside.

It was just like the time we broke into Mr Newton's house – when we didn't know it was Mr Newton's house – and it looked deserted and I knocked anyway. This time we knew Miss Slider wasn't home, but it seemed awfully impolite to just break in. What if she was at home and just hadn't shown up to school? I could understand that.

After a couple of minutes, with Michael shuffling his feet, and Hakeem taking his glasses off, polishing them on his shirt and putting them back on, only to do it again every fifteen seconds, I tried turning the doorknob.

Hakeem said, 'That's more like it.' It turned, but the door was locked.

Remembering our exploits at Mr Newton's, I led the way round the back. There was a high yew hedge, which hadn't been trimmed in about fifty years. It was all scratchy, but it did shield us from view. The back door was locked, and the windows all seemed firm. The house was in annoyingly good repair. We couldn't get round the other side of the house because the hedge on that side was completely overgrown and pushed right up against the building. It seemed hopeless.

As we stumbled past the overgrown yews again,

Michael swatted at a branch that caught him just below the eye. 'That hurt more than it should have,' he said. He turned back, grabbed the branch like he was going to rip it off, and something heavy fell off it, landing on his foot. 'Ouch … this bush is really out to get me.'

Before Michael could bend down to see what had hit him, I pounced on it. I held it up to get a better look in the poor light. In my hand sat an old leather pouch, tied at the top like a purse in a medieval movie.

'Open it.' That came from everyone, all at once. Of course I was going to open it, but I wanted to savour it – it felt like treasure. I tugged at the thin leather strap holding the top together and pulled the lips apart. What a disappointment. I fished inside to find a heavy, brass key. It was really old and bent. The brass was all tarnished.

'What's it for?' whispered Elemenope. I shrugged.

Hakeem said, 'I think I know. Did you see the lock on the back door? It's ancient. I bet it fits that. Lots of people leave an emergency key in a secret place outside. I'll bet that's what it is.'

It was.

Chapter Fifty-five

Miss Slider's house positively reeked of mothballs. Even though it was dim outside – that sort of soft, looking-through-cellophane, afternoon light – inside the house was dark. The windows were covered in heavy curtains, so the rooms were probably dark even in the brightest light. I tried to open one, then another, but each curtain was stapled to the edges of the window frames. Miss Slider obviously liked the dark. I had the strangest thought, and I couldn't keep it to myself.

'She couldn't be a vampire, could she?' That stopped everybody in their tracks. In the absence of any spoken response, I said, 'Just thinking out loud.' Still nobody said anything, but Elemenope held her hands in front of her, her index fingers forming a cross.

We walked through room after room; they were all dark and musty with a persistent smell of mothballs. The dining room looked like it had been set for a party; there were ten settings around a long oak table. All the cutlery looked really old and tarnished. The knives had bone handles and the forks looked like real silver. Everything was covered in dust. If Miss Slider had been expecting guests, I figured they never turned up – about a hundred years ago.

'What, exactly, are we looking for?' asked Michael.

I said, 'I don't know, but I'm hoping I'll recognise it when I see it.'

'How will you recognise something you've never seen before?' Hakeem had a habit of asking really logical questions – it was annoying.

I shrugged and sat on an over-stuffed sofa. Plumes of dust flew up and made me cough. We'd been in every room of the house, upstairs, in two bedrooms, downstairs in the dining room, the kitchen and this room – a lounge. I felt let down. I couldn't say what I had been expecting, but it wasn't nothing.

Michael spoke after a long silence. I'd thought he was just going through the motions, but he said something interesting. 'Has anybody else noticed there's no TV? Who doesn't have a TV? I haven't seen a computer, a laptop, a tablet or a phone either. Anybody else think that's odd?'

He was right. There was no form of technology at all. There wasn't even an old telephone.

Hakeem said, 'Well spotted. How does she keep in touch with people? I mean, she runs our school, so how does she contact anybody if she's at home? This is seriously weird.'

I said, 'Well … we're obviously missing something. But what?'

Michael's brain must have been working overtime. He said, 'Most houses in town have cellars, don't they? Maybe there's a trapdoor or something.'

That set us going back through the rooms we'd already been in. We lifted up carpets, poked about behind doors, but there was no secret door. Nothing. I felt frustrated and slumped down hard on the sofa again. Another cloud of dust flew up. Hakeem leaned on the edge of the fireplace. He slipped on the edge of the rug we hadn't put back properly and grabbed at the side of the mantelpiece. The fireplace groaned.

'What was that?' whispered Elemenope.

We'd all heard it. Michael went over to where Hakeem was standing and pushed down hard on the edge of the mantelpiece. The fireplace groaned again, and a shiny brass handle stuck out from between two bricks. It was the only thing in the house not buried in dust.

We all looked at each other, not sure what to do next.

Hakeem broke the spell with, 'What are we waiting for? You know what happens next … in the movies that lever always opens a secret door. Let's do it.'

'Go on, then,' I said. 'You discovered it, so you should pull it.'

Michael grunted, 'He didn't discover it – I did. He wasn't strong enough to make it pop out. I did that, so I should get to pull it.'

Elemenope whispered, 'No, you guys. Coming here was Martha's idea. She should pull it.'

So I did. I pulled it – nothing. I pushed it – nothing. I wiggled it from side to side, I rotated it, I pushed it in and out – nothing happened.

Frustrated, I slumped back down in another cloud of sofa dust. I watched as everybody took turns, doing what I had done, but nothing happened.

'That lever's got to do something,' said Hakeem. Just as he was taking his glasses off for their millionth polish since we started, I had a brainwave. I stood up, walked casually over to the mantelpiece and hit the other side of it really hard. The fireplace groaned again, and another lever shot out from the left-hand side. Now there were two identical levers, about three feet apart.

I said, 'Well, this doesn't take a genius,' and I grabbed

both levers and pushed them down hard. The fireplace groaned again, and this time a door opened in the wall on its left. A tiny door, just big enough for one short person to fit through. Fortunately, it was unusually wide, so a fat person fitted just fine. I didn't wait around for polite arguments about who should go first. This was my discovery. I pushed my way through, shoving aside a set of velvet curtains that hung in the way. The door slammed behind me. My eyes had to adjust to an even darker space, but that wasn't the weird part. Music. Gentle, haunting music entered my head. It was like pan pipes.

Chapter Fifty-six

The excitement of finding myself in that secret place with all its promise was matched by the marching butterflies that had somehow got into my stomach when the door slammed. I wanted to look around, but I wanted to do it with company. I looked at the door I'd come through, but there was no handle. I had to look really closely to see that there was even a door. The whole room was lined with the same dark, wooden tiles. The only thing that gave away the door was the pattern changing from a brick pattern to a herring bone. I couldn't even see a line around the door. Clever.

I was busy admiring the design, and talking to myself about it, when the door swung in, nearly knocking me flat. Michael bounced through, wide-eyed, fists ready, shouting my name.

He grabbed my shoulders and said, 'Wow, Martha, are you OK? You've been gone ages. Come on … we've got to go back. The others are about to call your parents.'

I said, 'What? I've only just got here. What are you talking about?'

'Seriously, Martha, you've been gone for half an hour.'

'Don't be silly … I've just turned around.'

Michael shook his head furiously and said, 'No. We've got to get back there. They're going to think something really bad has happened.'

'But I want to look around. I mean, look at this place … it's amazing.' The room was full of shelves, crammed with books. There was a small bench cluttered with odd-looking equipment, like old radio sets with tiny light bulbs sticking up. I wanted – no, I needed – to investigate.

I started to walk towards the bench, but Michael grabbed my arm.

'Ow. What are you doing?'

'Taking you back. The guys are worried about you. They're probably worried about me now too. This alien stuff is freaky.'

'It's not alien stuff. It's science stuff. I'll bet Hakeem would want to see it.'

'Only if he hasn't gone to find your parents … or the police.'

Michael started pushing on the herring-bone patterned tiles that showed where the door was. I hadn't noticed it had closed behind him. What was it? Was it designed to only let one person through at a time? They needed one of those at the Co-op to stop people barging through the door.

The door didn't move. We started feeling all around where the tile pattern changed, but the wall was smooth. There was no handle, no lever – nothing. We were trapped.

* * * * *

Michael and I took turns calling out. We couldn't even hear any voices on the other side of the wall.

'That's what I was trying to tell you, Martha. We couldn't hear you. We were calling out but you never answered.'

'Well, maybe *I* didn't hear *you*.'

'Come on. We've got to get out of here.'

The door suddenly shivered and swung in, pushing me over. Hakeem and Elemenope came through together, falling on top of me. Hakeem's foot was stuck in the door so it couldn't close. When he tried to pull it back, Michael pushed it further into the gap, wedging the door ajar.'

'Ow!'

'Oh, stop it, Hakeem,' said Michael. 'Your foot's going to save our lives.'

Hakeem stoically kept his foot in the door. I didn't think it hurt that much.

Elemenope stared at the equipment. She did her goldfish impression again.

Hakeem said, between little gasps of exaggerated pain, 'You've been here for ages, Martha. What have you been doing?' He looked accusingly at Michael and said, 'And you … you were supposed to bring her back. What took so long. Seriously, we were panicking in there.' Lying on the floor robbed his accusations of any authority.

I said, 'Well, for starters, I'd only just got here when Michael came charging in, so don't go off at me. And secondly, we'd been looking for how to get out for maybe a minute when you lot arrived. So, I think you should check your facts.'

'I have,' said Hakeem. 'And my watch. Seriously, Martha, it was over an hour.'

'Well, check your watch now, smarty pants.'

He did. Then he held his watch up for us all to see; the hands were racing around the dial.

Chapter Fifty-seven

My head was spinning, and not in a good way. Not like when you get off the Cyclone or the Octopus at the fair.

Hakeem said, 'This is seriously weird. It's like time is going faster in here. How is that possible?'

'I don't like it. I think we should get out of here … now.' I meant it. For all I wanted to know what had happened to Jemima and Miss Slider, I didn't want to spend my life in some weird speeded-up room.

Nobody spoke. We went back through the curtains into Miss Slider's sitting room – Michael grabbed a book off a shelf and shoved it in the door so it couldn't slam shut – and we stood perfectly still for a minute. It was a real minute. Hakeem held his watch out again so we could see the hands moving at normal speed.

'What just happened?' said Elemenope. She always whispered, but that question had an eerie echo.

Hakeem was taking his glasses off and on like his life depended on it. If anyone was going to have an answer it was him. I was happy to wait, but Michael chimed in first with, 'It's obvious, isn't it? This is alien stuff. This whole house is probably an alien spaceship, and we need to get out of here before the aliens get back.'

Again with the aliens. I didn't say it. Mr Newton would have told us if this was alien, wouldn't he?

Hakeem left his glasses on eventually and said, 'Well, I think Miss Slider has got some serious time-manipulating technology. I want to do some research before we come back.'

'Oh, I'm not coming back,' said Elemenope. Michael's face told me he wasn't either.

I said, 'Whatever we do, I think we should all go home now. Our parents will freak if we stay here any longer. My dad's probably looking for us already.'

* * * * *

Dad wasn't out looking for us. When I got home he had Bella on his knee, listening to her read her school book. He was asleep, and she was making all sorts of mistakes. I knew because I had read that book years ago. It was about a boy singing on a pirate ship. She was saying stuff that wasn't even in the book. I listened for a bit, but eventually I had to say something. 'That's rubbish, Bella, you're just making that up. Are you even reading?'

She snarled at me, 'Yes, I've read it, Martha smarty-pants, and it's really boring, so I'm making it better.'

Dad woke up at that point, put his arm around my little sister and said, 'That's great reading, sweetheart. I'll tell Mummy what a good girl you've been.'

Bella gave me a look that yelled, 'I'm his favourite!' and I fumed. How dare she? She was getting praise for the wrong reason. I was outraged, but for once I held my tongue. I had bigger problems.

* * * * *

It was ages – well an hour – until dinner. I attacked my biscuit tin. Three Jaffa Cakes and two Hobnobs later I was ready to think. Had that been time travel at Miss Slider's house? I didn't know. I only knew one thing: I had to go back. And I had to take Hakeem with me. OK; I only knew two things.

Mum had been at work all day, so Dad was getting dinner ready: frozen pizza. I loved pizza, and recently Mum had been getting great pizza from some online grocery shop. They delivered straight to our house, and that made me think we were living in a perfect time.

What could be better than having food, especially frozen pizza, delivered straight to your door?

Another great thing about Saturdays was we were allowed to eat the pizzas in the living room – on our laps. We didn't even get in trouble if we spilled a few crumbs. I loved Saturday nights. Once Bella had gone to bed I could sit up and watch some TV with Dad. The third great thing that happened that day was Dad said, 'Martha, I think you're old enough to watch *Doctor Who*.' I had no idea what that was, but if it was something I had to be old enough to watch, then I was definitely going to watch it.

What a revelation. I had no idea what half the stuff was, and I couldn't ask Dad because he kept shushing me. But I saw something that made me sit up and take notice: a time machine.

When I went to bed I couldn't sleep. Dad came up after about an hour, and said, 'What's all the noise?'

I didn't know I had been making noise but, apparently, if I moved my furniture around it sounded like a thunderstorm downstairs.

Dad looked at what I'd built and said, 'What's that?'

I thought it was pretty obvious. 'The *TARDIS*.'

'OK, but the Doctor's Tardis is blue, isn't it?'

I didn't think the colour was important, so I said, 'Well, mine isn't.' It was a hotchpotch of pink sheets, purple cushions and an upturned chair. It also wasn't bigger on the inside. I didn't know how to do that.

'Does it work?'

'I haven't tried it yet.'

Dad laughed and said, 'Come on … it's late. Back to bed, you.'

While he was hugging me, I asked, 'Do you think time travel's real, Dad?'

'That's a bit too clever for me. Maybe.' Then he asked, 'If it was, where would you want to go?'

I couldn't answer. I couldn't explain that I needed to find Jemima in a future I couldn't be sure even existed. I couldn't even explain it to myself.

Chapter Fifty-eight

When I went downstairs for breakfast, Dad was shuffling around in his ratty old dressing gown. I gave him a hug and said, 'I know.'

'What do you know, honey-bunch?'

'Where I'd go in my Tardis.'

Dad's eyebrows asked the follow-up question for him.

I said, 'I'd go and find Jemima.'

'Uh-huh.'

I wanted pancakes. Mum wasn't up yet, and I knew if I waited for her she'd say no. There'd be a long look at me, some sighing and, if I was extra lucky, a lecture about healthy eating. I really didn't feel like a lecture.

'Daddy, if I make them, can we have pancakes?'

'What's that, butternut?'

'Pancakes. Can I make them?'

'Do you know how?'

I gave him my most confident stare. 'Of course.' I didn't wait for an answer as I reached for Mum's old recipe book. In truth, I had tried to make pancakes before – a couple of times. One lot were terribly lumpy because I was too impatient to beat the mixture properly and the other time I made such a mess (nobody had ever got batter on the ceiling before, apparently) that mum banned me from ever making them again. I didn't need to remind Dad about that.

Bella even offered to help, which was annoying and OK in equal parts. I let her do the dry mixing, but I wanted to crack the egg. I was pretty sure a bit of egg white on the counter wouldn't matter too much. I spent ages whipping the batter. 'No lumps today,' I said to nobody.

'What's that, Martha?'

I hadn't noticed Mum coming into the kitchen.

'Oh … hi, Mummy.' I thought I'd turn on the treacle, try to bypass the whole 'healthy-eating-not-having-pancakes-for-breakfast' situation.

To my surprise, Mum said, 'Ooh … I'll have some of those.' I must have woken up in an alternate universe. Hakeem was always talking about those. Apparently, there are lots of different universes, and in some of them you live your life in parallel: the sky is green, the grass red and your mum is not a total control freak – that sort of thing.

Apart from putting her hand on my arm to stop the flood of maple syrup onto my stack, Mum was OK through the whole of breakfast. I liked that universe.

It even continued when Hakeem rang and suggested we go back to Miss Slider's house. To be fair, what Mum said 'Yes' to was a trip to the rec with my friends. She could be so nice when she didn't know the whole story.

Bella nearly ruined it when she asked if she could come too.

I said, 'Haven't you got some more homework to do?' The look I got could have cooked eggs, but I had guessed correctly and little-miss-make-up-the-words-to-what-you're-reading was going to get caught out.

* * * * *

It wasn't technically a lie. Hakeem was my friend and he did meet me at the rec. There was never anything in what I'd asked Mum that said we would stay there. So, when we skulked around the side of Miss Slider's house I hadn't actually done anything wrong.

The key was where we'd left it, in its bag on a yew branch. We wasted no time getting to the fireplace, thumping both sides of the mantelpiece and squeezing together through the weird door into the wood-panelled room. I wedged my left shoe in the doorway to make sure we could get back out.

It was exactly how it had been the day before, but Hakeem did something he hadn't warned me about. He said, 'I hope this works,' as he raced to one of the old screens on the bench.

I started, 'What are you …?' but he cut me off with a wave of his hand. I watched as he tapped an ancient keyboard – his hands flew over the keys. The screen showed a clock face, with whirling hands, but as Hakeem typed, the hands slowed down. Eventually they stopped. Well, not quite, but they turned super slowly. Hakeem turned and smiled.

'Phew … I wasn't sure that would work.'

'What did you do?'

'Well,' he said, 'I remembered something last night. I had trouble sleeping, and I couldn't stop thinking about what happened – you know – when my foot got stuck in the door. As I thought about it, I remembered seeing a clock-face somewhere in this room, and it occurred to me that maybe a computer was controlling the time in here, so I just had to come and see.'

'Clever.' I said. I was in awe of Hakeem's brain. I still

wondered why Mr Newton hadn't told him all about the newts first.

Hakeem said, 'Well, we'll see about all that. Now for the rest of my plan.'

'Hang on. If you've slowed down time in here, what's happening outside?'

'If I've got it right, that time will be normal, so we could be here for hours, but outside only a minute or two would pass.'

My head started to hurt.

Chapter Fifty-nine

As scary as the wood room was, it paled compared to the room we found next. Opposite the door we'd entered was another one. It had the same change of pattern, but no obvious knob or handle. It opened easily to Hakeem's touch. I shoved my right shoe in the doorway, just in case it was a slammer too. The floor was freezing, even through my socks.

The room was much more conventional. Its wood panelling looked like the old library I used to go to. There were heaps of ancient dark leather chairs, but they weren't set out like a sitting room, arranged for chatting or sharing drinks. The chairs were lined up along three walls, and above each one hung a painting of a woman.

It was the same woman – Miss Slider. She was different in each one, and she wore very different clothes. In the one closest to the door she looked like a young girl, with pigtails. She looked like she should have been in a *Heidi* film, or *The Sound of Music*. But behind her, instead of a Swiss mountain or a village, there was a shiny metal building with no windows.

Above the opposite chair, the painting showed her as ancient – even older than she looked in real life, with silver hair and so many wrinkles. She was standing in front of what looked like a mud hut with smoke coming out of its roof. It didn't even have a chimney.

I walked all around the chairs and studied the paintings. They showed a whole life, from the young girl to the crone, but the buildings were way off.

'Hakeem … these paintings are just wrong. Have you noticed?'

'Hmm? No. I've been looking at the chair lights.'

'What chair lights?'

'These ones.' He pointed to the chair in front of me. There was a tiny row of red lights running along the right arm. They were so dim, I hadn't noticed them.

I said, 'What about them?'

Hakeem changed the direction of his pointing finger and said, 'Look at that one.'

The chair was about halfway down the opposite row, about two-thirds of the way around the room. Unlike all the others, its right arm glowed a soft green.

'What do you think that means?' he asked me. I think he asked me, but sometimes Hakeem asked himself questions out loud, so I didn't answer straight away.

I looked at the picture above the chair with the green lights. There was Miss Slider exactly as I had last seen her: grey, wild hair, old-fashioned clothes – I could almost smell the mothballs – and standing outside the very house Hakeem and I were now inside.

'I think I know,' I could have shouted, but I was too scared to raise my voice. I did an 'Elemenope' and whispered it. My heart was racing. I was scared, but excited that I might have beaten Hakeem to the point.

'Could it be?'

'Could it be what?' I asked.

'This is crazy.'

'Can I tell you what I think?' I really had to get the words out before Hakeem did, so I just blurted out, 'These are time-travel chairs … or time-period chairs … or something like that … and Miss Slider uses them to come and go through – well – time.'

It was crazy.

Hakeem started his glasses ritual, so I knew I was right. Or at least close.

When he finally put them back on his head and kept them there, he said, 'I think you're right. But what's with the pictures?'

I had an answer for that, too, but I felt silly saying it out loud. 'Well, the buildings go from that one,' I pointed to the first picture, above the first chair, 'with the mud hut … to that one,' I pointed to the last one, with the really young girl, 'with the super-crazy modern building.' I waited for Hakeem to look at all the pictures in between.

He nodded, so I went on, 'But Miss Slider … if the lady is her – and I'm pretty sure it is – goes the other way.' I swept my hand from right to left, and watched Hakeem do the same with his eyes. The girl got older as the buildings got older, and she got younger as the buildings got newer. That was backwards.

I said it out loud, and it sounded as crazy as I feared. 'If that's Miss Slider, then she's getting younger as we get older. Or maybe that's not her at all.' I added the last bit so I didn't sound quite so crazy.

* * * * *

Hakeem started the whole glasses off–glasses on routine again.

He looked at me for a long time before saying, 'I think you're right, Martha. I was just thinking maybe she was a bad painter.'

'You're kidding, right?'

Hakeem said, 'If I was, I'm not going to admit it now. Your idea is genius. That makes these chairs represent different times in her own life … Wow!'

'So, what's with the different lights, do you think?'

Hakeem was back to his old self. 'Oh, that's obvious. This one here, with the green lights, is the current time – in Miss Slider's life.'

'And ours.' I added.

'Yes, and ours, of course.'

It might have all been obvious to Hakeem, but I had a real headache coming on.

Chapter Sixty

I didn't want to stay too long, my head was hurting – it felt like my brain was hurting – and I was hungry. I'd left some sandwiches and biscuits in my bag in the normal sitting room. Hakeem never thought of things like that, but he smiled when I told him. According to Hakeem's watch we had been gone about an hour, but when we got back through the white room, and stood in the dusty old sitting room, it had only been two minutes.

I sat on the old sofa, sending a cloud of dust flying up, and heard a thump from the corridor.

'Was that you?' asked Hakeem.

'No … I'm right here.'

Just then Mark One and Mark Two came bouncing in.

'What are you two nerds doing in here?' asked Mark Two.

Mark One said in his snide whining voice, 'Fatty's worth at least two, so you should ask what the three of them are up to.' They both laughed, but not with any real amusement.

Hakeem said, 'If you mean Martha's worth two of you, then you're right.'

That seemed to confuse the Marks. Mark One said, 'Well, there's nothing in here worth anything. Let's go.'

I said, 'Wait a minute. Why are you here?'

'Isn't it obvious,' said Mark Two. 'We're looking for stuff to nick.'

Hakeem said, 'You do know whose house this is, don't you?'

The blank look on the Marks' faces told me they didn't, so I answered for them. 'It's Miss Slider's … you know … the head. It's her house, and if you don't want her to find you in here uninvited, you'd better get out.'

That did the trick. The two Marks skulked off out the back door. They weren't very smart or they would have asked us what we were doing in the house. It was good they didn't, because I didn't have an answer ready. I waited for them to get clear before I turned the key in the lock. Why hadn't I done that before?

* * * * *

My heart was racing. I hated the Marks. I knew they were bullies, but they were obviously thieves too.

'That could have been nasty.'

'You're telling me,' said Hakeem. 'I suppose we're trespassing too; that hadn't occurred to me before.' He shuffled his feet.

'But we used the key. And we're not stealing anything. Anyway, how are we going to find Jemima?'

'I've been thinking about that. That room ... it doesn't fit with what you told me.'

'No ... so?'

'Well, if Miss Slider uses those chairs to go to different spots on her timeline she must have something else she uses to do what you said. You know, the flash of light and disappearing.'

I had been thinking something similar. 'You're right. She didn't bring Mrs Gnash back here, get her to sit quietly in a chair while she zapped her into the future. She must have, like, an actual time machine ... a Tardis.'

'You do know *Doctor Who*'s not real, don't you, Martha?'

I wanted it to be real.

Hakeem went on, 'I mean, things can't be bigger on the inside than they are on the outside. But she didn't go into any sort of box, either, did she?'

'No.'

'There's got to be something else here. Come on … we've got all the time in the world, now.'

I took my sandwiches back through into the first wooden room. We watched as the hands on the computer screen barely moved. Hakeem was right: he'd slowed time down in here. But that didn't stop me being hungry. My stomach moved in normal time.

Chapter Sixty-one

'Why didn't we see that before?' Hakeem was staring at a black sign hanging over another herring-bone tiled doorway. The sign said MUSEUM.

'I don't know.' I really didn't. I didn't know why anything was the way it was in this house.

Hakeem pushed the door and we stepped into another weird space. It wasn't like any other museum I'd been in before. There were no glass cases with boring signs you were supposed to read. There were no signs saying DO NOT TOUCH. There wasn't much of anything.

What caught my eye was a huge chair (Miss Slider really liked her armchairs) with a tray-table attached to its front. I thought it would be exactly what Dad wanted for watching telly.

Instead of a flat tray and helpful cupholders, the tray sported a bewildering array of dials and switches. Right in the middle were three clocks, all showing different times.

'Oh, wow,' said Hakeem. It was his turn to whisper. 'This is what I expected a time machine to look like.'

* * * * *

'D-d-d-dinosaurs …' Hakeem looked shattered. Quite literally – torn to pieces. He had a scratch right across his face, his clothes were in tatters, his hair was standing on end and his glasses – what was left of them – were sitting between his mouth and his chin.

I laughed, but I probably shouldn't have. I said, 'Well, that's what you get for charging off without me.'

Hakeem half stood, and fell sideways out of the time-chair. That's what we called it when Hakeem had climbed in and started fiddling with the switches and dials. For a scientist he was not very cautious. He'd smirked as he turned a knob beside the first of the clocks, which wound its hands backwards. Then he fiddled with the knobs beside the other two clocks and flicked the big red switch at the top. That's when he vanished.

I didn't have time to panic because he came back, complaining about dinosaurs, straight away. I thought he must have been playing a trick. But apart from all the physical damage he'd sustained, he was as white as a sheet.

'Did you really go back and see dinosaurs?'

'Uh-huh. Wow, Martha, this thing's really dangerous. They nearly got me. Lucky they were just little ones.'

'Did you get out of the chair?'

'No … I tried, but there's some sort of force field or something. I was stuck in the chair.'

I said, 'Maybe that's a good thing. Can I have a go now?'

'I think we should try to understand it a bit better first.'

'Oh, now you're all "mister responsible" when it's my turn. Come on, get out so I can get in.'

Hakeem was shaking his head, 'I really don't think that's a good idea.'

'You came back, didn't you? Why shouldn't I?'

I sat in the time-chair. It was surprisingly comfortable. 'What do the dials do?'

Hakeem couldn't help himself. Despite being scared, and angry with me (I didn't get why), he couldn't help trying to explain the science, even if he didn't understand any of it.

'These clocks, I think, represent the past, the present and the future.' As he said that, his fingers pointed to the three clocks in turn. 'These knobs adjust the time you want to go to, and this lever,' he pointed at the red switch, 'makes it go.'

I said, 'I thought it'd be more complicated than that.'

'Well, the science is all hidden away, "under the hood" so to speak … like a car. You can't see the engine, but the controls make it go. Same thing here, I think.'

I didn't want a science lecture from Hakeem. I wanted to find Jemima. I knew Mr Newton said Miss Slider could take Mrs Gnash to the future, so it seemed reasonable that Jemima and her dad would have gone there too.

I certainly didn't want to meet any dinosaurs, so I left the first clock alone. The second one Hakeem had said was the present time, so I left it too. The third one was weird. It had five hands. When I turned the knob they all went at different speeds. I decided to play it safe, and only turned the knob enough for the longest hand to move what looked like five minutes.

'That should be safe enough,' I said as I flicked the red switch.

I could just make out the start of something Hakeem said. It started with, 'No …'

* * * * *

I felt like throwing up. I probably shouldn't have made those tuna and mayonnaise sandwiches – I always used too much mayo. Maybe the eggs were off. My head felt heavy, then light, like it might fly off. I wasn't spinning, but it felt like I was being turned inside-out.

When I opened my eyes, I was still in the room, but the lights were off. I couldn't get out of the chair – not even a little bit. I couldn't even lift my bottom up. The door burst open. Literally. Hakeem stumbled into the room.

I called out, 'Hi … I'm OK. What's going on?' Hakeem kept saying, over and over, 'Honestly, Martha, I wish you'd listened to me. Oh my God … oh my God. Where is she?'

That's when I noticed Hakeem was in tears.

Chapter Sixty-two

I started to panic. I called out, but there was no answer. Hakeem came over to the chair and went to lift up the tray, but I watched as his hand shimmered and went through the space where the tray should be, as if it wasn't there. Had I disappeared?

Without warning the shimmering stopped, and my nausea with it. I don't think I've ever seen anyone jump like Hakeem did – straight up into the air with no preparation. Like a cat.

'Martha … thank goodness. What happened? You've been gone ages. I thought you were never coming back!'

'I've only been gone about a minute.'

'No …' Hakeem was shaking his head. His glasses were on and off his face so rapidly he couldn't have seen anything.

I tried to explain, but just as I opened my mouth he blurted, 'I told you to wait. I told you to let me explain, but you just pressed buttons and went off!'

'What, like you did? Don't yell at me for doing exactly

what you did!'

He calmed down and said, 'Alright, then. What did you see?'

'Nothing. Just shimmering lights, and I felt sick.'

'That would be the inertia control … it hasn't worked properly on that old thing for years.' Miss Slider! I hadn't seen her come in. Neither had Hakeem judging by his spontaneous jump – even higher than his last one.

Tiny Miss Slider looked us both up and down. I was still in the chair and I squeezed out to stand in front of her. I expected time to slow down, like it did whenever she was close, but it didn't. I was so shocked to see her; I couldn't get my words out. I said, 'What are you … why are you … we weren't …. well we were … but we didn't …'

'Relax, Martha. By now you obviously know a few things about me, and it's OK.' She smiled at me, and went on, 'I came home a few moments ago, and realised someone was in my house. All the dust on my furniture was in the air – it never does that for me – it usually just sits there.'

I found some proper words, 'Miss Slider, have you seen Jemima?'

'Jemima? Jemima Waddington-Clarke? No. Why would I have seen her, Martha?'

I gulped – *oh, no … if Miss Slider hadn't seen her, did that mean Jemima was in a different time?*

'But, she and her dad disappeared at the same time you did with Mrs Gnash – the manti-thingy – you know the alien you took off to a different time.'

Hakeem was just standing there, glasses in their now habitual state of off-and-on-again-ness. Not helpful.

Miss Slider furrowed her brow. 'Did you see that, Martha? You shouldn't have seen that. Tell me what you saw, exactly.'

'Well, I didn't actually *see* it happen … but I heard it. A huge bang and you were gone. So was Mrs Gnash, and so were Jemima and Gerald.'

'Who's Gerald?' she asked.

'Jemima's dad – her real father – not that horrible Mr Toilet.'

'Who's Mr Toilet?'

I was getting annoyed – we were getting off topic.

'The Toilets is what I call Jemima's mum and stepdad. It's not important.'

'OK, well, something obviously has gone wrong. Time travel – the way we time benders do it – is not the most exact science.'

Hakeem came out of his trance: 'But time travel must

be incredibly scientific. I mean we're not there yet, with all our advanced mathematics and research – NASA and SpaceX. I mean, if they haven't worked out how to do it, how is this even possible?'

Miss Slider snorted, 'Oh, we don't use science, dear. We tried that. You've seen the chairs, and this old thing.' She pointed at the chair I'd just climbed out of. 'They don't work … well they do a bit. For years a group of us had worked on time travel in secret. It started with Albert Einstein. He had a secret lab that my father worked in. He built this chair – the first of its type.

'My father was a very clever scientist. He taught at Cambridge university and tinkered in here on the weekends. He showed me all the secrets, but he could never get the scientific community to take him seriously. It eventually sent him a bit loopy and he went on a retreat in the Himalayas – somewhere deep in Nepal. My mother went to find him. It wasn't good. She found him all curled up in a cave, wearing rags and clutching this.'

She pulled a disc from the pocket in her cardigan. It looked like a small doughnut. A small shiny doughnut with pink icing. 'Oh, wait … that's my lunch. We don't use doughnuts; we use these.'

From her other pocket, Miss Slider produced another doughnut. This one was grey and furry. It still looked squishy, but not so delicious. The smell of mothballs was overpowering. 'This is a bender.'

Hakeem and I both gawped. No other word would do. Open-mouthed gawping was all we were capable of.

'How does it work?' were the first words out of Hakeem's mouth.

They collided with my first words: 'Can we use it to find Jemima?'

Miss Slider continued smiling as she said, 'I don't know how it works exactly ... I hold it and think where I want to go – I mean which time I want to go to. It gets a bit confusing. But it takes me there, and anything or anyone I want to take with me.'

'So we could use it to find Jemima,' I said. 'You must have taken her with you.'

Miss Slider stopped smiling. 'But I didn't want to take her or this Gerald with me, so they must have got hit with an accidental time-wash. That's what happens if the bender malfunctions. Which it does. A lot.'

Hakeem's glasses were back on, held firmly by the frown that was stuck on his face. 'I don't quite understand,' he said. 'If you can control the bender as you say, how can it not take other people with you.'

'Fair question,' she said. 'Let's discuss it over a cup of tea.'

Miss Slider led us into her kitchen. Dust was settled on every surface, but as she filled the kettle and moved about, it stayed put. It was only disturbed by Hakeem and me. Great clouds of it swirled about our feet.

As she put the cups and teapot on the little table in her sitting room, Miss Slider left the bender beside them. I couldn't help myself. I grabbed it; didn't get a chance to hear Hakeem's cry beyond, 'Martha … no …' I spun wildly. The room disappeared in a kaleidoscope of shapes and wild colours all crashing together. I wasn't thinking. That may have been the problem.

Chapter Sixty-three

I landed on my knees. My head was dizzy and I wanted to throw up. There was nothing to see at first, then a mist gradually cleared and I realised I was in a room I knew – sort of. It was Mr Newton's basement, and he was pacing, well kind of pacing, back and forth in front of a set of broken ropes. He was muttering to himself, 'Where will she take it? That was awful.'

I realised I had gone back in time, rather than forwards. *Ha! Hakeem was wrong about time travel only going forwards.* Of course, if I thought about it, you must be able to go backwards, or Miss Slider would never have been able to get back from the future. That made me think about a movie I'd seen, then I realised I must have been thinking about Mr Newton as I touched the time bender, and that was why I'd gone back to his house and back to when I'd last seen him.

As he turned to face me, I decided not to explain myself. I felt the time bender in my hand, and tried to think about Jemima. I was distracted by the thought of pizza; I smelled mothballs, and started to spin.

My knees were not happy as they crumpled beneath me again. The nausea was intense and I even felt a bit of sick in the back of my throat. My bedroom! But when?

I needed the loo – that was where it should be, but the door was locked. A voice I kind-of recognised answered with, 'Go away, Martha, it's my turn. Come back and vomit later.' Then there was a mumbled, 'Crazy cow.' It was Bella, but her voice sounded older.

I watched her come out and push past me. She was taller than she should have been. Sisters don't speak at bathroom switch-over time, so that was easy. The mirror must have been broken somehow, because the face looking back at me was gaunt. I stopped; the loo could wait.

My face. What had happened to my face? I looked like I'd seen a ghost; my eyes were sunken, there were big dark rings under my eyes, and my mouth looked like it was stuck in that stupid selfie-pout I hated other girls doing. I looked at my arms – skin and bone. I felt my bum – gone, just bony.

I walked to the kitchen, feeling like I was about to break in two. Mum looked me up and down – I was used to that look of disappointment, but something was different about that too. She gave a nervous laugh and said, 'So … breakfast?'

That was a stupid question. Of course, I wanted breakfast, but that was another thing: where was my appetite? I really wanted to eat so I made four slices of toast and loaded them with butter and jam. At the table, Mum's eyes were popping out of her head. I saw her give Dad a nudge. She had to do it again to get his attention. He looked at me, and my plate, and did a little double-take.

Raspberry jam – my favourite. I took a second bite while I was still chewing the first mouthful. But when I swallowed, something awful happened. I felt full. Not just full – too full. I raced to the bathroom and promptly threw up. It all came back. And some carrots. When had I eaten carrots? I don't even like carrots.

When I got back to the table, the sight of my uneaten jammy toast made me feel hungry and sick at the same time. I gave Mum a pleading look and said, 'Mum, am I anorexic? Or … what's it called … bulimic, or something?'

I got a sideways look from Dad; Bella snorted. Mum shuddered.

Whatever was happening in this future was all

wrong. I felt in my pocket and felt the surface of the bender. Just as Mum started to say, 'We've been through …' I closed my eyes and thought really hard about going back; I wanted the past, and I needed to talk to someone. I suddenly wanted to talk to Mr Newton as the smell of mothballs assaulted my senses and I felt like throwing up again.

I did throw up … right onto the floor of the strange wooden studio. That was what came to mind as I looked around. It was dark, mainly because I was under a table. A couple of candles burned weakly on a ramshackle desk. There were piles of paper strewn all over the desk and some had spilled onto the floor, right next to my hiding place. They were covered in drawings. An unfinished painting of an old-fashioned lady rested on an easel by the tiny window.

I found a rag and started to clean up my sick when I heard voices at the door. What was the language? Spanish? Italian?

The door flew open and two men walked in. The larger man was waving his arms and speaking rapidly … I couldn't understand a word. He picked up one of the papers, stared at it and screwed it into a ball.

The shorter man – and he was way shorter – shuffled

into view. He stood in front of my table, and I caught sight of his funny old shoes. They seemed to leave a trail of water wherever he went. His voice was familiar, even if the language was weird. It sounded like a machine. He held a piece of paper with drawings on it that looked like a bird's wing and he was trying to show the larger man something about its shape.

The larger man kept interrupting, waving his arms around. He strode over to where a large cloth hung over a strange shape. Still talking rapidly and shaking his head at the smaller man, he pulled off the cloth and finally stopped talking as he pointed to the wooden machine with a screw-shaped sort of sail on top. I suddenly knew what I was looking at. I'd seen pictures of this very thing. Leonardo da Vinci's flying machine!

I had gone way too far back in history, but then it hit me like a bag of potatoes. I'd been thinking about Mr Newton, and here he was (or they were) talking about flight with the greatest inventor of all time. I couldn't see the smaller man's face, but I knew it would be a mask.

The figure I now knew was Mr Newton turned to look under the table, clearly saw me, but didn't give me away. Did he recognise me somehow?

I had to get away, so I clutched the bender and

thought about the future. I just wanted to go home, so I pictured my family. That should have done the trick. It did – sort of.

We were at the dinner table. Good start. The food smelled delicious. Better. I looked at my plate, piled with green vegetables I couldn't name, lying beside the smallest piece of chicken I'd ever seen. I watched, distracted, as I piled the odd green stuff onto my fork. There was no gravy to soak it in, so I just put it straight in my mouth. It was disgusting. It tasted like grass clippings. I couldn't swallow it so I sat there chewing the revolting stuff, hoping to soften it up somehow.

Mum said, 'That's the way, Martha. The kale will take some getting used to. It's a great source of vitamins, and it might help with your diabetes.'

Diabetes? When did I get diabetes?

'Excuse me,' I said in my best-manners voice. 'I need the bathroom.'

The kale made an undignified exit. The mirror was all wrong again. I was a lot older … maybe five years older, and really fat. Even I wasn't comfortable with the reflection. How many chins? Three. My skin was all blotchy and I looked ready to burst.

Back at the table, I looked away from my plate for the

first time. Dad was now completely bald. He'd piled on the weight too. Bella looked – I hate to say it – beautiful.

There was another child at the table. Had we borrowed somebody's kid? I didn't have to wait long. The little boy threw his hands across his plate and knocked his milk flying.

'Jasper!' Dad still hated spilled milk.

Oh no! Was Jasper my little brother? When did that happen? This had gone far enough. I needed help badly. I grabbed for the time bender; it slipped in my sweaty palm and rolled onto the floor and under the table. Mum and I both went for it at the same time. Mum got there first and gave me a disapproving look. 'Martha, is this a doughnut?'

'No … it's the latest craze at school … I'll show you.'

Mum didn't hand it back – I didn't give her the opportunity. I snatched it out of her hand and thought ferociously about Miss Slider.

The spinning and the mothball smell was as bad as ever. It went on for ages as I tried to focus on the last time I'd seen Miss Slider.

There she was, standing in front of me. I knew where we were; it was her house. We stood in the dusty, unused dining room. The first thing I did was look down at my hands and feet. They seemed the right size. I felt my face – only two chins. I must have mastered the time bender!

Miss Slider adopted a kindly look as she said, 'Martha? My goodness. What are you doing here?'

'Oh, Miss Slider … I'm so sorry. I shouldn't have taken the time bender. I don't seem able to use it properly. I just wanted to get Jemima back and take her home.'

'I see. So you're the reason I've been having trouble with time management recently. Every time I try to go somewhere, at another time, something goes wrong. If an inexperienced person has been using a bender, it can change the shape of time.'

'The shape of time?'

'Yes … that's right. Time isn't a simple linear progression. It bends around and different times exist together in different places. Time benders take you from one place to another. But you have to know how to use them properly. Otherwise you bounce about, and it gets awfully confusing.'

I was awfully confused.

She went on, 'I have been having all sorts of trouble lately. I wanted to go to the palace to see the new Queen's coronation, but I wound up in Paris during the revolution. That was a close-run thing.'

I said, 'Oh, were you going to 1953?'

'No, I wanted to see Victoria … she's the new queen.'

I felt sick. I said, 'So … hang on … If we're in 1838 (those history lessons were really paying off), how do you know me? I won't be born yet … not for ages.'

'Oh, Martha. Time benders live across years. I go in and out of history, and in and out of the future all the time. Of course I know you.'

Miss Slider held out her hand and said, 'Now, may I see the bender you have?'

I pulled the strange doughnut out of my pocket, holding it out like an offering. Miss Slider pulled a bender from her cardigan pocket and placed them side by side. They began to vibrate and hum. I watched in amazement as they slid together and became one.

'Ah …' she said. 'That makes sense now. We have been using the same bender.'

It may have made sense to her, but I was just getting more confused.

'So, hang on. Are you a time bender or is this little machine a time bender?'

'I can see how this is confusing. I'm a time bender only because I can use a time bender. These little "machines" as you call them, aren't machines at all. They're living creatures. We don't know much about them. They're from high up in the Himalayas; they're very rare. They live across time as I said, and if you have the mental ability to communicate with them, they will take you anywhere you want to go.'

I didn't answer because I was thoroughly confused. I'd been communicating with a living creature which took me through time. Not an everyday occurrence. As I was thinking this, Miss Slider said, 'Wait … you've been using this bender, so you must be able to communicate with it.'

Normally I get annoyed when somebody says what I'm thinking before I get a chance to say it. But I was still thinking.

The next thing she said floored me. 'Martha, you must be a time bender.'

'How's that?'

'Well, you have obviously been using this bender to travel. How else did you come to this time? Tell me, have you been anywhere else?'

I felt guilty. I shuffled my feet as I said, 'I think I saw Leonardo da Vinci.'

'That's quite possible. Often we go to times and places which we've seen or read about.'

'But … Mr Newton was there as well, I think.'

She looked me in the eye and asked, 'And, had you been thinking about him?'

'Yes. I wanted help.'

'I see. And then did you think about me?'

I nodded. 'I also wanted to go and find Jemima, so I thought about going to the future. You know, where you took the Mantiform Caliopteryx.'

'The what?'

'Oh, maybe you haven't met her – it – yet.' I paused because what I was thinking was really hard. 'I went to the future, twice, and saw my family. It was really weird. Does what you see in the future always happen?'

Miss Slider laughed, 'Oh no … of course not. We can change the future by what we do in the present.'

That made me think even harder, and my head began to hurt as I said, 'So … can we go back and change things to make the present different?'

She laughed again, 'No, no, no. It doesn't work that way. Present actions can change the future, but it's not possible to change or undo things in the past. Well, not much – maybe a little. But you have to be very careful not to fracture the fabric of time.'

'Oh.' I was disappointed. I thought, briefly, that I could

go back and stop Jemima's parents getting divorced, but that wasn't going to happen now.

I focussed back on the problem that started all this.

'Miss Slider, how can I get Jemima back from the future?'

'Well, Martha, that is going to take mastery of the time bender, some practise and a lot of luck. Let's have a cup of tea.'

The kitchen was exactly as it had been when I was there before. The dust still didn't move for Miss Slider, and now it wasn't moving for me.

Chapter Sixty-four

'We'll do it together to begin with,' said Miss Slider, taking my hand and putting it on top of the time bender she was already holding. It began humming. 'The first thing is to clear your mind. Think emptiness.'

I tried to think of nothing, but my mind couldn't relax. The next thing I knew, we were standing in the hallway of our house. Not the new one, but our old house in London. It was the day the police came and I saw Dad crying. The look on my face probably told my travelling companion that this was not only *not* the time I wanted, but it was not a good time at all.

Miss Slider squeezed the bender through my hand and I felt the spinning nausea again as we jumped back out of that time. We landed back in her house, but it seemed different; it was colder. Miss Slider frowned and said, 'Obviously haven't been here for some time – the heating's off.'

I said, probably rather rudely, 'Don't you have control over where we go?'

'Of course,' she snapped, 'but you were looking distressed, so I just took us out of there – to somewhere safe. And here we are. You're welcome!'

'I'm sorry … it's just that was a particularly bad time for me.'

'And your father, by the look of things. I was letting you drive, but maybe you're not quite ready.'

'Can I please have another go? I really want to find Jemima.'

'Why is this so important to you, Martha? I didn't think you were friendly with the Waddington-Clarke girl.'

'I didn't think I was either – at first. You know, she was all snooty and rude, but then I discovered how very lonely she was, and we just sort of fell together. Anyway, whether we're friends or not, she's in trouble, in the wrong place, and she needs help.'

Miss Slider gave a kindly look and said, 'That's what I was waiting for. You can't use a bender properly for your own personal gain. They don't respond well to selfish thoughts. We might have a chance now.'

She took a deep breath and said, 'Take it very carefully, Martha. Before you hold the bender again, try to be clear about where and when you want to go. Think about Jemima and where you think she went. If she got caught up in the time I took the Mantiform Caliopteryx to, I might be able to help if I think about it too.'

I closed my eyes and formed a picture of Jemima in my bedroom. I thought about her real father and the moment I was sure they disappeared. I felt Miss Slider's hand close over mine, with the bender, and felt the spinning nausea and smelled mothballs again. How does anybody get used to that?

I opened my eyes to darkness. Not like night-time. Like all the light had left the world. It was cold and damp. Suddenly a blinding light was in my eyes and a scream filled my ears. It was an angry *I'm-going-to-kill-you* scream.

It stopped as quickly as it had started, to be replaced with a gentle, 'Martha? Is that you?'

My eyes were slow to react, but with the light turned aside I could just make out Jemima, and her dad. They both held pointed sticks and looked like they hadn't eaten in days. Their clothes were torn in places, and where their skin showed all I could see was caked mud. Gerald had a dark stain over his bandaged knee; I knew instinctively it was blood. Jemima's face had scratches across her nose and cheeks. There was dried blood on those too.

Gerald spoke, 'We thought – um – we thought you were that thing again.'

'What thing?' asked Miss Slider.

'That giant insect … it's attacked us twice.'

It had to be the Mantiform Caliopteryx. 'Was it Mrs Gnash?' I asked Jemima. She nodded and ran over to me. We hugged; she was crying, and snot dribbled out of her nose onto my shoulder.

'Oh, Martha … I can't believe you've come … it's been awful.' Each phrase came out between sobs.

We sat on the floor of the cave. It was cold and slimy. Jemima and her dad filled us in. Apparently when they had disappeared in front of me, they somehow landed in the woody bit of the old forest on the edge of our town. I'd never been allowed to go there. Kids at school told all sorts of rumours about the place. Scary stories of ghosts and werewolves. Mum said that was all nonsense – it was a hang-out for local drug addicts and drunks. Either way, I never wanted to go there, and yet, that was exactly where Miss Slider and I now found ourselves.

Gerald carried most of the story. 'I don't understand what happened. One minute we were leaving your house, then we were here, at the edge of this cave. Good thing, too. That creature can't quite fit in here.'

I asked, 'Do you know what year it is?'

Gerald gave me a strange look and said, 'Why?'

I gulped. 'Well, Miss Slider here … oh … sorry … I didn't introduce you. Gerald, this is Miss Slider – our head teacher. Miss Slider, this is Jemima's father, Gerald … um, sorry, but I don't know your last name …'

'MacArthur,' Gerald said, 'Gerald MacArthur.'

'OK. Introductions done,' I said. 'Important things now. Gerald, Mr MacArthur, Jemima, um … you'd better sit down.'

'We are,' they said in unison.

'Sorry … of course. The thing is … how to say this?'

'What Martha is trying to tell you,' said Miss Slider, 'is I am a time bender. I also use a time bender. Hmm, I see your problem, Martha. It's not as simple as I thought, is it?'

I picked up the thread, 'The thing is, Miss Slider can take herself, things, and apparently other people, to different times.'

Blank looks in stereo told me that neither Jemima nor Gerald had understood a word. In fairness it had so far been a pretty rotten explanation.

I tried again. 'When you left our house the other night, you got caught up in Miss Slider taking the Mantiform

Caliopteryx – Mrs Gnash – to the future. That's where we are now: the future.'

'And we're stuck here with that thing that's trying to eat us?' said Gerald. 'Great!'

'That was not meant to happen,' said Miss Slider quietly. 'I'm most terribly sorry. I think I can fix things, but you'll need to trust me. And Martha. Apparently, Martha has some time bending abilities as well.'

The air changed in the cave. There was a hot blast of stench. Gerald and Jemima backed up to the wall furthest from the cave entrance as Gerald said, 'Quick. Get back here. It can't reach this far.'

Miss Slider and I ran after them. I was very glad that the strange time-altering effect Miss Slider used to have on me had gone away. I didn't have time to mull on that as I leaped away from a flashing claw that scraped my leg.

We spread out, feeling the dank cave wall behind our backs. The smell got worse and we could hear the creature breathing. The light was out, and we were back in that fathomless darkness. I felt Jemima's hand reach into mine. I squeezed hard. She was shaking.

Nobody spoke. After what could have been five minutes, or an hour, snuffling noises slowly moved away from the cave entrance. We waited another age before Miss Slider finally said, 'Right, well we obviously need to get out of here and back to your own time. Martha, do you think you can get us to the right time?'

'Me? But I've only just started doing this. You have so much more experience.'

'The thing is, Martha, I think you have a better idea of when you all belong. I've been doing this so much and for so long I could misjudge where you should be.'

That didn't make much sense, but I was so keen to go, and get Jemima back safely, that I said, 'OK.'

Miss Slider fished in her cardigan pocket and brought out the bender.

Chapter Sixty-five

I never thought I'd be so happy to see St Finbar's. But there we were, right outside the school gates. It was night-time, and the wind was biting. Nobody seemed to care. All I wanted to do was get home. But when had we landed?

I asked Miss Slider, but she just stood with her hands on her hips and said, 'Well, you'd better get off home so your parents don't start worrying.'

'Yes, but how do we know if we're in the right time?'

'Oh, you'll work it out.' And with that she headed off.

I was still holding Jemima's hand. 'Where's your dad?' I asked. She turned through a slow circle, and her face started to crinkle. Gerald had been lost along the way. We called out his name, and that brought Miss Slider back.

'Is something wrong, girls?' Jemima was shaking and I had a horrible sinking feeling.

I asked, 'Um … Miss Slider, if we haven't come back after he disappeared, where would Jemima's dad be?'

'Wherever he was before. Honestly, Martha, am I going to have to explain it all to you again.'

I wanted to say that she hadn't explained it the first time, but intuition was kicking in. 'So, if he hasn't disappeared yet, he'll just be wherever he was?'

'That's what I said.'

The sinking feeling was getting worse.

I said to Jemima, 'Come on … I think we'd better hurry.'

We raced along the high street in the growing dark. There was Lumpy the cat. I swallowed, and watched in horror as a long claw stretched out and snatched him. Then it had me, and Jemima was beating the creature again with her riding crop. We kept running, back to Mr Newton's house, back into that cellar and we relived the whole tying-up-and-bizarre-feeding-a-pizza-to a Mantiform Caliopteryx.

It wasn't until we were sitting in Mr Newton's kitchen again, discussing pizza, that I realised fully that the time-slowing effect Miss Slider had on me had completely gone away. I asked her about that.

'I think,' she said, 'it must be that you really are a time bender, and it's taken a few uses of a bender to shift into your new reality. Welcome to the club, Martha Gibbons.'

I felt sick. I felt elated. I felt confused. I would have to process that later. Right then and there I had a daughter to return to her father.

Jemima and I went to my house, and relived the whole Dad-finding-the-freezer-defrosted fiasco.

Then I heard Mum: 'Hello, dear. Have you been over again?' She turned to ask Dad a question, saw his back retreating with a bag of spoiled food, and directed her gaze at me.

I said, 'Jemima's running away … she can stay here … can't she?'

I didn't wait for Mum to suggest it. I went straight on with, 'So, can we have Indian takeaway for dinner?'

Mum said, 'That's funny, I was just about to suggest that.' I heard myself asking if we could have butter chicken. Best not to leave anything to chance. So, Dad and Bella went off to get the food. That was the best thing about reliving this bit of my life. I knew I was going to get butter chicken and not be shamed when I asked for seconds.

'OK, you two … what's going on?'

I witnessed Mum's interrogation of Jemima again. It was exactly the same as last time. Word for word.

Jemima said, 'I want to live here, please.' It was like

she was saying it for the first time.

Mum sipped her tea, letting the words settle, 'Well, that's interesting, Jemima. Can you tell me why?'

'You don't fight.'

Mum said, 'Yes, we do … all the time.'

'No,' said Jemima, 'you don't. You argue. It's different.'

Like I said: word for word.

I thought Jemima was being a good actor, then, slowly I realised that she wasn't a time bender, so, maybe for her, this was the first time this had happened to her. That made me happy, because I realised she hadn't yet been to that terrifying cave with the monster trying to eat her.

When Mum said, 'Martha, could you get some water, please,' I knew what I would hear outside the door.

I waited until there was silence, so I walked in to find Mum comforting Jemima. Just like last time. I had to keep telling myself that it wasn't a repeat for them. I had forgotten to get the water, but Mum didn't notice. I had to listen to Jemima's description of her 'father' – the horrible Mr Toilet. It made my blood boil. More so since I knew how he would behave when he came round.

Mum finally said, 'I think you can stay here tonight … you can sleep in Martha's room. It'll be fun; let's call it a sleepover. I'll give your mother a call and see what she says. OK?' Jemima nodded.

I heard Mum's deep breath as she reached for the phone. We went to my bedroom and had the exact same conversation I remembered. Even the discovery of my biscuit tin, and Jemima's disappointing refusal to join me in a pre-dinner Jaffa Cake.

Mum was still on the phone as we got downstairs. I could hear Mrs Toilet shouting down the phone. I didn't want to relive every moment.

Chapter sixty-six

Jemima looked thoughtful. I thought about the discussion we had had the last time we sat here and made a monumental decision. I remembered Jemima didn't ask a lot of questions about Mr Newton, Mrs Gnash or Miss Slider. I steered the conversation to her family and for the first time lived a different timeline. I still expected a flood of questions, but it didn't happen. While Jemima told me the story of her real dad, I decided I could protect her even more. I didn't tell her about the weird teachers we had. She didn't need to know that Mr Newton was a hugely intelligent pile of newts, or that our head (and now I) could bend time, and she especially didn't need to know that an alien had been trying to eat her. I kept all that to myself. What memories she formed of our time in Mr Newton's cellar would sort themselves out. And if she asked, I could tell her a gentler version. Or I could ask Mr Newton to clear her memory if it came to that.

Mum called, 'Dad's going to be home soon with dinner, and we should be ready.'

Jemima said, 'Your mum's really nice,' and I agreed with her.

I had another huge plate of butter chicken.

The Toilets hammered on the door, and there was Mrs Toilet shouting, 'Come out here, Jemima!'

Mum dealt with her again, and proceeded to sit at the table, not eating.

Jemima rang her dad. I had seconds, but not a big serve this time, just as Gerald knocked at the door and we relived (well, I relived – the others were doing it for the first time) the beautiful reunion of Jemima and her dad.

I looked out the front widow just in time to see the Mantiform Caliopteryx being chased by Miss Slider.

As Gerald moved gently about our dining room, I grabbed an extra chair and put it between Jemima and me. Using my best waiter-style sweep of hands I gestured for Gerald to sit down.

He smiled his lovely smile as he looked over the remnants of the food. He said 'Mmm ... butter chicken – my favourite. But I think we should get going, don't you, butter-nut?'

I said, a little too forcefully, 'NO ... I mean, no ... please sit and eat with us.'

Mum gave me an approving smile and said, 'Yes, Gerald, please join us.' Then she looked pointedly at me as she said, 'But there's not a lot left.'

* * * * *

There was a loud bang and a flash from outside. Dad turned and said, 'What was that?' I didn't have to say anything because Mum piped up, 'Oh, John, you're so jumpy … just thunder. Really!' Time *had* changed. Just a little.

I smiled. I knew what it was. Mrs Gnash was gone and Jemima and Gerald were safe. We wouldn't have the horrible Toilets over again, accusing us of all things under the sun.

It was good to be me again. Really me – my age – with Mum and Dad and even Bella in their right ages. I looked at my not-quite-empty plate and pushed it away. I'd never left food before. I looked at my stomach bulging over my lap and asked Mum, 'Will you help me eat a better diet, please?' She looked like she was about to cry.

It was then I noticed the bulge in Mum's belly, and my eyes must have widened of their own accord, because

Mum said, 'Martha, have you noticed something?'

I couldn't speak; I pointed at the bulge and gulped. She nodded, and I said, 'Jasper.'

Dad said, 'Well, that's funny. That's actually one of the names we're thinking of, if it's a boy, of course.'

'Oh, it is,' I said before realising it.

'*We* don't even know,' laughed Mum. 'We want it to be a surprise.'

Bella was getting all excited and said, 'I bet it's a girl … a lovely little sister to make up for you!'

I said, 'Bet, eh? Let's say if it's a boy, I get your room.'

I felt something stirring in my pocket. I reached in and felt a now familiar furry doughnut. I started to think about the future; the room began to spin. I felt sick and the smell of mothballs filled my nostrils.

THE END?

Peter Hannaford was born in Newcastle, Australia. He now lives in Stratford-upon-Avon, building gardens and falling in love with the wildlife. He is fascinated by the life-cycle of ladybirds. When not writing, he plants trees for future generations.